Caution Hot Mess Ahead

Jackie Paxson

Contents

To my Aunt Linda
The songbird finally got her wings.
I can hear your laugh with each joke I write.
You will be missed.
Love you more.

Oᴛʜᴇʀ Woʀᴋs

<u>Dirty Laundry Series</u>

Tabloid

Scandal

Rumors

Secrets

Deception
<u>A Work in Progress Series</u>

A Work in Progress

<u>Standalone novels</u>

Unexpected

The Ugly Christmas Sweater

Born to Be My Baby
<u>Novellas</u>

A Bark in the Park

WALK OF SHAME

How do I get myself into things like this?

I crept through the apartment of my latest one-night stand. My mind ticked off all the items I'd brought. The last thing I needed was the awkward 'here's your underwear' talk with my boss. Did I forget to mention that? Yep. I fell into bed with my boss. Now, for my best friend Teagan, falling into bed with the boss turned out great. Her sexier than hell boyfriend was her boss and totally smitten with her. My boss, on the other hand, was married to the owner's daughter. I know. I know. It's not a good look. I'm not a homewrecker. I promise. This minor slip was a combination of tequila shots and a celebration high. With what little I can remember, the sex was best lost to the hangover headache. There was a lot of fumbling, drooling, and a peen that was of the itty-bitty variety.

Don't get me wrong, size really doesn't matter to me. My friends call me a cockaholic for a reason. If you know how to use what you were given and use it right, then I will ride it all night long. Unfortunately, my boss, Stan, had no clue what he was doing. I can't even remember feeling it go in. The blurry memories make me cringe as I'm tiptoeing through the apartment.

As I made my way through, I noticed things I didn't last night. There was a giant fish tank that had sharks in it. The blue glow of the tank made those fuckers look evil as shit. A shiver slid down my spine. I needed to get the hell away from those things before they decided they needed to break the glass and kill me. Picking up my pace, I saw pictures of sharks and mean-ass fish everywhere. What the hell was Stan into? Well, besides the whole cheating on his wife with his employee thing.

A frightening picture of a great white shark made me freeze. Panic took hold of my body. Did I forget to mention I am deathly afraid of all sharks? My mind was spinning with my fear. Before I could fall onto the floor into a fetal position, a bang alerted me that there was action in the back. And it was definitely the kind I didn't want to encounter.

Forcing myself to ignore the horrors on the walls, I managed to get to the door. More noises floated from the back of the apartment. I yanked on the door. It didn't budge. Of course, it wouldn't open, it was locked. Turning the lock as quiet as possible, I pulled on the door. It swung free, effectively slipping from my grasp and hitting the wall.

"Ember?" Stan's voice was distant but way too close for comfort.

I literally jumped out the door and slammed it behind me, then took a few deep breaths while I leaned against it. A moment later, I heard a crash behind the door. It sounded like one of the horrible shark pictures fell. At least I knew then that he wouldn't be chasing after me. He was going to be busy cleaning up broken shark.

"Ember?" A deep voice drew my attention from the door facing Stan's apartment.

"Bucky?"

Bucky, aka Robbie Thomason, aka the sexiest guy with whom I haven't had sex. I raked my gaze over him. His clothes were disheveled, and he had a bit of lipstick smudged near his mouth. His man bun was gone. Wavy hair framed his face in that just had sex look that men can pull off. When women try it, they end up looking like they have a bird's nest on top of their heads. Damn if he didn't make my panties melt standing there with a dimpled grin. As I stared at him, realization hit. He was doing a walk of shame as well. Blushing, I looked down at my bare feet.

"Whatcha doin?" He nodded toward Stan's apartment.

"Uhm...nothing."

He chuckled. "Yeah. I'm doing the same nothing."

"I have no idea what you're implying, Bucky." I crossed my arms, standing straighter.

"What's that?" He walked toward me.

"What?" I spun around, expecting to see Stan standing in his doorway. Instead, Bucky snatched my polka dot panties out of my hand. I blushed. They were a pair of my laundry day panties with a few very unsexy holes in them.

"Hey! Give those back," I whisper/yelled while trying to grab them, but he held them away from me.

"Well, well, well. Are you doing the walk of shame?" He examined my panties as if they were some ancient artifact. Then asked, "And are these laundry day panties? I've heard of these but have never seen any in the wild."

"All right, jackass. Give them back."

"Don't worry. I think they're cute. I'm wearing my laundry underwear too." He pulled down his jeans slightly, showing part of that sexy V. You know that weird muscle that makes women lose their common sense.

"Uhm...I didn't see any underwear," I mumbled the words, I think.

He smirked, then said quietly, "That's because there aren't any."

I sucked in air, then began choking as I drew my eyes to his crotch. Grimacing, I began breathing again without help from Mr. Too-Sexy-For-His-Own-Good.

A noise behind Stan's door made me slam myself against the wall next to it. Bucky looked at the door, then back at me. "I'm guessing you don't want what's behind door number one." His voice echoed through the hallway.

"Shh. Keep it down." I kept my back to the wall and began sliding down the hallway in a weird crouch.

He laughed. "This is great to watch, but I need to get home and change before meeting Xander. I already called for an Uber. Wanna share?"

Mid crouch/slide combo, I stopped and looked at him. "You already have a ride coming."

"Of course. I set that up last night before I hit the sheets with..." Bucky looked up at the ceiling. "Donna?"

I lifted an eyebrow. "Are you asking or telling me?"

He shrugged, then strode down the small hallway to the stairs. When he was a few steps in front of me, he turned and then said, "You coming?" He twirled my panties on his finger.

Dammit!

I sprang off the wall, trying to catch him. He easily dodged me, then ran. It was oh dark thirty, and he was running while laughing like a crazy person. Out of principle, I don't run. It had nothing to do with the fact that the only curls I do have cheese on them. Huffing out a frustrated grunt, I followed his loud guffaws down the stairs. What an idiot!

When I finally caught up to him, he was waiting for me and holding the building's door with a stupid grin. I was panting like I was about to die and a distinct odor was pouring off of me. It was sweaty tequila. I bent over, placing my hands on my knees, trying to catch my breath.

"You all right?" He let go of the door, then stood too close to me. It was distracting me from that whole breathing thing that was necessary.

"I'm...fine," I said between breaths.

"Shit, Ember. It was only two flights."

"Fuck off. I don't like to run. I like to run even less when I had too many tequila shots the night before."

"Still...we should work on your running. I can set up a time to coach you."

I looked at him like he'd just morphed into a three-headed monster. "Just because I chased you to get my panties doesn't mean I want to run a fucking marathon. Apparently, your brain is still on an O-high."

A small matchbox-like car pulled up and honked. Bucky waved at the driver. "Ride's here. Ready?"

Was I ready? Fuck yes. I needed to get home, wash the funk off, then take a tight fifteen-hour nap. "Yes, I'm ready."

"Good." He put his hand on my lower back as he guided me to the car. I could have sworn he was rubbing the top of my ass with his pinky, but when I shot him a look, he was looking at the car. Great. I was hallucinating.

I slid into the backseat of the world's tiniest car. The driver glared at me. His seat was pushed all the way back. If he leaned back, I would have been able to do his dental work. The seat spread my legs as Bucky got in next to me. He had much more room. His side looked almost luxurious. I gave him a glare as the car pulled away.

He smirked as he watched the city pass by.

"Why are you smirking?" I asked.

His hazel eyes sparked when he turned toward me. "No reason. I'll take you home from my house. Unlike you, I'm not hungover."

A growl escaped me. He was so fucking annoying when he was being sweet. My mean as a snake glare did nothing to wipe the grin that curled his lips. While squinting my death lasers at him, my reflection in the car window drew my attention. Thanks to the stupid driver having his seat pushed back, my dress had been forced almost to my hips. Bucky and the driver were getting the coveted gyno view. I slapped my hands over my almost exposed who-ha.

Bucky's laugh echoed through the car as it came to a halt.

"We're here." Bucky reached into his pocket to retrieve his wallet. After handing the driver a few bills, he stepped out of the car, then held out his hand to assist me. I placed my hand in his and let him yank me out of the clown car. As the car belched me out, I flew into his hard muscled chest.

Must not react. Must not. React. Must. Not. React.

"Damn you're hard." What the fuck just came out of my stupid mouth?

"Well, not completely, but give me a few minutes and I'll be able to hammer nails." His eyes sparkled with mischief.

Jackass.

I stepped away from him. Blinking the sun out of my eyes, I looked around the area. My brain was confused. I thought he said he was taking me to his apartment.

"I thought you were taking me to your place."

He had a confused look on his face, then looked around. "I did. We're here. This is my building." Bucky waved toward the ten-story apartment building. My apartment building.

"You can't live here." I shook my head.

"Uh...I do. What's the matter?"

"What floor are you on?"

"The fourth. Why?"

I let out a breath I hadn't realized I was holding. "Good."

"Good? Lucky number or something?" He laughed.

"No. I'm on the ninth floor."

Bucky looked at the building, then back at me. "Are you fucking with me right now?"

"Nope."

"How have I not seen you?"

I shrugged. "No clue. I'm just happy three floors separate us."

"Why is that a good thing?"

Fuck me and my big mouth. "No reason. Well, thanks for the ride. See ya later." I walked past him toward the building.

"I'll make sure I see you now, Ember," I heard him call after me.

I hurried through the lobby. Luck was finally on my side. The elevator door opened the minute I pressed the button. Leaning against the wall, I took a deep breath. It didn't take long to reach my floor. As the doors opened, I jumped out of the elevator, then marched quickly down the hallway.

In my apartment, I dropped my shoes by the door and my purse on my couch. I quickly cleaned up in my bathroom and put on comfortable pajamas. As I was pulling on my shorts, my lack of underwear was like a slap in the face. That asshat still had them.

Fuck my life. I really liked those panties.

1

A FUCKING WEASEL

"Repeat that."

Stan cleared his throat and looked down at his desk. "You're fired, Ember."

"That's what I thought you said. Why the fuck am I fired? I'm the best damn personal organizer you have on staff. In fact, I just landed that huge account." My barely contained rage was boiling over.

"I'll be handling that account." I heard a deep female voice from behind me.

I turned to find Eve Lane, Stan's wife, leaning against the door.

"Hello, Eve. It's good to see you," I said through gritted teeth.

"I'd say the same, Ember, but I don't give pleasantries to sluts who sleep with my husband," she said as she walked over to stand next to Stan.

The breath left me in a whoosh. Looking down, I expected the floor to open up and swallow me whole. Instead, I just stood there staring at the floor like an idiot.

"I see you have nothing to say for yourself." Eve placed her hand on Stan's shoulder. "You see, Ember, we don't allow people to climb up the ranks of this company by sleeping their way to the top, then blackmailing their bosses."

I blinked at her. What the fuck was she talking about? "Eve, that wasn't the case at all. It was a mistake, I admit. We had a bit too much to drink then—"

Eve cut me off. "I don't want to hear your excuses. Stan and I discussed it and he told me how you were blackmailing him to get the best clients. You threatened to out your affair with him if you didn't get them. Well, that stops here. You're out. While you've been in here, I had someone from human resources pack up your office. Security will escort you out."

"Is this fucking for real right now?" My laser focus was on that fucker Stan. Not only was he a horrible lay with a tiny peen, but he had no qualms in destroying my career by lying.

"This is very real. Now, please leave without a scene." Eve nodded to someone over my shoulder.

Bobby, our security guard, gave me an apologetic look. "Come on, Ember."

I ground my teeth. The little angel on my shoulder patted my back and said, "Be the better person. You may need to use them as a reference." The devil on my other shoulder said, "Shank the bitch. If not, then give her some much needed advice about her husband."

Taking two steps, I resigned myself to listen to the angel for once. Unfortunately, I saw Eve rubbing Stan's shoulder sympathetically in the window's reflection. The devil took hold. Spinning, I looked right at the two of them. "You know, Eve, I truly feel bad for you. Not only do you have to be married to a sniveling, lying weasel like Stan, but he was so impressed when I straddled him, he came embarrassingly quick. He mentioned something about you laying so still it was like fucking a corpse. No wonder he looked elsewhere. You may want to add a few or at least one more trick in bed other than the corpse pose. Stan and his tiny tool will end up looking elsewhere again. But don't you worry, he won't find a better lay than me, so you're safe there." I tossed my long hair over my shoulder and marched past Bobby, who stifled a laugh with a cough. I think I heard my little angel slap her head in exasperation while the devil held up his hand in a high five.

Without looking back, Bobby and I walked to the bank of elevators. Each step felt like a weight pressing down on me. What the hell was I supposed to do now? I was at the top of my game. Professional organizers were all the rage, and I was one of the best in town. Strike that. Not one of the best. I was *the* best in town. People loved my tough as nails, tell it like it is approach. After that scene, Eve was probably on the phone trashing my reputation to anyone who would listen.

"Here you go." Bobby held out a tissue after the elevator doors closed in front of us.

"What's this for?"

He gave me a confused look. "You're crying, sweetheart."

I touched my cheeks and was surprised to feel they were wet. Fuck me. I let them see me cry. I wanted to kick my ass.

With a dab, I said, "Thanks, Bobby. Always looking out for a girl who makes it a habit of making a fool out of herself." My voice came out too watery for my liking.

Bobby put his arm around my shoulders. "Not every girl. Just you, Ember. Sure gonna miss you around here. You always made my lunch break with your crazy tales. Drea is going to miss them too."

I smiled at him. "Well, I can always email your wife my tales so she doesn't miss out. Though they may be cut quite a bit with my lack of income now."

The elevator doors opened to the lobby. Immediately, I noticed the box setting on the security desk. Reality crashed down on me. When we got to the desk, I reached for the box. All I wanted to do was run out of there. It was beginning to feel as if my seams were about to burst. I wasn't about to let anyone see that. My luck they'd have it on tape and watch it over and over while having a good laugh.

Bobby stopped me from escaping with my career in a box. "Wait a second, Ember." I looked into his sad eyes. "Are you going to be okay?"

"Of course, Bobby. I'm just like a cat." My smile was so tight it hurt.

He raised an eyebrow. "What?"

Huffing out a laugh, I said, "I'm a pussy that lands on her feet."

Bobby shook his head with a smile. "I believe you will. But if you need anything, you call me. Drea and I will help." He pulled me into a hug.

I tensed. Hugging was not the thing I needed at that moment. My emotions were bursting out of my eyes involuntarily. When Bobby rubbed my back in a soothing motion, an ugly water breath escaped. Bobby pulled back, looked at my face, and grimaced.

"Sorry, Ember. I know you don't like affection, but I had to. It was from me and Drea." He stepped away, giving me space.

I waved my hand. "I'm gonna miss you the most." Finally, grabbing the box that I fully planned on burning later, I continued, "Well, I'll see you around."

Turning on my heel, I left the building. With each step away, my resolve wavered. Somehow, my legs got me to my car. I set the box on the passenger seat and secured it with the seatbelt. Thoughts spiraled around in my brain. I stared out the windshield at the concrete wall of the parking garage. What the hell was I going to do? My head dipped, hitting my forehead against the horn, making it beep.

After about ten minutes of blubbering into my steering wheel, I dug my keys from my purse. Inhaling deeply, I turned the car on. A small voice in the back of my head wondered if the vengeful bitch, Eve, planted a bomb in my car. When it turned on with no incident, I was weirdly disappointed. It was time to move on. I backed out and made my way through the parking garage and into the scary world that contained my unknown future. On that thought, my damn eyes sprang a leak again. Fucking emotions.

"That was it? They fired you because of your asshole boss?" Olivia asked.

"Yep. Granted, I was probably an asshole for sleeping with him."

"I will not dispute that, but it's not a fireable offense. Maybe I should do an in-depth exposé about Coordinator Lanes." Olivia paused, then continued, "That's still a stupid fucking name. It sounds like a lame bowling alley."

I laughed as I pulled into my apartment building's parking lot. "Thanks for the offer, but I'm not sure I want to be a subject in one of your stories. It's not really my thing."

Olivia snorted through the Bluetooth in the car. Recently, one of my other best friends, Teagan, was thrust into the limelight thanks to a story Olivia wrote about her. Well, she only had to write that story because Teagan and I got drunk and put a wildly inappropriate dating profile on a dating website. I would never own up to that, though.

"Teagan didn't want to be in the paper either. That was partially your fault. I just saved both of your—"

"Skrrr...Skrrr...oh goodness me...Olivia, you're cutting out. I'll have to call you later." I made unconvincing static noise.

"Jesus you're a horrible—"

I hit *end* on the call. Shoving my phone in my purse, I grabbed a permanent marker from my office in a box and wrote "*Stan the asshole has a tiny peen.*" It made me feel better to graffiti the box with some truths even if it didn't matter anymore.

I started toward the building when I noticed someone sitting on a bench outside of it. They were reading a newspaper. Who the hell did that anymore? I squinted through the leaves of my plant sticking out of the box. When the mystery reader turned the page, I froze. Son of a bitch. It was Bucky.

"Fuck me," I mumbled.

Just a day ago, I didn't even know he lived in my building. Now, I fucking see him every time I turn a corner. The last thing I needed was his sexy ass asking questions. My emotions were so high that I wasn't sure if I'd punch him or kiss him just for asking about my day. I was leaning toward the violence, but it was too close to call. Therefore, he didn't need to see me. Hefting the box higher, I covered my face with it while striding toward the door.

My determination not to let him see me was so focused that I didn't pay attention to where or how fast I was going. This need for invisibility made me miss the door and run into the wall of windows flanking the door. Bouncing off the wall, I lost my balance and landed on my butt only a few feet from the bench he was sitting on.

"Hey, Ember! Looks like you're falling head over heels for me." He laughed at his own dumb joke.

I rolled my eyes, then started picking up the scattered contents of the box.

"What do you have there?" Bucky picked up the box.

"Put that down!" I yelled.

He looked down at me, then at the box in his hand. A grin curved his lips. "Did you get fired?"

Snatching the box out of his hand, I scooped up the rest of the contents and put them in the box. I moved to stand and felt a hand on my elbow. Once upright, I yanked my arm out of his grasp.

"What gave you that clue, Captain Obvious?" I moved toward the door, but the box being yanked out of my grasp stopped me.

"I'll carry this for you." He smiled.

I squinted my eyes at him. Willing lasers to shoot out and incinerate him. When it didn't work, I huffed out a breath. When a girl needed superpowers, they wouldn't manifest. I grabbed the box, trying to pull it out of his grasp. He held tight.

"Give me the box, Bucky," I gritted out.

"Come on. Let me help you," he pleaded.

"I've had enough men 'helping' me for one day. Plus, I have the sneaking suspicion you just want to know where I live so you can move to sitting in front of my door with your newspaper. Who reads newspapers nowadays anyway?" He went to answer, but I held up my hand. "Scratch that. I don't care. I'm going. Don't follow me."

He let go of the box and took two steps away from me. Feeling triumphant in something, I moved toward the door. Stopping, I realized that because of the box, I couldn't open the door. As I was about to put the box down, the door swung open. Bucky stood there with a grin. He bowed, then motioned for me to enter.

Damn him for being sweet. The little angel said, "It was very nice of him. Maybe you should invite him up for some coffee." The devil countered with, "It was very nice. Maybe you should invite him up for some bedroom gymnastics."

"Shut up, both of you," I mumbled under my breath as I walked to the elevator. Glancing over my shoulder, I saw Bucky watching me from outside the building. He gave me a crooked grin and waved to me with his fingers. Spinning around, I stared at the elevators, effectively ignoring the sexy man checking out my ass.

The devil's voice echoed through my mind. I effectively shut that down. It was not the time for sex. That's how I'd gotten into the mess my life was in. Oh, but it would probably be a fun ride. Shaking that thought out of my head, I stepped onto the open elevator, successfully removing the sexy distraction that was still checking me out and waving my laundry panties in his hand.

Bucky was a dead man.

2

Goodbye Cockaholic

The noise in Midnight Sun was drowning out my thoughts. I took a sip of my water. Teagan, Olivia, and Nomi stared at me. They'd been sitting like that for the last ten minutes. I was feeling like a bug under a microscope. Nomi's sister, Nora, finally broke the weird silence.

"Why are the four of you so quiet? In all the years I've known you, I've never seen the four of you acting as if you're in a library. Even when you were in a library, you weren't quiet." Nora leaned against our table.

"Ember got fired a few days ago." Nomi took a drink while continuing to stare.

"Oh, yeah?" Nora looked at me and then continued, "That doesn't explain why you are all staring."

"She isn't drinking. She hasn't said one snarky remark. It's creeping us out. She is acting soooo..." Teagan looked at the ceiling while searching for an answer.

"Normal," Olivia said helpfully.

Teagan snapped her fingers. "That's the word. Normal."

Nora looked at them and then glanced back at me. She did this a few times, then said, "Yeah. Something is definitely wrong. I noticed she didn't even shake her tits at my new bartender."

I rolled my eyes. "Seriously? I don't need to shake my tits at every guy I see."

The four of them froze. Nomi had her glass halfway to her mouth, blinked a few times, then set the glass down. "Are you kidding us right now? That is the one thing we can count on. You're a cockaholic. We know this. We also know something is wrong when you aren't going after some strange sex."

I stared at the condensation on my glass of water. Using my finger, I drew designs through the droplets. Shrugging, I pulled my gaze from the glass to meet theirs. "I'm just not feeling like myself. Can you blame me? I did just get fired after all."

"Uh-huh. I think there's—" Teagan was cut off when two familiar faces walked up to our table.

"Hello, beautiful ladies." Bucky grinned at me.

"Hey, Bucky. Xander." Nomi smiled at the two incredibly handsome men.

"Hey, Olivia." Xander's gaze bore into Olivia.

I watched as she gave him a small wave while keeping her eyes on her phone. Xander deflated a bit. I felt bad for the guy. He had it bad for her and she was being pretty harsh. I knew I was a ball-buster and said whatever I wanted without a care about the person's feelings. What Olivia was doing was different.

"What brings you two to Midnight Sun?" Nora asked. She'd popped out her hip in a pose that had most men drooling.

"Well, we had heard this was the place to be after a long day." Bucky's gaze didn't leave mine.

He was so damn annoying. Couldn't the guy take a hint?

"It is. There are a lot of single ladies around here. I'm sure you'll have a good time." Nora smirked as she took notice of where his attention was focused.

"It was nice seeing you, Bucky." My voice carried over the white noise of the bar. Tables around us had stopped talking and stared at our little group.

His damn smile promised things I didn't want to learn first-hand. I blanched at that thought. When was the last time I didn't want to know how a man performed in the sack? As I thought about it, I couldn't come up with anything. Even when I was stealing kisses in kindergarten, I was curious. I just didn't know what that meant. Who was I kidding? I wanted to know what he was like in the sack, but there was a part of me that presses the pause button whenever he's around. If he ever discovered what apartment I was in, I wouldn't have the power to resist him.

"It was good seeing you, ladies." He winked at me, then dragged Xander away from the table.

"What's going on there?" Nora asked.

"Another one of Ember's hook-ups." Olivia stared down at her phone.

"No!" My voice was so shrill everyone winced.

"Come on, Ember. We saw how you and Bucky were at Grams and Vernon's wedding." Teagan crossed her arms.

"Plus, when was the last time you turned down a guy who looks like that?" Nomi pointed toward Bucky, who stood with his back to the bar and stared directly at our table.

I banged my fists on the table. "I did *not* fuck him." My voice was a bit too loud and the surrounding tables quieted. With a glance, I saw Bucky's smug smile grow wider. Fucker.

Olivia put her hands up. "All right, Ember. You can't blame us for being surprised."

"She's right. Even I'm surprised and I'm not really in your group of friends." Nora tapped the table. "Welp, gotta go check on the kitchen. As usual, let me know if there is a problem. I'll see you tomorrow at Mom's for dinner?" she asked Nomi.

"I don't know. I've got a big case coming up." Nomi looked down at her half full glass of wine.

"That's the third Sunday now." Nora prodded.

Nomi shrugged. Nora waited a moment, then shook her head in frustration. She walked away, shaking her head.

"What's that all about?" Teagan asked.

"Nothing. Weren't we talking about Ember and why she's acting so weird?" Nomi deflected.

"That was weak. I thought you were a high-powered attorney. You couldn't change the subject any better than that?" I clicked my tongue at her.

A flash lit up Nomi's eyes. Oh shit! I just fucked myself without even getting dinner.

"All right, Ember, why did you get fired? You had just told us all that you landed that huge client. What happened?"

I'd been under Nomi's lawyer scrutiny before. It sucked every time. She always made me feel like I got caught smoking in the bathroom, then sent to the principal's office. To bide my time, I took a long sip of my water.

"Quit stalling and spill it," Olivia said with her nose in her phone.

"You already know most of it." Olivia shrugged and made a 'get on with it' motion with her hand. "Fine. I slept with my boss after too many tequila shots."

"Okay. That happens." Teagan grinned.

I rolled my eyes. "Yeah, well, my boss is married to the company's owner's daughter. The schmuck told her or she found out. How she knew doesn't matter, but he told her some lame excuse and blamed me for the whole thing."

"Your boss was hot too?" Teagan asked.

"Hell no. That was one hundred percent tequila-induced madness."

"Ooo...that is not a good look." Nomi shook her head.

"Thanks, Nomi. I didn't know that." I snapped and then made the mistake of looking at Bucky and I wanted to punch his smirking face.

"Okay...well there are other places you can go, right? I mean, you're one of the most sought after professional organizers in the city."

With a shrug, I said, "I don't know. I have a few contacts at other companies. There are a few options. I've just been taking the last couple of days to wallow and languish in the pity party I was throwing. Tomorrow, I pull the big girl panties up and go on the hunt."

"That sounds like you on a Friday night, not job hunting." Teagan snorted.

"That's the other thing. If my need to have a taste of any hot guy was under control, then maybe I wouldn't have lost my job. I need to grow up and get my shit together."

The three faces of my friends stared at me slack-jawed. Well, I knew what they thought of me. Along with a new job, maybe I should find new friends too.

"Are you serious? You're giving up your cockaholic ways?" Teagan's eyebrows were so high they almost met her hairline.

"Yeah, Teag."

"How do you plan on doing it? It's like an alcoholic giving up alcohol. You gonna do a twelve-step program?" Nomi asked.

I shrugged. "I'm sure I can cut cold turkey."

All three of them snorted.

"That's not gonna happen," Olivia said.

"Thanks for the vote of confidence."

"Seriously, Ember. It will not be that easy." Teagan tapped my hand.

"Okay. So, what do you propose then?"

"We could always do something like we did for Teagan," Olivia offered.

"Hell no. I will not be in the damn paper. Plus, I don't think a dating profile would help with my problem."

"Hmm...I think we should think about it for a bit. In a week, we meet right back here and devise a plan to reform our friend the cockaholic." Nomi smiled.

I took in a deep breath. The brain trust that was Teagan, Olivia, and Nomi nodded. I was so screwed.

"Well, on that note, I am outta here. Gotta get up early to start the job hunting." I hip checked Olivia to get her to move out of the booth.

As I slid out, I glanced toward the bar and noticed Bucky had left. I took a deep breath, thankful for small favors. If I was lucky, he found someone else to sniff around. I looked at my friends, who had worried looks on their faces.

"What?"

"You sure you're okay?" Nomi asked.

I plastered the brightest smile I could muster on my face. "Of course. You know me. I'll be fine. See you guys next week."

The minute I turned away from the table, my smile was wiped off my face. Of course, I wasn't okay. I had no job, practically no savings, an apartment I wasn't sure I'd be able to afford after the month was over and the company car I knew was going away soon. I was so far from okay, I'd need to take a space shuttle to even be close to okay.

My worries consumed my mind so much that when I left Midnight Sun, I didn't notice I had a shadow. The crunch of gravel behind me brought me back to the present. I pulled the keys out of my pocket, making sure my car key was between my middle and ring finger. I wouldn't hesitate to do some eye gouging if necessary. The footsteps grew closer. As I approached my car, I spun on the intruder, holding my key like a weapon.

The creep halted with his hands in the air. It was Bucky.

"What the fuck, Bucky?" I breathed out while willing my heart to slow.

"I'm sorry I scared you. I wanted to make sure you got to your car okay."

I cocked an eyebrow at him. "Really?"

"Yes, really. By the way, what the hell were you going to do with your key?" He stepped closer.

"I was ready for some serious gouging action." I shot my hand out in a gouging motion.

"Scary. Is everything okay?"

"Yeah. Why?"

He shrugged. "I don't know. You seem upset."

"I'm fine. You can go back inside now." I made a shooing motion with my hand.

"Are you sure that's what you want?" He was in my personal bubble.

Involuntarily, I licked my lips. His eyes traced the movement. My lady bits stood at attention, panting for him. Stomping that feeling down with both feet, I cleared my throat and said, "Yes. I'm sure."

Damn if my voice came out wanton instead of strong. Bucky reached out and pushed a strand of hair behind my ear. Fuck me. That was the one move that usually had me melting with my legs splayed open.

No. No. No. I would resist.

"Are you sure? Because with your elevated breathing and dilated eyes, it tells me you want something more than a goodbye right now."

Damn right I did, but I needed to draw a line in the sand. I haven't slept with him and I wasn't planning on sleeping with him or any other sexy as sin guy for the foreseeable future.

"I'm sure. Good night." Opening my door, I quickly jumped in the car and slammed the door in his stupid, sexy face.

Bucky stepped away as I started the car. His smirk was still on his face. Lifting his hand, he waved as I pulled away. I almost slammed on my brakes when I saw the piece of cloth in his hand.

Son of a bitch. Why the hell was he carrying my panties around?

3

A Sunny Pines Horror

"Hey, Grams! I brought your...ahhh!" I turned my back immediately when I entered Teagan's grandmother's room in Sunny Pines.

"Oh, Ember, dear. Come on in. Don't mind Vernon. He's just playing around down there." Grams said matter-of-factly.

"Uhm...I don't know," I mumbled.

The view of walking in and seeing Vernon going down on Grams would cause night terrors forever. It was definitely something I could have lived my whole life without witnessing. I would share this horror with Teagan the moment I left the retirement home.

A slapping sound was heard. "Vernon, you've embarrassed Ember. Get out from there. It's already the third time today."

Third time! Damn. Vernon was a stud. The rustling of the sheets made me close my eyes tighter to banish the horrible images invading my brain.

"We're all clear, Ember," Grams said.

Hesitantly, I turned and got an eyeful of saggy old man ass. I spun back around. Vernon's laugh floated away as he walked toward the bathroom. A shiver rolled through me. Yet another image that would haunt my dreams.

Grams tapped the bed and then said, "Come sit. I promise these are clean sheets."

Turning toward her, I gave her a doubtful look, then shrugged and walked over. "I'd ask how you are, but you seem to be enjoying yourself."

"I love my Vernon. He is an insatiable animal, though." Grams covered my hand with hers. "How are you doing, sweetheart? Teagan told me about losing your job."

Sighing, I placed the plate of cookies on the bed. "Grams, I don't know. I tried to put on a brave face for the girls, but honestly, I don't know what I'm going to do. I've called all my contacts and apparently my previous employer has effectively blacklisted me. It will be a long time until I get a job as an organizer again in this town."

"Is there anything else you'd want to do? My Vernon has connections."

"I've done nothing else, and I feel like I'm getting to the age where they don't want someone like me." I shrugged.

"Oh pish. You are still a young chicken. Where is the Ember that wouldn't let anything get her down? That confident, ball-busting girl who came into our lives like a whirlwind."

"That girl is forty with no job, an apartment she can't afford, and a car that will get repossessed any day now."

"I can help you, hun." Vernon stood at the end of the bed, thankfully wearing a robe.

"I appreciate the offer, but I'm sure something will come up."

"All right, dear. I still have my fingers in a lot of pies. You just say the word and I will be on the phone." He took a cookie and then said to Grams, "I'm going to catch a game of pinnacle." He kissed her with a bit too much tongue for their age, but they both smiled as he left the room.

"Marriage looks good on you, Grams." I squeezed her hand with mine.

"He makes me happy. I'd like to see all you girls find that happiness."

I rolled my eyes. "Grams, a man is the last thing I need right now. That's how I got in this mess," I mumbled the last part.

"I know. Teagan told me about the married boss. Definitely not a good choice, sweetheart." Grams gave me a sad smile.

"Yeah, I should have known tequila was a bad idea. Oh well, I've cut men out of my life altogether. They are nothing but bad news."

"I don't know about that. Whatever happened to that boy you brought to my wedding? He's Edna's grandson, right?"

Inhaling a deep breath, I said, "He's not a good idea, Grams. Believe me."

Grams shrugged while grabbing a cookie. "I wouldn't discount him completely, Ember. That boy was clearly half in love with you then. It was adorable."

I stared at her, speechless. "Bucky?"

She grimaced at his name. "I can't imagine any mother naming their child that."

"If I remember correctly, that was all Edna's doing. His real name is Robbie."

"Oh, that's right. I'm still not great with names. Anyway, you should give him a chance."

Oh boy. It was a conversation I'd had with Teagan's grandmother since we were in high school. She never liked that I was open to something physical with no commitment. When I'd met Teagan and her grandmother, it was after I'd lost my grandmother and my mother left. Grams stepped in when I was at my lowest. She saw past the false bravado that I wore like armor.

"Okay, Grams. I'll think about it. Well, I better get going so you can go hang out with your crew of delinquents." I dodge a swat from her.

"Oh you. You're lucky I love you."

"Love you too, Grams." I leaned over and gave her a hug. "I'll be back again soon. Hopefully, with some good news."

"Good news, bad news, it doesn't matter. Your visit doesn't require any of it. I just like seeing your face."

A lump formed in my throat as I choked down tears. Damn Grams and her making me feel feelings. I hugged her tight one last time. Sniffling back some tears, I gave a little wave and then left the room.

When I ran into something, I was rubbing the tears off my cheeks. I blinked up with blurry vision and said, "I'm sorry. I didn't see you."

"That's all right, Ember. You can rub up against me anytime."

I jumped back. "Bucky?"

He sighed heavily. "Yep."

"What the hell are you doing here? Are you stalking me?" I whipped out my phone, ready to call the cops.

Bucky put his hands up. "Whoa. Whoa. Whoa. I'm not stalking you, Ember. I was here to see my granny. They called me about her."

I glared at him menacingly, but it must not have looked that way because he laughed. That just pissed me off more, but I felt I needed to be the bigger person. So, I suppressed the little voice telling me to throat punch him and instead asked, "Is everything okay with Edna?"

He ran his hands through his hair. "She's fine. They called because if she doesn't start acting right, then she's going to get kicked out."

"Kicked out? What the hell did she do?"

"Apparently, she likes one of the new orderlies. Whenever he's on duty, she fakes a fall, then when he helps her up, she gropes him."

A giggle escaped me. When he gave me a look, I bit my lip to stop from outright laughing in his face. These old folks were crazy.

"The guy is so fed up he's ready to file charges. If he does that, then she's gone. That means she'd be living with me and that can never happen. I love my granny but living with her on a day-to-day basis would kill one of us. And I'm too young to die."

The laugh I was holding in burst out.

"I'm glad you find this funny," he said flatly.

That made me laugh even harder. I had to bend over to catch my breath. When I finally pulled myself together, I stood. But one look at his face made me laugh all over again. I didn't know if it really was his face making me laugh, the situation or all the crap in my life finally making me lose my mind, but it took a good five minutes for me to finally pull myself together.

"Better?" He stood with his arms crossed.

I wiped an errant tear away and gulped in a deep breath. "Yep. I'm good."

"Anyway, I had to have a talk with Granny about her handsy ways. I advised her to keep it to willing elderly participants."

"Good advice. Well, I need to go," and I moved past him.

"I'll walk with you since I've had my scolding session with Granny already."

My strength to fight him off had drained away with my laughter fit. I just shrugged while walking faster than normal.

"So why are you here? Does your grandmother live here?"

"Nope. She's dead."

"Shit. I'm sorry."

"No problem. I'm past it. It's been over twenty-six years. I come here to visit Teagan's grandmother."

"Oh gotcha."

Silence slowly built around us like a bubble. It surprised me with how comfortable it was to be silent with Bucky. We walked together in that silence until we were blinded by the sun as we exited the building. Dots floated in my vision as I walked toward where I thought my car was parked. When they disappeared, I was pleased to see I was standing in front of my vehicle. My subconscious was a badass bitch.

"This is me. Thanks for walking with me."

He nodded while rocking on his heels. "Can I ask you something?"

Dread knotted in my stomach. "I guess."

"Wanna go out on Saturday?"

My lady parts perked up at the prospect of a date and hot, sweaty sex. Well, I couldn't guarantee the hot and sweaty part but definitely the sex. Who was I kidding? It would definitely be hot and sweaty with Bucky. Yes, was on the tip of my tongue, but when I looked at my car, I was reminded why sex with anyone at this point in my life was a bad idea.

"I can't," I answered to his sculpted chest. Had his shirt been that tight the whole time I'd been talking with him?

"Oh. If Saturday doesn't work, we can do—"

"Look, I'm not looking to date anyone. So, no day is good."

Bucky stared at her with a confused look. "Can I ask why?"

"No, you may not. Now, I've gotta go." I yanked open my door, then practically dove into the hot car. My eyes met Bucky's as I turned on the car. A memory flashed through my brain reminding me of something. I rolled down my window as my A/C was barely taking the edge off the sweltering heat. "I want my panties back."

Bucky grinned. "Sure. You just need to tell me which apartment is yours and I'd love to return them to you."

I let out a frustrated yell as I rolled the window back up. Throwing the car in reverse, I barely missed an elderly man wearing a robe that fluttered in the breeze. The breeze allowed me to see *all* of the old man since he wasn't wearing anything underneath.

Fuck my life.

There would be no way I was ever going to sleep again. My dreams would be filled with dancing elderly twigs and berries with the random flat old man ass thrown in for good measure.

4

From Bad to Worse

Tears streamed down my face as I watched the repo man hitch up my car. Well, maybe it wasn't the repo man since it was a company car, but it felt like it. It felt like the proverbial nail in the coffin. The tow truck driver kept glancing in my direction. He looked uncomfortable. I did not know what my face looked like, but it clearly bothered him.

"Hey! What's going on?" Bucky's voice carried through the parking lot.

Why was my life being targeted by karma? There was no way karma wasn't a woman riding the red dragon. That bitch.

"Everywhere I turn you're there. For fuck's sake, Bucky, can't you let a girl get humiliated without showing up to watch?" I angrily wiped the tears out of my eyes.

"Sorry. I was on my way out." He stood next to me quietly, and we watched the repo man finish up. "Are you okay?"

"Just peachy." I gave him a fake toothy smile.

"Damn. That's frightening." He grimaced at my face.

"If you don't like it, you are more than welcome to move on."

I watched silently as the tow truck pulled my only mode of transportation left. The weight of the world pushed down on my shoulders. It was too much. Just as I was losing my battle of holding things together, powerful arms encircled me. I crumpled into the embrace. Ugly crying was never my thing. I was never one of those girls whose emotions were on display. In that instance, over a stupid car, I lost it. Sobs racked my frame until I was completely spent. I stood in the powerful embrace until all the emotion was wrung out of me.

"Feel better?" Bucky's voice soothed like the hand that was rubbing my back.

"Yeah." I sniffled and looked into his eyes. An emotion I didn't want to define lingered there.

Pulling away to put space between us felt important. For good measure, I crossed my arms as well.

"What happened to your car?" He nodded toward the empty spot.

I gave him a strained smile, then said, "Thanks for the comfort. I'm sure I will see you around. You've been like a bad rash lately."

His deep laugh sent chills down my spine. My brain forced my legs to move away from him. That damn laugh followed me all the way to the doors of the apartment building.

"Hey, Ember!" Bucky yelled from the spot where he remained.

I turned with my hand on the door, holding it open for one tenant that was too busy on his phone to realize someone was holding the door for him. That little devil on my shoulder wondered what would happen if I'd let go of the door. The angel pushed the devil off my shoulder and just shook his head.

"Yeah," I yelled back, startling the texter who looked around in wonder.

"When do you want me to give you these back?" Bucky pulled out my panties and twirled them on his finger.

The texter looked at Bucky, holding my panties, and then at me. I felt my face flame.

"Mind your business," I snapped at the gawker, then yelled to Bucky. "Keep them. I have other laundry day panties." Not waiting to hear his retort, I escaped into the building while fury built in my veins.

Bang. Bang. Bang.

I blinked around at my surroundings. A home improvement show played on the TV. Squinting at the time, I saw it was almost five p.m. I rolled onto my back and covered my face with one of my throw pillows. After my repo experience with Bucky as a witness, I came back to my apartment, determined to find a new job. Unfortunately, there were a lot of cute dog and cat videos that were much more important for me to watch than to look for a new job. Once the videos ran out, I felt the need to binge home improvement shows to get ideas for a home I was probably never going to gain now that I was jobless.

Bang. Bang. Bang.

Lifting the pillow off my face, I groaned and rolled off the couch. I shuffled over to the door through the sleep haze that was still clouding all my thoughts. Opening the door a crack while keeping the chain across, I saw it was the property manager, Igor.

"Hi, Igor. Can I help you?" My voice came out funny.

Igor grimaced at me. "I heard you have no job. They have fired you."

I sighed. "Unfortunately, that is true, but I'll have something lined up shortly."

"No job. No apartment. Those are the rules." His Eastern European voice cracked like a whip.

"You will have your rent. Don't worry about it. Have I ever not paid?"

"I don't trust you. You have poor reputation." Igor squinted at her.

Rolling my eyes so hard I think I checked out my own ass, I said, "I'm sorry I offend your delicate sensibilities, but I'm just living my life."

Igor slammed his hand on the door frame. "Two months' rent by end of month or you're out."

"What? That's not right."

"Oh well. You can always find a new place." He smirked.

"Fucker," I mumbled under my breath.

"What?"

"Nothing. You'll have your money." I shut the door and leaned against it and listened to Igor's mumbled curses. Or at least I thought they were curses. I don't speak any Eastern European languages so I couldn't be sure.

I pressed my entire body against the door and waited for the ding of the elevator. When it finally came, I let out the breath I hadn't realized I'd been holding. That weight of the world feeling was back, and that bitch was heavy. I trudged over to the couch and resumed watching the home improvement show. My mind was a whirlwind of defeatist thoughts while I stared blankly at a couple trying to renovate a home. The sound of a screech owl broke through my thoughts about selling my organs for cash.

I didn't need to look at the caller ID when I picked up the phone. "Hi, Dad."

"Peanut, I've told you to call me Dennis. You are old enough now."

"And I've told you, that's weird. You may have been conned with all that hippie thinking, but not me. What's up?"

"Sherbert said he'd heard something about you losing your job."

I closed my eyes for a moment. I adored my father. He has been my rock my entire life. My mom left us for her tennis instructor when I was fourteen and I only hear from her when she feels the need to have a child in her life. Seeing as the woman was now in her sixties, it shouldn't even matter anymore. After my mother left us, we moved closer to my dad's family. That was when I met Teagan in high school. Dad worked hard his entire life, and I don't think I ever saw him on a date while I was growing up. It was only recently I'd found out he'd met someone named Starshine. I hadn't met her yet, but I just knew my father was getting pulled into a cult.

"Who's Sherbert, Dad?"

"He's Starshine's son. Apparently, he worked at one of your competing companies and it was big news." Dad paused, then said quietly, "Did you really sleep with a married man, Ember?"

I cringed. It was not a conversation I wanted to have with my father. "Dad, I really don't want to talk to you about this."

"All right. I understand. I'm just worried about you. Do you need money?"

Yes. Yes, I did. Was I going to say that to my father? Hell no.

"I'm good. I've got a lot in my savings so I can take my time looking for the best job I get offered. My landlord is even being understanding and working with me regarding rent." I smiled tightly, and though he couldn't see it, I hoped it sounded through my words.

Dad laughed. "You're a terrible bullshitter, Ember. But if you don't want to tell me the truth, that's fine. There is another reason I'm calling, though."

I relaxed against the couch. "What's up?"

"I need to send you Aunt Beatrice."

Shooting up to a standing position, I said, "What? Why?"

"Starshine and I are going on a cruise for a month. You know she can't stay here by herself."

"Can't you just set up one of those automatic feeders and waterers? That would work."

"She's not a dog, Ember. I'm sure it will be fine."

While I paced, I rubbed the bridge of my nose, trying to thwart the migraine that was speeding my way. "Come on, Dad. I won't be able to take care of her."

"Geez, Ember. It's not like she's a baby. All you have to do is make sure she's fed and takes all of her medication. And I mean all of it."

"Will I have to cut up a piece of hot dog and shove a pill into it for her?"

An exasperated sigh echoed through the phone. "As I said before, your aunt is not a dog."

"I know. I know." Falling back onto the couch, I knew I would not win. "When should I expect her?"

"We leave on the twenty-fourth."

"Of next month?"

"No," he said almost too quiet.

"Wait a minute, the twenty-fourth is Monday. Are you telling me I should expect Aunt Beat-Rice on Monday?" It was already Friday. That left me no time to prepare mentally for the eight-point earthquake that was my aunt.

"Of course not." Dad paused while I blew out a relieved breath. "She'll be there on Sunday."

Sucking in a breath a little too quickly, I choked. Who knew you could choke on air? "What?" I croaked.

"Love you, sweetie. I'll try to check in during the cruise. Have fun, Peanut."

"Dad! Dad!" I yelled into the phone and desperately said, "Dennis? You better not have hung up."

Pulling the phone from my ear, I saw the call ended. Dammit. My too clever father knew exactly what he was doing when he dropped that Beatrice news on me. Immediately, redialing only sent me directly to voicemail. Out of frustration, I yelled incoherently, and then threw my phone. I watched in horror as it bounced off the couch and rocketed toward my kitchen island, crashing into the granite countertop and falling down to the tiled floor in pieces.

I rushed over to the destroyed phone. The last thing I needed to do was buy a new phone. Taking the three pieces over to the counter above my junk drawer, I yanked out the duct tape. I was going to make the damn phone work if it was the last thing I did.

5

THE PROPOSITION

Walking into Midnight Sun, I was stunned by how empty it was. On a typical Saturday night, they would pack the place asses to elbows. If we wanted to come in on any other Saturday, we'd have to call Nora ahead of time to save us a table. I had no idea if Nomi had called her sister for this Saturday, but it appeared it wasn't necessary.

"They aren't here yet," Nora said from the hostess stand.

"What the hell is going on here?"

Nora lifted one shoulder. "There's a new bar down the street that just opened. They have an adult arcade, sports bar and restaurant."

"Shit. That's some hefty competition."

"Ehh. It'll be fine. It happens when you own a bar. It's a fad. You might as well have a seat at the bar while you wait."

"Okay. I'm sure they will see me when they come in."

Nora punched me in the arm. "Don't be flying your bitch flag in here, Ember."

"What? I wasn't being sarcastic." For once, that was true. It seemed Nora wasn't as unaffected by the empty bar as she pretended to be.

I walked quicker than normal to the bar. Nora was shooting me an identical look Nomi had. It was scary. She looked ready to kick my ass. Plopping on the stool, the bartender stopped wiping the bar down and approached me.

"Hello there! What can I get you tonight?" He smiled with really bright white teeth. It was almost too much to look at.

"A glass of Merlot."

He nodded, then went about filling the glass.

I watched him closely. He was totally my type. He styled his short-cropped hair to perfection to give him the look of having just had a woman run her hands through his hair. The white button-down shirt was tight across his muscled chest and he had the sleeves rolled up enough that I could see a bit of a tattoo on his right arm. When he placed the glass in front of me, I slid my credit card to him. My eyes trailed down his back to his tapered waist that only highlighted the perfect ass, making my mouth water. I closed my eyes, forcing myself to resist the urge to whip my tits out and entice him out back.

"Here you go, ma'am."

Fuck me. He used the m-word.

"Thanks." I took the card and shoved it in my clutch.

"Are you okay?" he asked as he went back to wiping the bar top.

"I guess."

"Is there anything I can do for you?" He batted those too pretty to be real eyes.

I took a big gulp of my wine. The devil on my shoulder was back and encouraging me to tell him exactly how, where, and with what he could help me. The angel stared slack-jawed at the gorgeous bartender, then preceded to remind me what happened the last time I sided with the devil.

Shaking my head, I took a deep breath. "As much as I'd love to take you up on your offer, I can't." I held up a hand when it looked like he was going to speak. "Don't get me wrong. You are a fucking perfect specimen and if I weren't in such a fucked-up place in my life, I'd take you out back and let you screw my brains out against the wall next to the trashcans. Unfortunately, that isn't something I need to be doing right now."

My devil slapped his forehead while the angel gave me a standing ovation.

The bartender had turned an interesting shade of red while I'd been turning him down, and I felt a bit bad. I was sure he'd never been turned down before. Giving him a reassuring tap on the hand that was on the bar top, I said, "Sorry. I'm sure you don't get turned down very often."

He looked down at the bar top. "I can honestly say that doesn't happen often. But I was referring to getting you something off the menu."

It was my turn to blush. I quickly finished my wine. "I'm sorry. I just made a fool out of myself."

He gave me a grin. "It was very flattering. My boyfriend is going to love this story. Believe me, if I were single and straight, I'd be all over you."

Boyfriend? When I thought it couldn't get worse, it did. Of course it did. I should probably bring my caution cones with the disaster my life had become. Before I could apologize again, a voice burst my bubble of embarrassment.

"I'll volunteer for that job."

I spun toward the voice. "What the fuck are you doing here?" Shaking my head, I continued, "Scratch that...I don't care. You're stalking me and now it's time to call the cops." I pulled out my duct-taped Frankenstein of a phone. The damn thing wouldn't wake up when I tapped the screen or pushed the on/off button. Somehow, with one of the taps or shakes, I got the flashlight function to turn on. The bright LED light flashed all over the bar while I hit it against the side of the bar.

"What the hell is that?" Bucky pointed to Franken-phone.

"My phone...ah ha." I rejoiced as the phone finally worked.

"I get that, but when did you run into a giant to crush it like that?"

Pulling the phone closer to me, I glared at him. "Franken-phone is fine. Especially for calling the cops on a stalker."

The phone powered down again. Dammit! "Come on, Frank. Don't make me look like an asshole," I whispered to it.

"Were you just whispering sweet nothings to your phone? I'm guessing it's got a kick-ass vibrate setting." Bucky laughed at his joke.

I rubbed my forehead. The wine was finally kicking in, but it didn't make Bucky disappear. "I will ask you again. Why are you here?"

Bucky shook his head. "Ease up, Ember. I saw the parking lot was pretty empty, so I stopped by for some dinner and a beer." A mischievous glint sparked in his eyes. "When I saw you from the hostess stand, I decided to come over. Just in time to hear you give one hell of a memorable speech. That was really award worthy."

Have I said how much my life sucked in the last ten minutes? Well, I'm going to say it again. My life sucked the big hairy one.

"Fantastic." Over Bucky's shoulder, I saw Teagan, Olivia, and Nomi walk up to Nora. "Well, it's been a slice of horrible. I'm sad I won't be able to enjoy any more of your annoying company, but my girls have finally arrived." Giving him a finger wave, I said, "Tootles."

Tootles? When the hell did that fucking word join my vocabulary? I'd wonder about that while I lay awake unable to sleep tonight. The girls waved at me. I joined them without another look at Bucky and his stupidly handsome smirk.

"Do you want him to sit with us?" Nomi asked.

"Who?" I blinked at her, making myself focus on our conversation.

"Bucky."

"No, why?"

"You haven't taken your eyes off him since we sat down," Olivia said with her face in her phone.

"How the hell would you know? You haven't even put down your phone since we sat down," I snapped.

"I've got something brewing. Gotta make sure it doesn't get snatched away from me, but I'm all yours now." She put her phone into her purse.

"Let's see how long that lasts," I mumble.

"We aren't here to talk about Olivia's love affair with her phone. We are here to discuss how we can straighten out your life." Teagan smirked.

She was fucking loving all of this. Teagan had been waiting for the moment for some payback for the mess we made of her dating life. I'll be damned if they were going to do the same to me.

"Yeah okay. So, what do you have? Who wants to go first?" I made the gimme sign with my hands.

"Well, you see, we have only one plan for you. It's more of a proposition. If you can do it, then we will go to that comic thing with you," Nomi grumbled the last part.

"You guys want to go to Comic Universal with me?" My voice was a bit too loud and drew a few stares from the surrounding people.

"Nomi didn't say we wanted to go. She said if you manage to do what we propose, then we will go," Olivia clarified.

"Dress up?" I asked.

Teagan cringed. "Yes."

"Anything I want?" Looking at them, I was already planning the perfect outfits.

"Yes," they said together.

"All right. I'm in." I smiled.

"You haven't heard our proposition yet." Teagan had a confused look on her face.

"It doesn't matter. I've got this."

Nomi smirked. "Let's give you the details before you go all in."

I sat back in my seat and crossed my arms. "Fine. Go ahead."

"First, no sex. None until the comic thing," Olivia said. "This is a no break rule."

I forced myself to keep my face neutral. "No problem." With me out of work, it would be no problem to stay away from men altogether. I wouldn't even be tempted.

"Second, you will have to do platonic activities with men or a man of your choice. It doesn't matter who, but it can't end up in sex. Ever." Teagan stared at me.

Maybe I was a little too cocky. Then an idea hit me. I could just hit up one of the oldies at Teagan's grandmother's nursing home, and I know nothing would happen there.

"Easy."

"Third, they have to be close to your age. They can't be someone's five-year-old kid or one of those horny men at Sunny Pines. Also, though I know we don't really need to mention this but they can't be married or in any other re-lationship," Nomi added.

That feeling of the weight of the world was back. Who the hell could I find to do these stupid things with, pay for them and not expect some sort of sexual gratification in return? Were there even men out there like that?

"Okay." I ground out.

"Fourth, you—"

I cut Olivia off. "How many fucking rules are there? Do you have them written down? How is all this nonsense going to change my life?"

Olivia glared at me and continued, "Fourth, you will start a diary about these interactions and how they make you feel. They don't have to be detailed, but we need to have documented proof that you did these things."

"Why don't I just fucking scrapbook about them?" I snapped.

"You can do that too." Teagan gave me a smirk.

"Wait a minute, is this diary going to be published for another exposé care of Olivia? I told you I'm not down for that. You also didn't answer how this was supposed to help my life. Doing a bunch of dumb activities with some rando will not get me a job to keep my apartment." I felt heat rise up my neck when I just realized I'd shared a bit too much. I didn't want them to know about the apartment.

"Hold on. Are you losing your apartment? We will not let that happen." Nomi smacked the table, making us all jump.

"Not exactly." I bit my lip, debating how much to share.

"Spill it, Ember. We are always here for each other no matter what. Let us help." Teagan gave my hand a squeeze.

"Fine. The fucktard that manages my apartment building found out I'd lost my job. He's demanding two months' worth of rent by the time the next one is due."

"Can he do that?" Olivia turned to Nomi.

"I highly doubt that." Nomi bit her lip. I could practically hear the gears moving. "Get me a copy of your lease. I'll handle this. Don't worry. As for how this is going to help you. Well, first of all, it is going to show you that men can be more than a penis to use and then throw away. It will also show you that you are worth more than what's between your legs."

A very unladylike snort escaped me. "I already know that."

The three of them gave each other an unreadable look. A thought hit me like a bolt of lightning. They didn't think I was worth more. Some friends they were.

"It sounds like you question what I'm worth." I bared my teeth at them like a wild animal.

"That's not..." Teagan sputtered.

Olivia just rolled her eyes, then grabbed for her phone.

Nomi had a look I couldn't identify. "You know that is bullshit. We love you. We couldn't care less if you fuck everyone and anyone. You said you wanted to straighten out your life. Sex has finally backfired on you. You need to rebuild your confidence, find kick-ass Ember, and in the process breakdown that wall around your heart. Sex has always been what you used to keep men at arm's length or further. You won't have that now. Now, it will just be you. It will work, Ember."

Tears threatened to spill. Dammit. Emotions were not a thing I wanted to have right now. I cleared my throat. "I'll try it. How long does this have to go on?"

"Until Comic Universal," Olivia said.

Three months. Ninety days. Two thousand one hundred sixty hours. One hundred twenty-nine thousand six-hundred minutes. And an ungodly number of seconds.

I swallowed. "All right, I'm game." Pausing, I forced the lump of dread in my stomach further down. "So, what happens if I lose? I mean, I don't think that will happen, but in the event it does, what are my repercussions?"

Nomi smirked. "You will have to go on a two-week cruise."

I blinked. A cruise? Hell, it would be a win-win. I smirked back, but Nomi continued, "A Sunny Pines cruise and you will bunk with Edna."

My stomach dropped. Horrible scenarios flashed through my mind. I shuddered at the thoughts.

"Are you fucking serious?"

Teagan nodded and pulled some papers. She slid them over to me. It was a paid receipt for the cruise.

"Holy shit! You already bought the ticket? You're betting I'm going to fail?"

Teagan took the paper back and shoved it into her purse. "Not at all. It's refundable, but we knew we needed to be prepared. Plus, according to Grams, these spaces were going like hotcakes."

With a glance over to Bucky, who was deep in conversation with some girl wearing a tube top, short skirt, and sky-high heels, an emotion that felt a lot like jealousy coursed through me. I said, "Okay. When does this begin?"

My so-called friends said together, "Now."

6

Beat-Rice and the Menagerie

I sat at my kitchen table with my first cup of coffee of the day. It was going to be a multiple pot kind of day. After our drinks and dinner at Midnight Sun last night, I had Olivia drop me at my apartment. The wine stopped working once I watched Bucky walk away with Ms. Sky-High Heels. I refused to look deeper into my reaction to that. There were plenty of other thoughts to keep my mind from shutting off. Unfortunately, it was only that thought that wouldn't let me rest and when I did finally succumb to sleep, I dreamt about Bucky screwing that girl against the wall next to the trashcans behind Midnight Sun.

I brought my nearly empty cup to my mouth when a tremendous bang sounded. I jumped out of the chair and frantically looked around. When another bang didn't immediately come, I sniffed the air. No smoke or ozone detected. My heart eased when another bang sounded again. It shook the vase on my table next to the couch. Something was going on and I needed to figure out if I needed to run out of the damn building. Rushing over to the door, I swung it open and immediately got knocked on my ass by an enormous suitcase.

"Careful with that one, Ember. That's got my liquor in it."

"Aunt Beatrice."

I shoved the suitcase off and heard the clanking of glass. At least I wouldn't have to buy her liquor.

"Why are you still laying on the floor like a two-bit whore? We are Tylers. We are at least worth fifty bucks." Aunt Beatrice cackled while dropping two more suitcases.

Holy shit! How much did she pack?

Standing, I moved to shut the door but was stopped by a sneaker-clad food. "Hold up! There's still more."

Dammit, I knew that voice. Fortunately for me, he was carrying two carriers with holes and two more suitcases. He couldn't see me because I was hiding behind the door, hoping he wouldn't see me.

"Ember! Did you see the nice young man who helped me? I told him about you."

Sweet mother of God. What the hell did my aunt say to Bucky?

"Ember?" After setting down the luggage and carriers, he turned toward the door.

"Know many other people named Ember?" My voice was flat.

Aunt Beatrice waddled over to me and grabbed my hand. "This is my niece, Ember. She's easy." She leaned closer as if to whisper a secret and then continued, "It runs in the family."

Bucky smirked. "Well, I think that's everything, Beatrice. I'm sure I will see you around the building."

"Wait a minute. I promised to give you something for helping me." She waddled back over to another piece of luggage.

We watched as she practically dove into the bag. My aunt was a little person. She only grew to be four-foot-five inches tall. Though once you met her, you understood that her height didn't matter. If people were judged by how big a personality was, she would have been a giant. Nothing gets her down. If you know the old saying, where there's a will, there's a way. Well, I think it was written specifically about my aunt.

"What is she digging for?" Bucky whispered to me.

"No fucking clue."

I blushed as I watched Aunt Beatrice pull out sex toy after sex toy. Dildoes, vibrators, and bullets. Oh my!

"Aunt Beatrice, what are you looking for? Maybe I can help."

She came up for air and placed her hands on her hips. "Son of a bitch. I think I left it at your father's house."

"That's okay, Beatrice. I told you I didn't need anything."

"Oh, shut up!"

Bucky blinked.

"Here, I want you to have this." She placed an oddly curved vibrator in Bucky's hand.

He stood frozen. The vibrator wasn't in any kind of packaging.

"It's got fresh batteries. Maybe if you work it right, you could use it on Ember." She slapped my ass.

"Ow." I rubbed my butt cheek.

"You gotta get used to spanking, Ember. Most men like to do it. And if they do it right, it makes the sex even hotter." She wiggled her bushy eyebrows.

"Can I give you the vibrator?" Bucky's voice shook.

"Hell no. I don't want a used vibe. You touched it. You keep it. And don't get any ideas about using it on, with, or around me." I crossed my arms over my chest.

"It's barely used. A little soap and water and it'll be good as new." Aunt Beatrice waddled over to my kitchen but stopped and snapped her fingers. "Word of advice: Make sure all the soap is off. It can really sting the lady parts."

"Can I leave now?" Bucky muttered.

"I wish you would."

Bucky sped out of my apartment with his hand outstretched. He looked like he was in one of those egg-on-a-spoon races. I bit my lip, attempting to hold back the giggle that wanted to burst out of me. With a shake of my head, I shut the door and turned from it toward the inside of my apartment and froze.

The apartment looked like a hoarder's paradise. Suitcases and sex toys were strewn everywhere. Aunt Beatrice sat at the kitchen table holding a mug. Mentally, I was calculating what needed to be done in order to get everything organized and Aunt Beatrice settled in her room away from me. My train of thought was broken when the carriers shook and a small paw reached out.

"What the hell is in there?"

Aunt Beatrice put down the mug and hopped off the seat. She waddled over, then crouched down in front of the carrier. With a click, she opened a little door. Reaching in she grabbed a furry kitten that was striped like a tiger. She held him over her head like she was in *Lion King*.

"This is Ransom." She placed the little kitten on the floor and reached into the carrier again.

"This is Gerald." This kitten was all black except for a small spot of white on his nose and front paw.

Aunt Beatrice grunted as she attempted to pull something out of the carrier. Holy hell! How many kittens were there? The carrier was like a clown car for cats.

"And...this little bitch is Princess." An enormous ball of white fur yowled as it exited the carrier.

When Aunt Beatrice placed Princess on the ground, I blanched. Princess had a scar over an eye that looked weird. It also had one long canine that hung over its bottom lip. The cat looked like it was about to mug me or beat me over the head, then make me join the French Foreign Legion.

"What is wrong with it?" I stared at the cat, and it stared right back at me. It was definitely plotting my demise.

"Nothing. He has a glass eye because he was apparently one hell of a fighter on the streets." She stroked the pissed-off cat.

"Uh-huh. Wait...did you just say he?"

"Yep, Princess is a boy."

Okay then. Before I could ask more questions, the other carrier rattled and a clicking sound followed by a groan.

"Oh, my goodness, how could I forget you?" Aunt Beatrice walked over to the cage

I jumped back. "What the fuck?"

The animal lumbered from side to side trying to escape the carriage. When it finally emerged, it looked directly at me and made a clicking sound again.

"Aww...I think Cuddles likes you."

"What the fuck is Cuddles?"

"Don't you know a porcupine when you see one?" Aunt Beatrice asked.

"Yeah, but not one covered in packing peanuts." The poor animal had packing peanuts all over its back. It seemed unfazed by them.

"Oh that. Your father made me put them on there because Cuddles kept tearing up his couch. If you ask me, if Cuddles did that dirty work, it was only because he hated your dad."

I opened and closed my mouth a few times. There were so many questions that all wanted out at once, that it caused a question back up. A few shakes of my head and I finally settled on one.

"Why do you have a porcupine?" Yep. That was a good one.

"He's my emotional support animal."

Of course he was. Couldn't she get anything more practical? A dog. A cat. A boa constrictor. Nope. She landed on porcupine.

"I think I need something stronger than coffee," I mumbled.

"I've gotcha." Aunt Beatrice reached into the nearby suitcase and pulled out a bottle of vodka.

I made myself a promise in that moment as I took the vodka from Aunt Beatrice. I will never question if my life could get worse. Worse had a basement level called Hell.

7

A Fist Full of Furries

"Thanks for keeping me company." Olivia smiled while she drove.

"What the hell else did I have to do?" I shrugged in the front passenger seat.

"Well, you got me there, but it's so much better going to these things with someone else." She drummed her fingers on the steering wheel.

"Where are we going, anyway?"

Olivia called me the night of Aunt Beatrice's arrival asking if I'd accompany her to some function she had to cover for the *Central Times*, our local newspaper. It was one step above pamphlet if you asked me. Her misogynistic boss always gave Olivia the fluff pieces. It was usually a cat show, a little miss beauty pageant, or some local veteran celebrating his hundredth birthday. After her award-winning series of articles about Teagan's dating life, she really thought her career would take off. It didn't. In fact, she tried dragging each of us to her stupid assignments so she wouldn't have to suffer alone.

"Uh—" Olivia mumbled.

"What?"

"So, how's the job hunting going?" Her voice was shrill and mixed with desperation.

"It sucks. You already know this. Why are you deflecting?"

"Who's deflecting? I'm not deflecting. You are. Found a guy friend yet?"

"How the hell have I had time to do that? I have a whole damn menagerie in my apartment, and I'm including Aunt Beat-Rice in that."

"You better get on it." She smirked.

I glared at her. "Where are we going, Olivia?"

A tense smile curled her lips. She pulled her little car into the convention center. Cars were everywhere. After about ten minutes of circling the convention center's parking lot, Olivia stalked someone who was leaving and finally parked the car. Looking around, I was really confused. There were people dressed up in what appeared to be mascot costumes. An array of animals were represented. Bears, lions, tigers, and even something that looked like a demented mouse milled about outside of the center.

"Is this some sort of mascot convention?" It would figure she'd take me to a convention where people dressed up but it wasn't a comic convention. My luck was shit.

"Sort of. Let's go." Olivia grabbed her camera and satchel before getting out of the car.

I shrugged, then got out of the car. Olivia walked quicker than normal. Something was going on with her. I cleared my throat to get her attention. She slowed a half step so I could catch her. "You know you could have asked Xander to come with you. If you gave that guy half a chance, you wouldn't have to drag your innocent friends to these things.

Olivia's eyes widened. "I'd never bring Xander to this."

"What? Why? He looks like a sporty kind of guy. He probably knows who or what all these mascots are."

"I don't want to talk about Xander." She took that half step back and increased her speed by five.

Sweat was pouring down my back. I could even feel it pooling in my cleavage. Being a curvy girl was really hellish at times. Boob sweat was a real thing and if I wasn't careful, everyone would see the boob sweat rings.

We passed by the mascots standing outside. Each of them nodded at us, but I got the distinct impression they were checking me out. It was weird. An icy blast from the air conditioning chilled the sweat that had to be covering my body. A huge banner read *Welcome Furries*.

"Furries? Is that what they are calling mascots now?"

"Wait here while I check in at the press table." Olivia strode over to the press table without answering my question.

While I waited for Olivia to come back, I looked around the area. There were many people in these mascot costumes, but not everyone. I wandered over to a board where there was a list of activities.

9:00-Breakfast with Melvin (picture of a happy badger)

10:30-Panel on coming out to your family as a Furry (Hosted by Boomer and Bounce)

11:00-Furry Fifty Yard (Raising money for the Red Cross)

12:00-Lunch

1:30-Melding your Furry life into the every day (Speakers Dash and Flower)

3:00-Finding the perfect mate (Hosted by Bailey)

6:30-Disco Queen Furry Finale

"Which one are you going to?" a muffled voice said next to me.

"What?"

"Which one piques your interest? If you don't mind, I'd like to sit next to you."

I looked up at a smiling otter.

"Uhm...I didn't plan on going to any. What mascot are you?" I asked.

The otter tilted his head. "Mascot?"

"Yeah. Isn't this some kind of mascot convention?"

"No," he drawled. "This is a furry convention."

"I got that. I can read. Why is everyone dressed up as school mascots then?"

If an otter with a fake smile could look uncomfortable, he did. "Well, uhm...a furry convention is for people who enjoy anthropomorphic animal characters with human characteristics."

I furrowed my brow. "Are you telling me you're into animals that look like people?"

The otter shrugged.

"Does this include everything?" I looked around and noticed an art stand nearby that had half animal people having sex.

"Well, not everything. I mean, I wouldn't be opposed to getting a blow job while I'm Ozzy."

I blinked at him. "Ozzy?"

"That's my otter character. I'm Ozzy." He motioned to his suit-covered body and then held out his hand.

As if on automatic pilot, I put my hand in his furry paw. He jerked me toward him. The suit he wore smelled a bit like cheese. I held my breath, but it was too late.

"What do you say about that blowie?" He put his otter mouth near my ear.

I pushed away from the cheesy otter. "Yeah, that ain't happening."

"Ember?" Olivia approached us.

Both relief and anger surged through me. I knew she knew where we were going. My bitch of an ex-best friend withheld that information conveniently. I left the otter standing there and walked the five steps over to Olivia. Grabbing her arm, I dragged her toward the door.

"You fucking knew where we were going."

"Of course I did. It's my assignment." She shrugged, unashamed.

"So, what? You have to interview these people to ask why they have sex in these costumes?"

Olivia blew out a breath. "I actually did a lot of research. There is only a small percentage that actually finds this all sexually stimulating. Most just like dressing up in these costumes to become something they enjoy being. There is also a lot of art and crafts along with other activities."

"Well, I found one of those small percentages. That otter over there that smells like cheese wanted me to give him a blow job." I pointed toward Ozzy, who waved back. I gave him the finger and turned my back on him.

"Oh." Olivia bit her lip. "What did you say?"

"WHAT?!" My voice rang through the convention center, causing people and animal people to stare at us. "I told him to go fuck himself." I turned away from Olivia and began muttering to myself. "What the fuck else did she think I'd say? I'm not into human-like animals. I've had enough boyfriends who acted like animals to hate the whole idea. What did I say? Pfft."

Olivia touched my shoulder, making me jump. She shot her hand in the air in surrender. "Sorry, Ember. I didn't mean anything by it. But you have to admit at one time you would have taken a guy up on that."

I looked at Olivia as if she'd grown three heads. "I would have never dropped to my knees in front of a guy in some animal suit."

"What about our high school mascot?" She sighed.

I blushed. It was the one time I screwed the guy who played our high school mascot. It just so happened our mascot was a wolf. I gritted my teeth. "I screwed him because the guy in the suit was hot. It wasn't because I found the suit hot. You know what? I'm outta here."

"Wait! I can't leave without my story." Olivia pulled me to a stop.

I yanked my arm from her grasp. "I didn't say we. I'm calling a taxi and getting the hell out of here."

Leaving Olivia standing there, I walked outside into the heat. Furries were outside smoking cigarettes. They watched as I stopped on the curb to wait for my ride. My anger was almost too much. By the time the taxi arrived, I was overflowing with anger at myself and my so-called friends. I finally knew what they really thought of me. As the taxi pulled away, I could see Olivia talking to someone in a bunny costume. An angry tear slid down my cheek.

8

WE'VE GOT A WINNER

"Ember! You have some visitors. They told me not to tell you, but no one runs my life," Aunt Beatrice yelled through my door.

"I don't want anyone here. Send them away."

My bedroom door swung open and banged against my wall, lodging the doorknob into the sheetrock.

"I ain't nobody's messenger either," Aunt Beatrice called as she walked away, allowing Olivia, Teagan, and Nomi into the bedroom.

I turned my back on them.

The bed shifted as someone sat on the end. "I'm sorry, Ember." Olivia's voice wobbled.

A snort was my only retort.

"We're all sorry, Ember. We're all guilty for being judgy." Teagan sat next to me.

"What are the three of you doing here besides being a sorry bunch of friends?"

"We all came to apologize and to give you this." Nomi handed me a notebook.

A laugh escaped when I read it. On the cover written in a funky scrawl was *I'm a Hot Mess. You don't like it, you can go fuck yourself* with a unicorn giving two middle fingers.

"We thought this was right up your alley," Nomi said as she sat on the floor in front of me.

"It is pretty on point. Could have done without the unicorn, though."

"He is giving the middle finger." Teagan tapped the cover.

"The only redeeming part." I sighed. "Look, I know I've done a lot of fucked up things—most of them were of the sex variety—but that doesn't mean I want to be reminded what a slut I've been in the past. I'm honestly determined to become better. Balance my life better. Beat my terrible reputation into shape and earn back the respect of my friends."

Olivia, Nomi, and Teagan grabbed my hand. "You have our respect, Ember. We have always respected you for being so open and out there. Frankly, I've been jealous as hell about it."

"We want you to respect *you*. And it doesn't seem like you do that anymore," Nomi said.

"You're right. Sex has always been my thing in our group. Nomi is the ultra-successful one. Teagan is the innocent one. Olivia is the driven one. I've been the cockaholic as you guys like to put it. When I'm no longer that, what will I contribute?"

The three of them looked at me strangely, then started laughing. "You'll always be the hot one, Ember. Just maybe with her legs closed a bit more often," Nomi teased.

I swatted at her. "Hey! Bitch!"

"Also, Teagan is no longer the innocent one. She works for a sex toy manufacturer and is banging Grayson on the regular," Olivia pointed out.

"Oh, so very regular," Teagan said dreamily.

We grabbed pillows and pummeled her with them. Teagan fell off the bed. We all landed in a heap next to her, laughing like lunatics.

"What the hell are you four doing in here? Some sort of weird orgy thing?" Aunt Beatrice stood in my doorway.

"No, Aunt Beaty. We are just horsing around."

"Yeah well, if it was an orgy, I'd expect to be included," she huffed and stormed off.

"That is a bit gross." Olivia wrinkled her nose.

I raised an eyebrow at her. "A bit?"

She sighed. "I was trying to be nice."

"Yeah well, don't worry about nice with Aunt Beat-Rice. She won't be nice to you." A clicking sound came from the hallway and entered the room. "Get out, Cuddles."

"Is that a porcupine?" Nomi squinted at the door.

"Apparently, it's her emotional support animal." I leaned my back against the bed and watched as Cuddles sniffed around my room.

"I thought those were supposed to be dogs or cats," Teagan said.

"She's got cats too. They aren't supportive, though. More like plotting death while knocking everything and anything off any flat surface."

Cuddles left, and Olivia turned to me. "Are we okay?"

I shrugged. "Of course. You know I'm too damn lazy to find new friends."

Nomi, Teagan, and Olivia hugged me. It had only been two days since I'd stormed away from Olivia, but it felt like ages since I'd been around all of them. I smiled for a moment and then pulled away.

"All right. Enough of this mushy shit. You all need to go have your own lives so I can figure out how I'm going to win this bet."

They laughed and stood up from the floor. As they pulled themselves together, Teagan smiled at me. "I still think you should use Bucky."

I took the pillow laying on the floor and chucked it at her. "Get the hell out of here before I really need to find new friends, or at the very least teach that porcupine that you three are the enemy."

They laughed as they walked out my bedroom door. I looked at the journal that was lying on the floor. There were a lot of fucking pages in that thing. Grabbing it, I put it in my lap and flipped through the blank pages. The feeling of being watched drew my attention to my doorway. Princess was slowly walking past while staring at me with one good eye. I held the notebook up to my chest as if it were a shield. That cat had murder on its mind and no one could tell me different.

I wiped my hands on my yoga pants for the fifth time. All I had to do was reach up and knock. It shouldn't have been difficult. Though it felt way too major to be just a knock on a door. Chewing on my lip a bit too hard, I could taste the coppery tang of blood.

Come on, Ember! Don't be such a pussy.

I bounced on my toes and cracked my neck. It looked more like I was ready to go to battle instead of just knocking on a door. With one final deep breath, I raised my hand. As soon as my knuckles landed on the door, it swung open, causing me to fall forward into a very hard and very shirtless chest.

"Well, hello." Bucky smirked as I pulled away from him.

"Hi," I yelled. What the hell was wrong with me?

He winced. "Everything okay?"

Suddenly, my mouth felt like sandpaper. "Uh, yeah. I kind of have something I'd like to propose."

"Proposing? So soon? I'm kind of old-fashioned. I'd like to be the one to do that. However, if your proposition comes with a princess cut diamond, flowers, and fireworks, I just might be convinced to say yes."

I was reminded why this was a bad idea.

"Never mind." I turned to go.

"Wait! I'm just messing with you, Ember. You looked so serious. I mean, it took you like ten minutes to just knock on my door. I was trying to lighten the mood."

"You knew I was out here the whole time?"

Bucky bit his lip. "Yeah. My neighbor texted me saying some strange chick was outside my door."

"Strange chick?" I looked around the hallway. "Which neighbor?"

"Why do you want to know which neighbor?"

"Because I want to have a friendly chat with them to explain how not crazy I am."

Bucky laughed. "I'm pretty sure that conversation would just prove they were right."

I popped out my hip and said, "I can be very convincing."

Before Bucky could respond, the door across from his swung open. "Buck! Did you finally see the crazy—"

"Xander?" I looked back and forth between them.

Xander, Bucky's best friend and business partner, blushed. "Uhm...hi, Ember." He gave a small wave.

Furrowing my brow, I turned back to Bucky. "Was he the neighbor who called me crazy?" I turned back toward Xander ready to show him how not crazy I was.

Bucky grabbed my arm and dragged me into his apartment. Before he shut the door, he said, "See ya later, Xan."

I crossed my arms. "Was he?"

"Does it really matter, Ember? You are acting insane right now."

Sucking in a breath, my gum welded itself to the back of my throat, blocking my airway. I panicked and tried to desperately suck in air. When I only lodged the gum further, I scratched at my neck. It would be my luck that I die from a piece of Fruitstripes that was at the bottom of my purse.

"Are you fucking around right now?" Bucky had a confused look on his face.

I shot daggers at him the best I could, but my lips turning purple finally clued him in. In a blink, he spun me around and performed the Heimlich. It only took two swift upward movements to dislodge the gooey substance which ricocheted across the room and landed on a framed picture.

"Holy fuck balls." I breathed.

Bucky rubbed my back while a little nervous laugh escaped. "You can say that again. I thought you were fucking around being all dramatic, but then when your lips changed color it scared the hell out of me. Are you okay?"

"If by okay, you're asking if I can breathe again, then yes. If you're asking about anything else, I think that is up for debate."

He pulled away from me with a smirk. "Would you like something to drink?"

"Yes, please. Water would be great."

I followed him to an impressive kitchen. It definitely put mine to shame. It was a cook's wet dream. State-of-the-art appliances shone with a new appliance sheen. A copper or tin backsplash that mixed a vintage and modern look perfectly accented the dark granite countertop. I approached the island, pulled out a stool, and sat. He busily filled a glass with water from a pitcher he'd retrieved from the fridge. I forced my eyes to look anywhere than at the gorgeous specimen that was Bucky.

He slid the water to me, then leaned against the island. "So, what brought you to my neck of the woods?"

I gulped the water slower than necessary. The reality of what I was about to ask burst the short-lived near-death bubble I had temporarily resided. Also, I didn't want to choke again.

Once my drier than the desert mouth was lubricated, I placed the empty cup on the island. My eyes met his. Why did they have to be so damn pretty? Using that frustration, I fortified myself.

"Well, it's complicated."

He folded his arms, then laid his head on them. Bucky looked like a kid waiting for story time to begin. "I'm listening."

After a few nervous seconds, I started from the beginning. He already knew some of the story, but I filled in some gaps with half-truths, creatively worded truths, and a fuck-ton of omissions. When I finished, I took a deep breath and watched him. He wasn't laughing, smiling, or even having any kind of reaction. It confused me.

"Well, that was an interesting story. However, I know probably," he scratched his chin and looked at the ceiling, "oh, about ninety-five percent of that was bullshit. It was pretty bullshit but still bullshit. Just tell me what you are doing here."

My jaw hung open. He was calling me on my bullshit. No one did that. Ever. I was an outstanding bullshitter.

"I'm not joking," I squeaked.

"Oh, I believe that. It still doesn't answer my question." He stood straight, then walked around the island to stand within my personal space bubble, trapping me and staring at me.

Seconds ticked by as we stood there staring at one another. Finally, I looked at my hands in my lap.

"I need to do stuff with somebody." I could have punched my own face for the stupid sentence.

"Why not ask your friends? They seem up to *stuff*."

"I need to do stuff with a guy."

He stepped closer, leaving only mere centimeters between us. "I can do stuff. In fact, not just me. My hands. My lips. My tongue. My co—"

"Whoa, horsey!" I said a bit too loudly while shooting my hands up between us.

"What?" A confused look marred his pretty face.

"Everything needs to be platonic. This is a no dating, no sex, no physical contact kind of thing."

Bucky cocked his head and glanced at me. "Okay."

"Okay?"

"Yep. Okay."

This idiot was confusing me.

"Okay what?"

"Okay I'll do it." He pulled out of my personal bubble, finally letting me breathe.

"You'll do it? You don't even really know what you're saying okay to."

"It doesn't really matter. I'm looking at this as a way for us to get to know each other while I charm you. Once you win whatever this is for, we can go at it like bunnies." He smirked.

A tornado of emotions spun inside me. However, it was dread that won out. One thought floated through my mind. I'd made a horrible mistake.

9

Creepy Fucking Cat

D *ear* ~~Diary~~ *Journal?*

First and foremost, I am not addressing you as Diary. That makes me sound like some little girl writing in a glittery notebook instead of what this really is. A woman looking down the barrel of middle-age with a notebook bound in a sarcastic cover. Anywho...eww...did I just say anywho? Yuck! What in the world is happening to me? No sex must really be doing a number on my vocabulary. Who would have thought the penis would affect basic English language usage? I knew they could make guys stupid and a good one could leave a woman speechless but not having access to one...

Anyway, I'm here to tell you I had a completely platonic inter-action with a mega hot guy. Hey! Don't give me that look. I'm still allowed to appreciate without touching. And there was no touching. Except when he helped me from dying, but I figured that was an exception. Well, none of that matters because Bucky agreed. He has his own agenda, but as long as it doesn't fuck with me winning...I don't care. Bucky had one stipulation. I wasn't allowed to call him by his childhood nickname anymore. Oops...already fucked that one up. Oh well, it's not like he's going to see this. Now, I have to remember to call him Rob or Robbie. I'm leaning toward Robbie because I can probably play off an oopsie of using Bucky easier with Robbie than with Rob.

So...that's it. Totally platonic. Totally going to make Teagan, Nomi, and Olivia dress up as the Powerpuff girls.

That's all you're getting today. Later, ~~Journal.~~ Nope...not using that either.

Ember

"You're really counting that stupid interaction with Bucky?" Olivia said through the phone.

"Absolutely. It was completely platonic, and no sex was involved. Not even a handshake."

"First, platonic means no sex. Second, you've had sex from a handshake?"

I blushed, then cleared my throat. It was a good thing Olivia couldn't see me. "So, I've been looking at jobs. Do you think I have a shot at being a secretary?"

"Hmmm...nice deflection. I'll let it go since I know getting you working is way more important. A secretary? I don't think so. Do you really think you could be at someone's beck and call?"

I cringed. "How about—" I scrolled through the job website I'd been obsessing over the last couple of days. "A daycare teacher."

A choking noise came through the phone. "Holy shit! My latte just went through my nose and cinnamon burns like hell. You. A daycare teacher. You know that means taking care of little children with sticky fingers and snotty noses, right?"

"I used to babysit when I was in high school."

"Sitting with some kids while you did your nails is completely different from being responsible for how kids become little humans."

I shrugged, knowing she couldn't see me. "It could just be temporary until this mess blows over."

"Your funeral. Well, I gotta go. I have a meeting with my editor and I have a story that is going to blow him away."

"All right, good luck."

"Thanks. Talk to you later."

I put down my phone and looked at the screen advertising the daycare teacher. Before I'd settled on being a professional organizer, I had thought of becoming a teacher. Kids and I had always gotten along. My dad teased I knew just how to get on their level. With a smile, I hit send, submitting my resume for their consideration. I knew it was a distant chance, but my savings was getting low and if I had to be kept locked in the apartment with Aunt Beatrice any longer, one of us would not be leaving in one piece. I wasn't totally confident that I'd be the one leaving.

A hand slapping the table next to my laptop made me jump.

"Call this number. Get this job. I pulled some strings with one of my male friends." Think of Aunt Beatrice and she appeared.

"Where is it?" I looked at a piece of used receipt paper from a sex shop. Flipping it over, a number was scribbled.

"Does it matter? You being around all the time is cramping my style. I need to get my rotation back in order." She walked away.

"Rotation?"

She sighed dramatically. "You know I have to get my Monday man back on Monday, then my Wednesday man back on Wednesday and so on."

I blinked at her. "When's Dad coming back?"

She shrugged and then left her menagerie following close behind, except for Ransom, who was rubbing against my leg. I leaned down and picked up the cute little furball. Petting him absently, I could feel my sinuses tightening as the minutes passed by. Damn allergies. My eyes watered as my phone vibrated on the table.

Stalker with my panties: You have a black dress?

Me: Of course.

Stalker with my panties: Good. Our first buddy activity will be tomorrow at noon.

Me: What?

Stalker with my panties: Just be ready by 11:30.

Me: All right. What is it we are going to do?

Stalker with my panties: Why do you need to know? Can't you just trust me?

I sighed through my mouth since my nose was closed up.

Me: I just need to know if I should wear heels or flats.

Stalker with my panties: Heels. Definitely heels.

Stalker with my panties: Scratch that. Wear ugly shoes with possibly a potato sack.

Me: What?

Stalker with my panties: Or a moo-moo. Yes. That would work better. A moo-moo with house shoes. Perfect.

Me: Are you high right now? Been huffing too much aerosol spray?

Stalker with my panties: What?

Bucky, aka Robbie, was really making me regret asking him to do this stuff with me.

Me: What is wrong with you? I'm going to wear the black dress as you initially asked. I don't own a moo-moo or potato sack, so you are shit out of luck.

Stalker with my panties: Damn...well can you at least try to look frumpy? I don't need to be getting a chubby or having impure thoughts about my buddy.

A laugh escaped.

Me: You're an idiot. I will be ready by 11:30.

Putting down my phone, I carried the sleeping kitten over to one of the pillows the animals had made their own. When I stood, the world spun. I needed to get more oxygen to my brain, and only some allergy medicine and nose spray were going to work. Leaving the sleeping kitten, I made my way to the bathroom to take care of the stupid allergies. As I shut the water off from the bathroom sink, I heard a strange sound. The thought of something happening to Ransom made me pick up speed. A ripping sound drew my gaze over to the couch. Standing on his hind legs was that menace in white fur, Princess. With his creepy glass eye staring at me, he ran his claws down the edge of my couch.

"Stop that, you little bastard," I yelled and ran toward the little prick.

Princess brazenly slid his claw down the edge, managing to rip out a piece of stuffing before walking away with his tail in the air showing me his butthole. It took everything in me not to punt that asshole across the room.

"Beaty! Beaty!" I yelled.

"Jesus Christ, Ember. What?" She breathed heavily from running down the hall.

"That little fucker destroyed my couch." I pointed at Princess, who was innocently rubbing against Aunt Beatrice.

She squinted at the couch. "How do you know Princess did that? It looks like it was a shitty couch to begin with."

"I watched him do it. He made creepy eye contact with me with his glass eye."

"You know he can't actually see out of that one, right?"

I stomped my foot out of frustration. "You are going to have to buy me a new one."

"Fine. Let me get my change purse. I'm sure I have quarters in there. That's all that shitty couch was worth anyway." Aunt Beatrice and her minions followed her down the hallway.

I picked up my phone.

Me: How long until you come back? Beat-Rice is not going to survive this visit. Neither is that devil spawn Princess.

I stared at the message I'd sent to my father. When ten minutes passed, I chucked my barely usable phone onto the couch. The Franken-phone's duct-taped backing slid from it showing its innards. Poor Franken-phone always took the brunt of my anger. I gently put the phone back together, then turned it on. As I waited for the darkened screen to brighten, I cooed soothing words while petting it. The cracked screen lit, allowing me to let out a breath.

"You need a fucking job."

Aunt Beatrice's voice made me jump, almost losing my grip on my phone.

"Dammit! You're like a damn ninja."

She lifted an eyebrow and turned away from me. Princess Asshole stared at me, then followed Aunt Beatrice with his tail in the air and his butthole on display.

"Creepy fucking asshole cat," I mumbled.

He turned at my words. His cloudy glass eye stared at me while his permanent snarl threatened retribution for my comment. On the couch, I turned away and watched the little asshole retreat down the hall in the TV's reflection. But not before it gave me one last threatening glance. I shivered.

"The sooner Dad comes home, the sooner I can get rid of the crazies." I slumped against the couch and pulled out the sex shop receipt.

10

Putting the Fun in Funeral

The silence in the car was almost unbearable. The clock on the dashboard read 11:35. I'd been around Bucky, or should I say Robbie, for five minutes. He was already being unbearably insufferable. I watched the scenery pass by and contemplated doing a tuck and roll escape from the car. That option went out the window when I realized I really liked the dress and heels I was wearing. I'd need to reuse it when I killed Bucky and went to his funeral. A loud sigh broke me out of the enjoyable thoughts of killing him.

"What?" I snapped.

Robbie adjusted his white-knuckled grip on the steering wheel while grunting something incoherently.

"I don't speak pissy male grunts. You can pull on your big boy panties and tell me what's got them in a twist or you can turn the car around."

He glanced over at me, then down at my crossed legs.

"I was serious when I said don't dress sexy."

A blush flamed my cheeks. "I didn't. This is perfectly acceptable. All important parts are covered."

"Are you serious? Look at all that." He waved his hand frantically in my direction. The car swerved erratically with his movement.

"Whoa! Keep the car on the road, cowboy. So, you're upset I'm showing my legs?" I shook my head. "What do you think a dress shows? It's not Victorian England. I don't have high neck dresses with equally high boots. It will be fine."

"Don't blame me if people get upset with your dress that's on you." He shrugged but continued his white-knuckled grip.

"If by people you mean you, then you can go straight to hell. No one is going to blame the way I dress on how they act. You are a fucking grown up. Act like one." I crossed my arms and went back to staring out the window.

Every known curse word, and some newly invented, flew through my mind. The silence that built in the car amplified my anger with the asshat. It was so bad I had to close my eyes to keep myself from seeing his reflection in the window.

"Look, I'm sorry," Bucky grumbled.

"Whatever, Bucky."

"I thought we agreed you'd call me Robbie."

I turned toward him to look at his stupid face. "I'll call you Robbie when you want to act like a damn adult. An adult who can think past his dick. Until that happens, I will call you Bucky."

"Fine. We're here."

I blinked a few times. People walked around dressed in black while gripping tissues in their hands. For a tiny moment, I was confused as hell. That moment fluttered away in an instant when I saw the hearse.

"A funeral? You brought me to a funeral?" My voice rose higher with each question.

"Granny's...uhm...man friend? Well, he kicked the bucket."

"Uh...that sucks."

"Yeah." He looked down at his phone and cursed. "Granny's waiting for us. She can't wait to see you."

Bucky got out of the car. I sat there for a moment, but then the idea of Edna getting pissed at me because I made her wait got my ass in gear. I jumped out of the car and quickly pulled my skirt down as far as it would go. There wasn't a reason for me to be worried. Not one person did a double take. Well, one person did, but he wasn't supposed to.

Holding my head up, I walked past Bucky and waited for him to catch up. "Let's pay our condolences." I leaned toward him, then said for his ears only. "If you keep eye fucking me, we are going to be paying condolences to your balls when I rip them off with my bare hands."

I gave him my sweetest smile. For a moment, something flared in his eyes. I wasn't sure if it was fear or desire. I didn't want to find out, so I walked away. A loud, obnoxious laugh echoed through the parking lot. One heeled foot pivoted slowly as I looked at Bucky. He was at least silently laughing. Wiping away a stray tear, he slapped his knee before walking over to me.

"You are too much sometimes, Ember." He slung an arm around my shoulders.

I quickly shrugged it off, but before I could tell him about the next appendage I'd be removing and shoving somewhere, I heard my name.

"Ember?"

I let out a relief breath at the sight of Teagan's Grams. In two strides, I walked over and gave her a hug.

"Hey, Grams. Vernon."

Grams' husband nodded to me and took Grams' hand.

"What are you doing here, sweetheart?"

"I'm with Bucky."

Bucky had approached while I hugged Grams.

"Mr. and Mrs. Roberts. How are you?"

Grams pulled Bucky into a hug. A laugh almost escaped at the uncomfortable look he had on his face. Grams kissed him on his cheek and took his face in her hands.

"You're a good boy being here for Edna. Now, I'm going to borrow your date. Though I must say you young people are very unorthodox when it comes to your dates." She shook her head and then linked arms with me.

We walked arm in arm into the funeral parlor. I held back a laugh when I finally saw the name of the funeral home. *Bundy, Gacey, and Manson Funeral Home.* Then under that, a flashing sign said *0 days since death visited.*

"Holy shit, Grams. I didn't realize this place was named after serial killers. It's actually pretty awesome."

Grams gave her a confused look. "It's not that strange. It's their names, after all. Bobby Bundy, Greg Gacey, and Matilda Manson run this place."

"Wow. That's one heck of a coincidence. Though their slogan is pretty funny." I pointed to the flashing sign.

Grams winked at me. "I'm sure you could come up with a funnier one."

I shrugged. "We put the fun in funeral?"

Grams smirked. "Much better."

We approached Edna at the entrance of the funeral home. Grams let go of me and walked over to Edna, pulling her into a hug. It lasted only a couple of seconds before Edna pulled away dismissing Grams. Relief flowed over her features as she saw Bucky standing behind us. In two steps, Edna was embracing him. Grams linked her arm with Vernon, then whispered she'd see me inside. I nodded absently but was mesmerized watching Bucky comfort his grandmother. It was so sweet he almost earned back Robbie.

"It's about damn time you got here, Bucky. I've been waiting for ages." Edna dabbed at her eyes.

"Granny, I saw you get out of your car when we pulled up."

She waved her hand in dismissal. "I'm grieving, Bucky. How can you expect me to be concerned over something so inane as time?"

Bucky made eye contact with me and then rolled his eyes in exasperation. "All right, Granny. Are you ready?"

Edna straightened her back and said, "You bet."

I took that as my cue to say hello to her. "Hello, Edna. I am so sorry for your loss."

"Oh, Ember. I'm sorry I didn't notice you there. It's the grief. Thank you for coming with Bucky." Edna looked down at the flower she was holding and let out a breath. "Thank goodness my flower is okay. If that ninny Esther had damaged it with her stupid hug, I would have had to take it out on her hide."

Without another word, Edna and her single yellow rose marched into the building. Bucky and I had to speed walk to her while dodging walkers, wheelchairs, and many, many slow movers. When we finally caught up to her, she was seated a few rows behind the family. Grams and Vernon sat one row behind her. I slid in front of Edna, making enough room for Bucky to sit next to his grandmother. Watching other funeral attendees, I saw a pattern of sobbing women holding yellow roses.

"What does the yellow rose mean?" I whispered to Bucky.

He shrugged. "No clue." Bucky leaned toward his grandmother and asked, "What's with the yellow rose?"

Edna sniffled. "My beloved Frankie asked that upon his demise I bring a yellow rose as a sign of my undying love."

Oh shit. Frankie was clearly some kind of Casanova and from the looks of it, Edna thought she was the only one. With all the yellow roses around them, she clearly wasn't.

"Do you think..."

"Nope. She has no clue. This could get ugly." Bucky's leg bounced nervously.

A tapping on a microphone drew our attention to the front. The quiet chatter stopped as everyone gave their attention to the priest.

"Hello, everyone. Thank you all for attending the sendoff for our beloved Frank Salerno. He was loved by many and an upstanding member of our community. Over the years, it privileged me to see him frequently as he volunteered at many of the church's fundraisers. He particularly enjoyed the spaghetti night." A laugh broke the tension. "That being said, he asked that we not dwell on his passing but celebrate the life he lived. Frank did not want a long, drawn-out eulogy. He specifically said, 'Father, don't go blathering on like you do. Get in. Get it done. Get out.'" More laughter rang through the funeral home. "So, as he said, I will be done now. He had one last request. He asked that I welcome his love to come and pay their respects first. Frank was always a cryptic one. Will his beloved please come pay their respects?" The priest left the podium.

Edna rose with the yellow rose in her hand. Bucky and I watched her walk up to the casket. But just as she approached the casket, another woman joined her. Then another and another. They lined up, each holding a rose. We held our breath and waited for Edna to realize the other women around her. Edna placed the rose on Frank's chest. The woman next to her did the same. Edna's head snapped to the woman next to her.

"What the hell are you doing, Alyce?" she asked, then looked at the other women around her. "Are you fucking kidding me right now? You bitches slept with my man?"

"He wasn't yours. He was mine," a woman with a bob cut said.

"Bullshit, Karen. He was mine." A woman with a ponytail shoved the other woman.

"All of you are wrong. He was mine," Edna yelled and went into attack mode, shoving women left and right.

Bucky and I watched in horror as elderly women screamed and scratched at each other. Wigs flew along with a few pairs of false teeth. The ball of women moved in front of the casket.

"Should you do something?" I asked Bucky.

"I don't want to. Who knows what they'd do to me."

"Chicken shit," I mumbled.

He cocked his eyebrow at me, then we heard a crash. The ball of elderly women had rolled into the casket. Frank's body went flying and hit the people sitting in the front row. Frank's ejection didn't stop the brawl. When the priest attempted to break it up, the angry women brought him into the fray.

"Oh shit." Bucky shot up and ran over to Edna, who was holding a folding chair over her head.

Before Edna could bring the chair down on one woman, Bucky plucked the chair away from her and grabbed her around the waist, dragging Edna out of the funeral home. I grabbed our things and awkwardly followed them out. It was surprisingly easy to leave because of the melee.

"Ember!" Bucky yelled as he struggled with an angry Edna.

"I'm coming."

"Can you drive Granny's car back to Sunny Pines? Her keys should be in the glove compartment."

"Yeah. Have fun." I waved as I ran over to Edna's car.

The keys were exactly where he said they'd be. Who the hell left their keys in their car? Apparently, Edna did that's who. Sunny Pines was only a few minutes away from the funeral parlor. I sped out of the parking lot, narrowly missing some of the elderly attendees. Somehow Bucky beat me there. I got out of the car, and Bucky motioned for me to give him a few minutes. I pulled my phone out of my purse while I waited.

Me: So...I just went to a funeral that had a brawl due to the dead guy being a Casanova of epic proportions

Olivia: What?

Me: Yep! Looks like Viagra is a hell of a drug.

Olivia: I guess so. Haven't touched Bucky, have you?

Me: No! But apparently my most conservative LBD is enticing to him.

Olivia: LOL...you're so mean.

Me: How the hell was I supposed to know he can't handle himself over a little leg?

Olivia: No matter what, it should be one hell of a diary entry.

I cringed. I'd almost forgotten about that part. Dammit.

"Ready?"

I jumped. "Geez. You scared the crap out of me."

Bucky had a boyish smile on his face. "Sorry. Didn't realize you didn't hear me. Ready to head home, or did you want to grab some lunch?"

"I think I've had enough excitement for the day." I got into Bucky's car.

"Do you mind holding on to this for me?"

He handed me a plastic bag I hadn't even noticed him holding.

"What's in this?"

Bucky pulled out of the parking lot of Sunny Pines. "Go ahead and look what Granny gave me."

I opened the bag and pulled out a cylindrical crocheted bag with a bow at the opening and at the tip.

"What are these?"

Bucky bit his lip and said, "Cock cozies."

I dropped the offending object back in the bag and threw the whole plastic bag on the floor. Bucky's laughter filled up the car.

"What the fuck?"

"It's not like they were used, Ember. Apparently, that is Granny and her group's recent activity. They plan on having a craft sale with all the inappropriate goods."

"Why did she give them to you?"

He blushed. "She wants me to try them on. Make sure they work."

It was my turn to laugh. "That's both hilarious and twisted. Good luck with that."

Bucky pulled into the parking lot of our building. With a mischievous look, he said, "Want me to do a fashion show."

I shuddered my gaze. "No!"

Stepping out of the car I could hear his laughter following me. I marched to the elevator to take me back to my apartment and the X-rated thoughts about him wearing a colorful cock cozy.

11

Choking a Chicken

Dear Suzanne,

I'm calling you Suzanne today after the stuffed skunk I had when I was little. You may be wondering why. Well, it's because all of this stinks. Ha. Ha. Ha. Yeah, I know. It was lame, but so is this dear Suzanne thing too. Anyway, so I had another very platonic interaction with the increasingly annoying and sexy Bucky. Though I was quite distracted from his sexiness thanks to the old lady brawl at the funeral he took me to. Yes, I said a funeral. You can't get any more platonic than that. Anyway, before Edna could turn it into a wrestling match, we left. But not before the dead guy took out the front row. After this funeral, no other ones will ever live up to these expectations. I really hope mine ends up like this. Maybe I'll rig my coffin to pop me out like a jack-in-the-box. That would be awesome. Anyway, everything was very platonic and non-sexual until he offered to model cock cozies his grandmother crocheted. Ever since then my damn dreams have him entering my bedroom wearing only the cozy. A very large one.

Maybe this is going to be a bit more difficult than I'd thought. I'm definitely going to need to buy stock in batteries with the way these dreams are going.

All right talk to you later, Suzanne. You probably won't be Suzanne after today. Oh well.

Ember

I was already regretting calling the number on the back of the sex shop receipt Aunt Beatrice had given me. After the day of the elderly rumble over the dead Casanova, I knew I had to buckle down and find a job. The daycare had called, but I was on the fence about the idea of working with children. So, I went with Aunt Beatrice's suggestion. After all, part of cleaning up my hot mess of a life was getting a job that paid money.

Unfortunately, the job that Aunt Beatrice had suggested wasn't what it had seemed. When I'd called the number, a rough-voiced man answered. After two brief questions, he told me to come in the following day for an interview. The night before I'd gotten my best suit out and let it air in my bedroom. I was going to land the job no matter what. It never occurred to me I wouldn't want to land the job.

Nerves swirled around in my stomach as I rode the bus to the address the man had given. A horrible smell permeated the air. When I stepped off the bus and walked a block to the address, I double-checked that what my phone said was the same as the address the man had given me. It was the same. A chicken plant emanated the smell of death and chicken shit.

I gagged and almost ran back to the bus stop. I could find better. The angel on my shoulder gave me a pep talk. The devil puked into a bucket.

I sucked it up without taking too deep of a breath and walked into the office. The office was a special kind of hell. It was at least ten degrees warmer than outside. The smell was amplified and a strange odor of fried chicken mixed in with the death and shit. I wanted to punch the little angel in the throat.

"Yeah," the gruff voice from the phone call yelled out.

"Hi. Uhm...I'm Ember Tyler. I believe I spoke with you on the phone."

A horrible coughing and then silence was the response. I really didn't want to see what had happened. The coughing started again after I took two steps. I sighed, feeling glad I would not have to be on some true crime documentary.

"I'll be right out. Have a seat."

I looked around for a seat, finding mismatched chairs lined up against a wall. They were covered in feathers. My stomach flipped again. I decided standing was my better option. Looking around the office made me cringe. There was a mess everywhere. My inner organization queen wanted to jump out and fix everything. I gripped the sides of my pencil skirt to keep my hands from acting on their own. To take my focus off the mess, I looked around the walls. There were typical human resource posters, government notifications, and other pertinent information. However, it was the instructions about what happened to the chicken in the plant that froze me in place. The detail was impeccable for what looked to be a poster from the 1940s. It was a bit graphic, and I decided in that moment that I was going to become a vegetarian.

"I'm ready for ya." The man made me jump.

He stood next to me as I looked at the poster. The man was rotund, with an out-of-control beard that only stressed the lack of hair on top of his head. He was also about a foot shorter than me. It didn't help that I had some impressive heels on.

"Okay." I plastered on a smile.

He grunted and walked toward his office. I cringed as I entered. The mess was even worse. How in the world could he find anything in there?

"So you want to be a plucker?" he grumbled.

"A what?"

"The term is plant associate, but around here we call them pluckers. They make sure all the feathers are off the dead birds. That's what you came here about?"

I blinked at him in confusion. "Uhm...no. Well, actually, I wasn't sure what I was coming here for. My aunt just gave me a number to call about a job. I thought it might be office work."

He waved his hand around. "I've got everything handled on that end. We are short a plucker thanks to Hank losing his hand."

"Oh my God. He lost his hand plucking feathers from chickens?"

He gave me another look like I was crazy. "No. It was a wood chipper accident. I kept telling him to keep his damn hand out of there. He isn't the brightest. So, are you interested?"

"Uhm...I don't think I'm qualified. I've done nothing like that."

"Any idiot can be a plucker, girl. I just told you about Hank. Beatrice told me you were desperate." A soft smile curved his lips. "That Beatrice is one hell of a woman. I'd do anything for her."

What the hell was happening?

"Yeah, she's great. Are you sure there isn't any office work? Also, does it always smell like this and is it always this hot?"

His eyes flashed. "No office work, I told you. That smell is always around. You'll bring it home with you. As for being hot, this is pretty cool, actually."

"Oh. Well, can I get back to you about the job?" I stood from the chair.

"Well, I have a lot of people interested. I won't be able to save it for you, but I gave you the first shot because of Beatrice."

"I understand, and I promise I will call you today with an answer."

He shrugged.

"Thank you for your time." I held out my hand.

He took my hand in his, and I had to hold back the gag. It was slimy. How the hell was his hand slimy? I pasted on that fake smile again and slid my hand from his slimy one. The clicking of my heels was everything I concentrated on. I wanted to run from the building like my hair was on fire. Instead, I walked briskly while holding my breath. I did that the entire way to the bus stop.

Huffing in deep cleansing breaths, the few people waiting for the bus looked at me, then moved away. I must have looked like an idiot. Relief was palpable when the bus arrived. I hurried to the back. People sucked in their breath as I moved past them. I tried to smell my clothes to see if I was the reason. To my dismay, I was the reason people fled to the front. All I wanted to do in that moment was put my head down and cry. Instead, like everyone else, I held my breath.

A half an hour later, I was walking toward my apartment building with my heels hooked onto my purse while I ate a quickly melting pint of ice cream. It wasn't even my favorite, but after the disaster of the chicken plant interview, I needed some comfort.

"You okay?" Bucky asked.

I jumped. Damn him and his ninja skills. "Yep. Don't I look it?"

"Honestly, no. In fact, you look like hell and smell like death." He scrunched up his face.

"Thanks. Your charm is endless," I deadpanned.

I kept walking toward the building. He followed along. Sometimes I wondered if he was actually a giant puppy.

"What happened?"

"Bad interview," I said around a mouthful of melted ice cream soup.

"It couldn't have been that bad. I mean, interviews suck no matter what. That's why I own my own business." He puffed out his chest.

I was not in the mood for Bucky. If he didn't leave me alone so I could wallow, I was very likely to do something mean that I wouldn't regret. Well, maybe I'd regret it a bit many years from now. Probably on my deathbed.

"That's nice." I puffed my chest out, proud that I didn't throw my ice cream soup at him.

Ice cream soup was precious. I wouldn't waste it on the imbecile.

"What kind of job was it?"

"Chicken plant production associate." No way was I saying plucker.

"A plucker."

Mother plucker! I ignored his spot-on answer.

"If you need a job so bad, why don't you come work for me?"

I sucked the soupy ice cream and immediately regretted that when the ice cream did a reappearance by way of my nose. I started coughing while my eyes watered. Ice cream burned like a motherfucker the second time around.

"Shit. Are you okay?" Bucky slapped my back.

"Yes, I'm fine. If only an idiot would stop slapping my back."

He stopped immediately, then took two steps away from me.

"That was pretty impressive. I've never seen ice cream come through the nose. Hell, I think I saw chunks."

I gagged and walked over to the trash can to toss my precious ice cream soup. Great Bucky just ruined my beloved ice cream soup.

"Thanks for ruining that for me. Is there something you need? I mean, you said you have a job, but for some reason, you have been around so much lately I'm starting to think of you as an oozing sore that antibiotics can't cure."

"Yikes. Didn't realize I was that bad. I was actually on my way to work when I saw you. I wanted to make sure you were okay. We are friends, after all. Friends do things like that."

"Not my friends." That was a total and complete lie. Teagan, Olivia, and Nomi would totally be here if I needed them.

"Oh." Bucky looked down at the ground.

"I gotta go. See ya later."

The sooner I got away from him, the better my day would be.

"Okay. Well, think about the job offer. It's better than being a plucker." He smirked.

"Thanks, but it would be a cold day in hell when I came to work for you."

His smile fell as a wicked one curled my lips. My little bit of bitch boost put some pep in my step. The day was already on the rise.

12

Ass Emergency

"Hello Happy Little Rainbow Academy. This is Larissa. How may I help you?" The sugary sweet voice practically gave me a toothache.

"Hi, Larissa. I'm returning a call from Corrine."

"All right. May I ask who is calling?"

"Ember Tyler."

"Great. Let me put you on hold."

Nursery rhyme songs played through the phone. A crash from the back of my apartment made me jump.

"Aunt Beatrice? Are you okay?"

That was the last thing I needed. An injured Beat-Rice would be the nail in my coffin.

"What are you doing?" she called out.

"I'm on the phone."

"Oh good. So nothing. I need you to take me and a friend somewhere." She marched out with Cuddles following her.

"Aunt Beatrice, I am on the phone. We can talk about this when I am finished."

"No. I need you to take us now. Your phone is mobile. Get your ass out of the chair." She tugged on my arm.

Yanking my arm back, I said, "No. Plus, how do you expect me to take you anywhere? I don't have a car, remember?"

"Well, shit. I forgot how much of a loser you are." Aunt Beatrice turned toward the hallway. "Willie! We are going to have to call an ambulance." She turned back to me. "I need your phone."

"I'm on it. Do you have someone here?" I looked in horror as a short, rotund man waddled out of the hall wearing my robe and nothing else. Wonder how I knew about the nothing else? The robe didn't close and just fluttered around him.

"Of course I have someone here. Didn't you see the panties on the doorknob of the apartment when you came home?"

"I just thought you dropped them when you did laundry."

"Yeah well now you know. We have to call the paramedics."

I looked between them. Nothing seemed wrong with either of them. "Neither of you look sick. What's wrong?"

Rotund Willie blushed while Aunt Beatrice cocked her hip out. "We had a bit of a bedroom accident. If you'd had a better supply of lube, this wouldn't have happened."

Too many questions swirled through my mind. Before I could narrow it down to one, I heard laughing on the other end of the phone I was holding.

"Hello?"

"Ember, I've heard plenty. I want you to come in for a formal interview."

"Really?"

"Absolutely, and I will expect to find out why in the world your aunt's friend needs to go to the hospital."

I felt my face flame and gave Aunt Beatrice the evil eye. "Thank you. When do you want me to come in?"

"How about tomorrow at one? Most of the kiddos will be down for naps."

"That sounds great. I will see you then."

"See you then, Ember."

I placed the phone down and looked at Aunt Beatrice. "I got an interview."

"That's great. You can stop mooching off me."

I blinked at her. "What?"

"Uhm, Bea, I don't mean to be a party pooper, but I still need some assistance." Willie motioned to his back.

I choked on air when he moved to the side and I could see something tenting the back of my robe.

"What the hell happened?"

"Like I said, you didn't have enough lube available and your brush is currently stuck in Willie's rectum."

It took a monumental effort to hold back the vomit that threatened to make an appearance. Instead of hurling, I picked up my phone and dialed 9-1-1. I stood with my back to the pair until the paramedics arrived.

I was sitting in the emergency room playing a game on my phone while I waited for Aunt Beatrice. After the ambulance retrieved Willie from my apartment, Aunt Beatrice and I called an Uber to take us to the emergency room. During the ride, she explained that Willie wasn't her normal Monday guy but because she had to relocate he got moved hence the butt activity. I had no clue how those things connected, and I wasn't about to ask. I just stared out the window and daydreamed of a day when my life didn't suck as much as it did at that moment.

"We got it." Aunt Beatrice walked out of a set of double doors holding a bag.

"Great. What?" I blinked at her.

"They removed the brush with minimal damage." She held up the bag that contained the odd-shaped object.

"What had minimal damage?" I immediately regretted the words when they left my mouth. No answer to that question was going to make me feel better.

"The brush has minimal damage, Ember. Willie's butt hole is definitely damaged. I had that thing wedged in there good."

Jesus. I needed a drink. I stood from the chair and walked to the doors.

"Where are you going?" Aunt Beatrice yelled.

"I need a drink. Take an Uber home or better yet, have them put you in the psych ward."

Marching out of the emergency room, I looked around to get my bearings. Midnight Sun was only a few blocks away. It was only two in the afternoon, but day drinking was definitely something that was needed.

When I arrived at Midnight Sun, I just nodded to Nora while making a beeline to the bar. It was fairly empty. Thank goodness. I didn't need a witness to the level of shitfaced I needed to get. The daytime bartender was in front of me before my ass was fully seated on the stool. I ordered two fingers of whiskey. It didn't even hit the bar top before I emptied it and requested another. The bartender stared at me in shock, then refilled the whiskey.

"So...what's going on?" I blinked at Nomi, who was sitting on the stool next to me.

"How long have you been sitting there?"

She looked at her expensive watch and said, "About fifteen minutes. I was wondering how long it would take you to notice me. I got impatient and a little worried when you continued to stare unblinkingly into the whiskey."

"Yeah well, it's been a hell of a companion."

"I get that. So, what's up?" Nomi sipped on a straw as she stared at me.

"Did Nora call you?"

"Of course. Now, tell me what's up?"

I tipped back the rest of the whiskey and held it up for the bartender to refill. When the bartender moved to approach, Nomi shook her head and the traitorous bartender walked to the other end of the bar.

"Bitch."

"I've been called worse. Are you going to tell me or do I need to get Olivia and Teagan here too?"

I crossed my arms but continued to stare at the glass. "What the hell has happened to my life, Nomi? I was successful. I enjoyed men on my own terms. I was able to pay my bills with a comfortable salary and, most importantly, I lived alone. I didn't have a crazy aunt, with a menagerie of weird animals, that needed to stay and help pay rent or I'm going to get evicted. What happened?"

"Hmm..."

"That's all you've got to say? You whiskey blocked me for hmmm. I'm wondering what kind of lawyer you are," I snapped.

Nomi let out an exasperated sigh. "I don't know what you want me to say. You're having one hell of a pity party right now, and I forgot to bring my party hat."

"Fuck you, Nomi."

We sat in silence for a few minutes. I really was having a spectacular pity party.

"Feel better?" She finished her drink.

"No. Yes. I don't know."

"Why are you at Midnight Sun day drinking? I know you have alcohol in your house."

"The apartment is infected with Beat-Rice. Plus, I just came from the emergency room. Midnight Sun wasn't far."

"Oh my God. Why didn't you start with that?" Nomi's eyes frantically looked over me.

"I'm fine. One of Beat-Rice's male companions had an accident."

"Is he okay?"

"They managed to remove the object."

A confused look crossed Nomi's face. "I'm lost."

"He got something lodged where the sun doesn't shine."

"How the hell did that happen? Did he fall?"

"Nope. Apparently, Aunt Beatrice got him good with the object. According to her, it is my fault it got stuck because I don't have enough lube on hand."

"Wow." Nomi waved at the bartender, motioning for another round. "What was the object?"

"My hairbrush. They removed it and gave it back."

"Ew. You're really going to have to wash that off good."

It was my turn to give her a strange look. "I'm never going to use that thing again. Are you insane?"

Nomi shrugged and then asked the question I wish I didn't know the answer to. "Which end was it?"

"Bristles first. No amount of lube would have made that slide in easy." I shot the whiskey, trying to banish the image of Willie in my robe with my brush sticking out of his ass.

13

The Happy Little Rainbow Academy

It was day two of my attempt at getting a job. The Happy Little Rainbow Academy was two bus transfers away from my apartment. I was dressed in another suit because the one from the chicken plant was contaminated with that horrible smell. My fingers drummed nervously on the satchel laying across my lap.

"Cheese?" an elderly woman offered from across the aisle.

"No, thanks." I gave her a tight smile.

"It's diet," she offered again.

What is with the world? A girl has a few curves and she must automatically be on a diet.

"No, thanks."

"That's for the best. It's not like she was offering you a salad," a man sitting a few seats away said.

"Excuse me?" My bitch level was rising fast.

"I was just commending you on your decision to get healthy. Cheese isn't an option for a person like you."

I gave the arrogant prick a sweet smile. "Thank you. I guess you can relate, huh?"

He blinked at me in confusion. "What do you mean? I'm perfectly healthy."

My sweet smile turned sharp. "Well, clearly condoms aren't an option for someone like you, a dickless sack of shit who feels their opinion is something that should ever be shared. Whew...I'm glad I met someone who can relate to me."

The female bus driver snickered as an awkward silence filled the bus. Before dickless could share any more of his opinions, the bus stopped across the street from the daycare. I exited it with my head held high as the remaining riders erupted into laughter.

With some pep in my step, I crossed the street to the brightly lit building. My little bitch pick me up allowed me to ignore the sweat pooled between my breasts and all the other parts of me that anyone else skinnier wouldn't have. With a deep breath, I pushed open the door. A lullaby was playing over a speaker. A woman at the front desk hit a buzzer to open an inner door. They impressed me with their level of security.

Approaching the desk, the woman stood with a smile. "Hello. How can we help you?"

"I'm Ember Tyler. I have an interview with Corrine."

"Perfect, I'm Corrine Lavender." She held out her hand.

I blinked. There wasn't any way that Corrine was the owner. She looked to be twenty-five at the oldest. I shook my head, banishing the thought, and focused on the woman before me.

Shaking her hand, I said, "Nice to meet you."

With a smile, she cocked her head and said, "Follow me."

Corrine led me down a dimly lit hallway that had colorful pieces of paper hung on the walls. I'm sure if the lighting was better I'd be able to see drawings by little kids. A lullaby played over the speakers. Each room we strolled past was darkened except for one. As we passed one classroom, a small face appeared in the window, scaring the life out of me.

"Oh my God."

Corrine stopped and looked at me, then the room. She shook her head and walked over to the door. Shaking her finger at the little face, it disappeared.

"That's India. She's allergic to naps. Come on, let's get this interview on its way." She continued further down the hall to a well-lighted office.

Following her into the office, I looked around. Pictures of smiling children were everywhere. There was even a scattering of children's artwork. I couldn't hold back the giggle when I noticed a picture of a child making a face.

"Have a seat, Ember. I hope you found us all right."

"I did. It's quite convenient you are across from a bus stop."

"Now, we have to get down to a very important question." Corrine leaned over her desk. "What happened with your aunt's friend?"

A loud laugh escaped. I immediately slapped my hand over my mouth. Corrine sat back in her chair and smiled. I blushed while filtering what exactly I felt comfortable telling a potential employer. When I finally figured out what to say, I opened my mouth and *all* the gory details tumbled out. When I say everything, I mean, I even talked about not having enough lube. As the last word left my mouth, I knew I blew the interview. Who the hell goes to an interview and tells them all about the dysfunction that is their aunt and her sexual proclivities? Apparently, I was self-destructive that way.

Corrine shook her head, then burst out laughing. I watched as she howled with laughter. It was so contagious that I joined her in her hysterical laughing. Finally, she wiped her tears away.

"That is fantastic. I can't wait to tell my husband about that. He's going to love it."

"You're married?"

She huffed out another laugh. "Yes. I am married. I know I look young, but I'm almost forty."

"You're what?" A horrible screech left me.

"I'm not sure if I should take your screech as a good thing or bad. I'm overly optimistic, so I will say a good thing."

"Sorry."

Corrine shook her head as she stood. "Don't be sorry. It was wonderful meeting you. I hope you will consider joining us here."

I blinked at her. "Wait. What? You want to hire me? You haven't even asked me any job-related questions. You don't even know if I'm good with kids. All we talked about was my dysfunctional family." I wasn't sure I wanted to work for someone who would just hire anyone off the street to care for children.

She sat back down and pulled out a folder from her desk. Opening it she began. "Ember Tyler, aged forty. Has a dual degree in interior design and early childhood education. Few people know that because she doesn't put that on any resumes. Growing up, she was the main child caregiver to many of the neighborhood children. No black marks on her mandatory reporting. Only a few indecent exposures and one minor incident of stealing a cop car while naked." Corrine looked up from the paper and said, "I want to hear about that, by the way." She looked back down at the paper. "Recently, Ember was fired from her very lucrative professional organization job. No one would elaborate on the whys on that one, but from the tone of your ex-employer, she seemed pissed."

"Wow. How did you get all that information?"

Corrine smiled. "My husband is a lawyer. He does all the thorough background checks on potential employees before there is even an interview."

"Yeah, but that doesn't explain some of the information you got."

"Well, it seems a friend of yours works with my husband."

I grit my teeth together. "Nomi."

With a nod, she looked at me seriously. "I can't pay you what you were making as a professional organizer. However, I can give you a challenge every day. A guarantee that every day will be different. We are a growing daycare that is promoting learning at all levels, leading into elementary school. If you want to feel fulfilled every day, then this is the place to work. If you are looking to become rich, this is not the place for you. I will give you time to think about it."

Corrine stood to leave, but I stopped her. "I don't need any time. I'd love to work here."

She smiled at me. "Good. You start Monday morning at five a.m."

"Five a.m.?"

"We start early here. Come on, let me get you started on some paperwork, then get you on your way so you don't miss the next bus."

"Sounds great."

We walked toward the front of the building. The lights were brighter and the sounds of children playing filled the rooms. Nap time was over and from the sounds coming from the rooms, it was time for some energy exertion. Corrine grabbed a thick, colorful folder.

"I will need you to have this to me first thing Monday. If you have any questions, I put my card in there with my cell."

"Thank you. I'm really excited." I hugged the folder to my chest.

"I'm excited to see you get started. I think you will be a great fit here. Now, get out of here before you have to wait another hour for a bus."

I smiled. "Thanks, Corrine. I won't disappoint you."

Rushing out the door, I got to the bus stop just in time for it to arrive. When I sat on the bus, exhilaration and triumph I hadn't felt in a while flowed through me. I was employed again. My future was beginning to look a lot shinier. That meant I needed to celebrate. I pulled out my phone from my purse. Only one person came to mind.

Me: Hey! What are you up to?

Sexy Idiot: I'll give you a hint. It involves lotion and socks.

Me: Eww...forget I texted.

Sexy Idiot: What? I'm giving myself a pedicure. You've got to pamper yourself sometimes.

Me: Hmmm...I'm not buying it.

Sexy Idiot: Why, Ember, is your mind in the gutter?

Me: Bye, Bucky.

Sexy Idiot: Wait. Sorry. I couldn't help but tease you. What's up?

I took a deep breath. Why in the world did my mind choose him to text? Why didn't I immediately call or text the girls?

Sexy Idiot: Ember?

It was too late to back out now.

Me: Fine. I want to celebrate.

Sexy Idiot: You chose me to do that?

Me: Yeah. Don't get all excited. The girls are busy, and I need to do these activities.

Sexy Idiot: Awesome. Their loss is my gain. I have the perfect place. I think you will love it. The minute I saw it I knew it had your name written all over it.

Me: You better not be talking about your penis.

Sexy Idiot: Why, Ember...you really have a dirty mind. And no, this has nothing to do with my penis.

Me: Good. Pick me up at 6. This place better have wings. Any celebration needs wings.

Sexy Idiot: They do and I will.

Me: Great. See you then.

Sexy Idiot: Oh and Ember...

Me: Yeah?

Sexy Idiot: I was talking about playing my skin flute earlier.

My face flushed when I read the last text. I held back the urge to throw Franken-phone, but instead shoved it in my purse. How the hell was I going to see him without imagining him jerking off? This was going to be a disaster.

14

FUCKING LUMBERJACK ASSHOLES

"This place has my name written all over it?" I looked around the enormous building.

"It mixes booze and violence. I'm pretty certain this says Ember all over it." Bucky placed his hand on my lower back and led me to a desk where a young girl sat.

When Bucky had picked me up, he was dressed like a lumberjack. He wore worn jeans, boots, and a flannel on top of a white tee. His hair was pulled back in his usual man bun. He looked sexy as hell. He grimaced when he saw the dress and heels I was wearing.

"You're going to want to change."

"What? Why? Where are we going that I need to change out of typical bar attire?" I put my hands on my hips.

"Sweetheart, just take my advice and put on jeans and sensible shoes. As much as I am enjoying the view, where we are going, you will not want to be wearing heels and a sexy dress. Trust me."

I glared at him, threw my arms up, and let him in. "Fine. I will be a few minutes. Next time, I need to wear something more specific text me ahead of time."

Marching into my bedroom, I rummaged through my closet. Luckily, I had just done laundry and one of my favorite pairs of jeans was clean. After throwing them on, I slipped on some comfortable flats and a flattering shirt and was ready in record time.

"I'm read—" I stopped in my tracks.

Aunt Beatrice's menagerie were curled up with Bucky on my couch. Princess took up prime real estate on his lap as Cuddles snuggled next to him. He absently pet them.

"What in the world?"

"What?" Bucky turned and Princess hissed at me for disturbing his pampering.

"How did you get that asshole to not be one?"

He shrugged. "I've always been good with animals."

I shook my head, not believing my eyes. "Are you ready?"

"Yep."

He gingerly placed all the animals back on the floor. He said to each one, "Thank you for letting me care for you. You're all very sweet."

Who would have thought Bucky was a baby talker?

"Are you okay? If you want to stay with the menagerie, you can."

He gave the clicking Cuddles one more pat on the head, then walked to the door. Opening it, he waited for me to walk through. "You know, Ember, I do love you in dresses, but those jeans make your ass look fantastic."

I snapped my head toward him as I locked the door. "Friends, Bucky."

"It's Robbie, remember?"

"It's Bucky every time you want to be a pervert."

"Well, shit," he mumbled under his breath. "You have a lot of stipulations."

"They are for both our benefits."

"I doubt that."

We walked up to a station where a woman who was dressed like a cross between a stripper and a lumberjack stood examining a tablet. She glanced up and saw Bucky and me approaching. A big smile curled her lips. Her squeal of excitement possibly ruptured my eardrums. She ran up and jumped into Bucky's arms. He swung her around as she squealed again.

"Robbie! Oh my God! It has been forever. What in the world are you doing here?"

"Well, I thought I'd introduce my friend to the art of drinking and ax throwing." Bucky looked at me, then said, "Ember, let me introduce you to Nova. Nova, this is my friend Ember."

Nova held her hand out to me. "Nice to meet you."

I took her hand in mine and gave a strained smile. "Nice to meet you too. You two look very close. How long have you known, Robbie?"

She grinned and winked at Bucky. "Our families grew up down the street from one another. I would always tag along when he and my brother would go off on an adventure."

Bucky leaned close to me. "Nova's brother, Blaze, owns this wonderful establishment."

"Yes, he does and if you think your ass is getting a discount, you have another think coming." A man in a tight black tee and equally fitted jeans walked toward us. His hair was pulled up in a man bun while a thick beard covered his face. The sexy lumberjack looked me up and down, then said, "Now her ass could get a discount."

"Aww...thank you," I said in my sweetest tone.

"Nova, can we have a station please?" Bucky said flatly.

The man was standing stiff as a board. I held my hand out to the newcomer. "I'm Ember."

He took my hand and kissed it. "Well, my beautiful Ember, I'm Blaze."

"Yeah. Yeah. Yeah. We all know each other now. Can we throw some axes?" A tinge of jealousy colored Bucky's words.

"Nova, can you put them in my reserved spot? I'll take them there."

"Sure, Blaze. It was good seeing you, Robbie. Nice to meet you, Ember."

Before I could say a word to Nova, Bucky had his hand on my lower back, pushing me toward a loud bustling area. We walked behind a row of stalls that had a bullseye at the end. Two axes were jammed into a stump just inside each little area. Tall empty tables stood three feet behind the opening to the stall. A long piece of white tape indicated the entrance.

"Here we are." Blaze gestured to a stall with a reserved sign over it. "Have you ever thrown an ax, Ember?"

"Not that I can remember." I could feel Bucky's eyes bouncing between Blaze and me.

"Let me show you, sweetie." He grinned.

If I wasn't supposed to be wearing a chastity belt, I would have taken him into the nearest closet. I was beginning to dig the beard too. I watched as Blaze removed the ax from the stump, and the muscles in his back made me all tingly.

Suddenly, I realized why exactly my friends called me a cockaholic.

"Here you go." He held out the ax.

Taking it from his outstretched hand, they forced me to step forward thanks to the heft of the thing. "Wow. Didn't expect it to be this heavy."

"It's all right, sweetheart. Blaze will help you." He stood behind me.

Well, there went any attraction I had for him. Talking about yourself in the third person was a turnoff. My douchebag alarms were going off. I kept my mouth shut since he was a friend of Buckys. Glancing over at him, I got the feeling Blaze would not be his friend for much longer. A vein was ticking in his forehead and his arms crossed over his chest bulged with tension. His jealousy was pretty hot.

"Okay. Hold the handle with two hands." Blaze put his hands over mine. "Then you're going to lift it over your head."

"Okay." I tensed when his hands left mine and latched onto my hips.

"Now, take a step and throw."

I did as he said but forgot to let go until it was too late. The ax flew from my hands backward and landed in the wall between two men talking outside of the men's room. Their eyes bulged when they realized how close they'd come to being castrated. The ax was shaking in the wall at waist height.

"Shit," Blaze said.

"Sorry. I think I let go too late."

Blaze swallowed, then said, "It's okay, sweetheart."

"Damn, Ember. You gave those guys quite the scare." Bucky laughed.

"Shut up, asshole."

He just grinned. Blaze returned with the ax after apologizing to the two men. I didn't feel that bad. Why the hell were they standing back there chatting, anyway? They were practically asking for it.

"Do you want me to help you again?" Blaze asked.

"I'm sure she will be fine, Blaze," Bucky snapped.

"Do you still want my help? I can stick around," Blaze pressed.

"She's celibate," Bucky blurted out.

Blaze and I snapped our gazes toward him. I felt a blush creep up my neck. Fucking Bucky.

"That's great," Blaze gritted out between clenched teeth.

"Yep. Her business is closed for business. Zero traffic going there. She's a friend zone only gal." Bucky kept talking.

"There's a—" I began.

"I guess I should leave you two to your fun. I will stop over before you leave." Blaze smiled at me and nodded at Bucky before leaving.

"What the fuck is wrong with you?" I spat.

"What? It's the truth. At least that's what you keep telling me."

I looked up at the ceiling in exasperation. "This is a jealousy thing?"

"No. I'm just looking out for my friend, and I didn't want him to get the wrong idea with all the eye fucking you were doing."

I picked up the ax. "I can't believe you. Maybe I should rethink our friendship."

He held up his hands as if he were innocent. "I was just trying to make sure you didn't go fuck him in some closet. That sure looked like what you wanted to do."

"Fuck you, asshole." Without looking at the target, I flung the ax toward it in frustration.

"Holy shit." Bucky's eyes were wide. "That was—"

I punched him in the face before he could say another word. As he cradled his cheek, I marched out of the place. With my phone in hand, I called a taxi. Anger coursed through my veins. Fucking Bucky and throwing my past in my face.

15

EQUAL PARTS ANGEL AND DEVIL

Hey Karen!

I'm calling you Karen now because I feel like you'd be the type to want to speak to the manager. I went with fucking Bucky last night to throw axes. His jealous ass humiliated me, so I punched him in the face.

In my opinion, it was a successful friend date.

That is all for today, Karen. Now, you can go talk to the manager.

Ember

"Ember! Someone's at the door," Aunt Beatrice shouted.

I dropped my pen on my notebook. "Aunt Beaty, you are out in the kitchen. The door is right there."

"I'm busy. Now, will you please answer the damn door? It's really making my hangover worse."

Marching out of my bedroom and to the open area where my kitchen and living room met, I saw Aunt Beatrice making a Bloody Mary.

"Seriously? You think drinking more alcohol will make things better?" I asked as I approached the door.

"Of course. Hair of the dog and all that." She raised her glass in cheers.

Shaking my head, I opened the door without looking to see who was knocking. "What do—"

"Hey, Ember." Bucky was holding a gigantic bouquet.

I slammed the door and began walking back toward my room. The banging started up again.

"Who was that?" Aunt Beatrice asked as she took her drink to the kitchen table.

"No one."

"It's Robbie," Bucky called through the closed door.

"Who the hell is Robbie? Have you finally gotten laid, Ember?"

"It's Bucky, Aunt Beaty. And as I told you before, my love life is none of your business."

The banging started up again. Maybe the punch in the face damaged something last night. Mental note: kick him in the nuts next time he's a jackass. Less likely he'd be at my door banging like a crazy person.

"Wait a minute. Wasn't Bucky that hunky boy who carried my boxes up but refused to play with mine?" Aunt Beatrice looked eagerly at the door.

"That's the one. Do you want me to let him in for you? I'm sure he returned because he realized his mistake of turning down your advance."

Aunt Beatrice fluffed her hair, and then grandly gestured at the door. "Let him in. He better be good on his knees for me to take him back."

I bit my lip as I walked back to the door. Opening the door, I didn't see Bucky there anymore. I stuck my head out the door and saw him with his back against the wall next to the door.

"Come on in. She's waiting for you."

"You know I came to see you," he whispered.

I grinned and leaned against the door. Looking closer, I saw a light bruise under one eye and he looked a bit disheveled. If he wasn't annoying the shit out of me, I might have felt bad. Who am I kidding? I wouldn't have felt bad for his dumbass. He deserved it.

"I know but she wants you to come in. She said you better be good on your knees."

Bucky paled. "Are you fucking with me, Ember?"

"Nope. In fact, this feels like the perfect payback."

"Is he coming or not, Ember? Wilber just texted for a booty call. If I can get that hottie with the nice ass, I'm not going for Wilber and his wrinkly one."

"He's coming in." I pulled on Bucky's shirt and dragged him into the apartment.

"Hello, handsome," Aunt Beatrice purred.

"Uhm..." Bucky froze like a deer caught in headlights.

"Welp, I gotta catch the bus for work. You two kids have fun." I grabbed my bag on the floor by the door.

"Wait. I can take—"

Slamming the door behind me, I cut off Bucky's words. A small part of me enjoyed making him squirm. The large evil part of me wanted to rub her hands together and relish the torture I'd just put him through. With some pep in my step, I entered the elevator to make it to my first day on the job.

"How old are you?" A little girl in pigtails pulled on my shirt as I cleaned up a spilled juice box.

"Forty."

Her jaw dropped as she stared at me. She solemnly nodded and walked away. It had been the weirdest afternoon. I haven't worked around children since my student teaching days. I'd forgotten how noisy and messy they were. My need to organize everything crawled under my skin.

"How are things going, Ember?" Susan, a young teacher who was responsible for getting me settled into my role, asked.

"Okay, I guess. This is just a lot different from my last job."

She nodded. "Yes, but it is so rewarding."

I gave her a sideways glance. Rewarding wasn't what I would've described it as. In that moment, I could see three boys picking their noses, two girls doing some very provocative dancing and one child running around with a trashcan on his head. Reward was definitely not the right word.

"Loving things?" Corrine asked.

Throwing the juice-stained rag into the laundry bin, I pasted on a fake smile. In all honesty, I'd been rethinking my decision of taking this job because the moment I walked into the room, a kid threw up on my shoes. But I needed a job. I would make this work.

"It's been great." I hoped the face I was showing illustrated the greatness.

Corrine and Susan had funny looks on their faces. They glanced at one another, then started laughing.

"What?" I asked.

"You're terrible at acting," Corrine said, wiping a tear away.

"I'm not acting. It really has been…" I swallowed, then continued, "great."

"It's okay that it's been a rough day. We don't judge. As much as these are our little angels, they are equally little devils," Susan said.

Just as Susan finished, the little girl who asked how old I was walked over dressed in black construction paper holding a piece of paper with flowers drawn on it. She handed me the flower paper.

"Thank you. What's this for?" I asked.

She gave me a sad look and said, "I'm attending your funeral. You're pretty old, so I wanted to make sure you had flowers when you died."

I gave the little girl a flat look as she somberly walked away. I turned toward Susan and Corrine. They were both holding back their laughter.

"Still great?" Corrine asked.

I scratched my nose with my middle finger as I walked over to the children's cubbies and began organizing them. Susan and Corrine's laughter echoed through the bustling room.

16

Fishbowl Margaritas

"Will we see you tomorrow?" Corrine asked from the front desk.

Exhaustion rained down on me. I'd forgotten how much energy little kids had coursing through their itty bitty bodies.

I nodded. "Yep." Looking down at my watch, I grimaced. I had five minutes to catch the bus home. "I'll see you tomorrow. Gotta catch the bus."

Corrine cocked her head. "You mean to say that's not here for you?"

I looked to where she was pointing and I saw Bucky leaning against his driver's side door. He looked like he was straight out of one of my favorite '80s movies. Involuntarily, my heart did a little flip. I gave myself a mental slap. That's not what he was here for. Just friends. Nothing more

"I suppose he is."

"Hmm...well have fun tonight." Corrine grinned and waved me out the door.

When I exited the daycare, Bucky pushed off his car and waved to me. In my head, some '80s music played. What the hell was wrong with me?

"Hey. What are you doing here?"

He shrugged and pushed his sunglasses on top of his head. I discreetly took him in. The bruise from my punch looked like a shadow under his eye. His hair was pulled on top of his head in a man bun. A tight gray T-shirt contoured his muscles that led down to low-slung jeans. I snapped my eyes higher before I wondered what he looked like out of those jeans.

"I thought I'd pick you up and take you to dinner."

"We aren't dating, Bucky." I sighed.

"You promised it would be Robbie."

"Yeah, and you promised not to act like a dick. Looks like we both broke our promises."

"Look, let me take you to dinner, Ember. I promise it is friends only. No expectations."

"Where do you want to go?"

"I have just the place."

Pursing my lips, I mentally weighed my options. When I looked up to see the bus pulling away, I knew he was my only option.

"Okay."

Bucky looked over his shoulder. "Missed your bus, huh?"

I shrugged and walked around the car to the passenger side. He raced around the front to open the door before I got there. Swinging the door open, I sat in the seat.

"I'll take being your knight in shining armor any day of the week."

"What exactly do you think you're saving me from?"

"I'm saving you from walking home."

"That's not—" He shut the door before I could refute his claim.

Jumping into the car, he started it and took off in record time. He zipped through traffic as if he didn't have a care in the world. More than one person flipped us off as we buzzed their car.

"What in the hell are you doing?"

He looked over at me with a grimace. "What?"

"You're driving like an asshole. I know this isn't how you always drive."

"Sorry. We're kind of on a time crunch for this restaurant." The car slowed, but his tapping on the steering wheel increased.

"What is so special about this place?"

"You tell me. We're here."

I blinked at the blinking sign. Señor Cervasas sign had a dancing mariachi guy as their mascot. I could hear the loud music in the car with all the windows rolled up.

"This place? Really?"

"What's wrong with this place?" He looked at his watch and cursed. "Come on. We have to get in the doors now." Bucky jumped out of the car and sprinted to the door.

I watched as he made it through the entrance at breakneck speed. He almost knocked over a lady in a walker. I got out of the car and saw him waving inside the restaurant. Looking around, I had no clue where we were in the city. Dammit. I was ready to leave his crazy ass there if he kept waving his arms in the air.

"Hurry up, Ember. They can seat us now."

The small crowd of elderly patrons trying to enter the restaurant turned to glare at me. Shifting my bag on my shoulder, I jogged to the door. I was not wearing the sort of bra for this kind of activity.

"I'm sorry. He's an idiot." I smiled at the group of blue hairs as I passed by them.

"Come on," Bucky whined.

"Cool your tits, Bucky. Geezus. I'm here."

"She's here. She's here." He held up my arm as if I'd just won a boxing match.

The hostess gave me a strained smile. "Come with me."

She wove us through the bustling restaurant. Each booth had intricate Mayan carvings. Colorful murals were painted on the wall. I was so enthralled by the murals that I didn't know she stopped. Bucky's hand on my shoulder stopped me from slamming into her. Blinking out of my awe, I saw we were at a corner booth. It could have easily seated ten people.

"Are there more people coming?" I asked Bucky.

"Nope. It was the only table they had available." He turned to the hostess. "Gracias, Señorita.."

She rolled her eyes and walked away. Bucky got in on his side and moved all the way to the back. I stuck to the edge of the horseshoe-shaped table. We were sitting in this weird diagonal that wasn't comfortable.

"I'm so glad we made it." Bucky wiggled in his seat.

"I can see that," and I opened the menu, immediately overwhelmed.

"Everything is wonderful here. Xander, Blaze, and I come here all the time. Their chimichangas are their specialty."

"All right, I suppose I will get that. I've never really eaten in a Mexican restaurant before."

Bucky stared at me. "Hold up. You've never had Mexican food?"

"I've had Mexican food. I'd just never been to a Mexican restaurant to eat that food."

"Oh. That's weird."

"Says the guy who practically ran over a group of old folks to get into the restaurant and then waved frantically like a lunatic."

He looked sheepish. "I guess I get excited about their fishbowl margaritas. They only have them once a month and you have to be in the door by five-thirty or you can't order them."

"What the hell is a fishbowl margarita?"

"That is." He pointed to something over my shoulder.

A waiter was carrying an enormous glass barely held up by a stem, filled with a rainbow of colors and the rim covered in an inch-thick crust of salt. I watched it float by. As it floated by, a familiar face caught my attention.

"Fuck me," I mumbled.

"I would, but you keep saying just friends." Bucky laughed at his joke. "Are you getting one?"

I gazed down at my menu. If I didn't look up, they couldn't see me. That's how those things worked, right? I glanced up and saw the two people walking toward us I'd hoped never to see again. Stan and Eve.

"What's going on, Ember?" Bucky said only inches from my face.

"What the fuck? Why are you sitting so close?" I shoved his shoulder with mine.

"I just wanted to see what was bothering you. Do you know those people?" He pointed toward my ex-boss and his wicked wife.

"Put your arm down, sit still, and shut the fuck up," I gritted through my teeth.

"Wha—"

"Well, hello, Ember. Fancy seeing you here." Eve's voice grated on my nerves.

"Hello, Eve. Stan."

"Don't address him, homewrecker," she spat at me and then noticed I wasn't alone. "Another marriage you're wrecking?"

"I'd say it was a pleasure to see you, but I don't like to lie, unlike the two of you."

Eve glared at me and then looked at Bucky. "Sir, I don't know if you are aware of the woman whom you are with. She is a notorious slut who tries to steal husbands. From my understanding, she is also unemployed. I mean, look at her. Who would hire someone like that?"

Unconsciously, I patted my hair down. Bucky took my hand in his, kissed the palm, and slid his arm around my shoulders.

"Ma'am, I think you may have the wrong person."

"I surely do not. I—"

"What I meant is I think you have the wrong person who would give a shit about anything like that. Ember is the sweetest, most brilliant, and loyal person I know. If anything happened between her and—" Bucky looked at Stan hiding behind Eve, "him, it would have been his greatest achievement."

Eve opened and shut her mouth like a goldfish.

Bucky snapped his fingers. "Hold on. Ember, sweetheart, was this the guy with the micro penis who cried after you fucked?" He laughed. "Shit. We've had a lot of laughs about that after I made her come over and over again screaming my name."

"Well, I have never been so insulted. Stan does not have a micro penis. It is perfectly adequate."

"Yikes, man. I don't think I've ever had a woman call my package adequate. Would you describe it as adequate, sweetheart?"

I grinned. "Adequate is not what I think of when I think of your package."

Eve huffed then stormed off with her little lapdog Stan following in her wake.

"I think we pissed her off good." Bucky laughed.

"I think we did."

We laughed. I stopped and leaned over, planting a kiss on his smiling lips. I only meant it to be a small peck. Instead, it turned into something so much more. His hand wound in my hair angling my mouth for better access. Just as his tongue slid into my mouth, someone cleared their throat next to the table. I pulled away to see the waiter looking uncomfortable.

"Are you ready to order or will you need a few minutes?"

"I need one of those fucking fishbowl margaritas," I said, pulling away from Bucky.

"Make that two," he said breathlessly.

17

CLOSE ENCOUNTERS OF THE NUT KIND

*O*kay, Karen,

This is an unplanned addition to this journal. I made a big ole oopsie. I planted a big one on Bucky. In my defense, how does one just ignore a man like that defending your honor and he did it in such a sexy way? How did that happen you ask? Well, we saw that turd and his bloody tampon of a wife at the Mexican restaurant. My coward of an ex-boss hid behind that shrew while Bucky decimated her. It was magical. That's if most little girls dreamed of becoming a princess and having a prince kiss them while forest animals sang songs. I was not like most girls. I dreamt about a man eviscerating someone on my behalf. In my fairytale, I'd marry the dragon.

All for now,

Ember.

"Earth to Ember." Teagan waved her hand in front of my face.

"Uh, yeah…sorry what were we talking about?" I looked over at Teagan in the pedicure chair next to me.

"You heard nothing Teagan just said?" Olivia asked.

"Sorry I spaced out." I looked at Olivia. "You heard her? You never hear anything unless it's on your phone."

"We all heard her," Nomi added.

"Well, excuse me." Turning back to Teagan, I said, "Please excuse me, but could you repeat what you said?"

"Grayson asked me to marry him, and I said yes," she said flatly.

"What?!" I squealed, kicking my feet and effectively splashing the woman who was trying to give me a pedicure.

Teagan grinned and held out her hand which had a massive rock on it. I took her hand to inspect it. Grayson did a hell of a job. It was the perfect mix of ostentatiousness and class. It described Teagan to a tee.

I whistled, then met her gaze. "You're not knocked up, are you?"

Teagan pulled her hand out of mine and swiftly smacked me in the middle of my forehead.

"Ow. What was that for? It's a valid question." I rubbed the spot she smacked.

"You deserved it," Nomi said with a shrug while Olivia nodded in agreement.

"Sorry, Teag. The question just popped out. So, how did he do it?"

Teagan smiled. "Well, we went on a walk with QD on that path near the river. Grayson was acting funny. He was fidgeting, and I wondered if the latest sex toy we tried had an ill effect on him."

"Too much info." Nomi grimaced.

"I didn't say which toy." Teagan blew out an exasperated breath, then continued, "Anyway, we stopped to look out at the sunset. QD was acting weird, and Grayson nudged her toward me. She came over and I pet her. Grayson gave me an odd look and then asked if I saw what she had."

"Aww...that's sweet," Olivia cooed.

"Uhm...not quite."

"I knew it wasn't going to go that smoothly," I said.

"Shut up, but you're right. The only thing hanging from her neck was a chewed ribbon. Grayson freaked out so much that he picked up QD and ran all the way back to the car. I still had no clue what was going on. We ended up at the vet and had to wait a few hours before she passed the ring. When the vet gave it back to Grayson, he dropped to one knee and proposed."

"Please tell me you washed that ring off before he slipped it on," I begged.

"Of course. Isn't it sparkly?" Teagan wiggled her fingers, making it glitter. "Now, tell us how things are going with you and your friend Bucky."

I groaned. "Can't we go back to talking about Teagan and her dog poo ring?"

"No," the three of them shouted, making all the pedicurists jump.

"Hi, Dad," I answered my phone as I got off the elevator to my floor.

"How's it going, Peanut?" he asked cheerfully.

"It's going okay. I have a new job."

"Oh really? What is it?"

"I'm working at a daycare."

"I always knew you'd do well with kids."

"They may just be the death of me."

"Wait until you have your own. How are things going with your aunt?"

"They are—" I stopped because I saw a pair of skid-marked tighty-whities hanging from my doorknob. "Gross" I mumbled.

"Everything okay, Ember?"

"Yeah. Looks like Aunt Beaty has another gentleman caller here."

"How can you tell?"

"Well, there is underwear on my doorknob and sounds that are similar to a monkey are coming from my apartment. Why in the world did you think this was a good idea?" I slid down my door and sat on the floor.

"What are you doing?"

I looked up to see Bucky standing over me.

"Dad, I gotta go. I hope you're having fun on the commune."

"Ember, wait—"

I hung up the phone before my dad could ask any more questions.

"What's it look like I'm doing, Bucky?"

"I thought we'd agreed to you calling me Robbie? I mean, after that kiss…"

"Nope. We aren't talking about that. What do you wan—"

Before I could finish that thought, I was laying flat on my back looking up at a pair of saggy testes.

"Oh God!" I sat up a little too quick and got a wet, limp dick slapped on my forehead.

"Pardon me," the old man said, grabbing his underwear.

"Why are you sitting in the hallway, Ember?" She looked past me to Bucky. "Oh, I see now. I'll leave you two alone."

I sat frozen on the floor. "I swear if I look up and see you laughing, I'm nut punching you."

"Haven't you had enough close encounters of the nut kind today?" He laughed loudly and ran.

"You better run," I yelled after him. When he disappeared down the stairwell, I wiped the wetness off my forehead. I refused to think about what the stickiness was. With a groan, I stood and then marched into my apartment. They could have been doing some intricate sex maneuver for all I cared. I needed a shower and a hard drink to erase the past ten minutes.

18

Arts and Farts

*D*eadman walking: *Next adventure begins Friday.*

    Me: What is it and what do you mean begins?

Deadman walking: It involves staying outdoors overnight.

Me: I don't do camping.

Deadman walking: It's not camping.

Me: Fine. I'm done work at 3 on Friday.

Deadman walking: See you then, Lipton.

Me: Lipton?

Deadman walking: Yeah. You know tea bag.

I'm truly going to kill him. He probably won't be surviving this excursion.

Me: Please tell me this weekend is me hunting you with an actual weapon. I'm down for that. I'll stay out in the woods with bugs for that.

When he didn't answer right away, I shoved my phone into my pocket. I needed to pay attention to the hellions. They were painting today. If I was lucky, I'd only have a few splotches of paint on my clothes.

"Who makes you smile like that?" Corrine asked, sidling next to me.

"What?"

"You don't smile like that all the time. Is it that guy who picked you up the other day?"

I felt blood rush to my face. "He's just a friend."

"Uh-huh. I get it. Most relationships are complicated. However, that guy from the other day really has the hots for you."

"I can't be in a relationship right now."

"Okay. Keep your secrets."

"Ms. Ember?" A little voice called for her.

It was one of the little terrors, Lilith. "Yes, Lilith?"

"I'm finished painting."

"All right. You can leave your painting there and go wash up."

"Don't you want to see it?" She batted her bright blue eyes at me.

I glanced over at Corrine, who was biting her lip to keep from laughing.

"Sure." I marched over to the little psychopath's easel. Lilith grinned as I looked at the black and red mess.

"That's very nice."

"Do you know what it is?"

I had no fucking clue what it was. It looked like an abstract painting. I couldn't say that to her, though.

"Is it a dog?"

She furrowed her brow and looked at her painting. "No."

"Well, sweetie, no matter what, you did an excellent job." I smiled at her.

"It's a painting of you."

"Well, thank—"

"...dead while crows eat your eyes."

What the fuck? I heard a snort from behind me. Corrine was walking as fast as she could from the room.

"Uhm."

Lilith grinned. "Do you still find it pretty? I made sure to put in a lot of blood."

I stared at her and realized in that moment she was either going to write horror books or she was going to be a serial killer. My money was on the latter.

Taking two steps back, I said, "It's still lovely. Now, go wash up."

Lilith giggled then skipped away. Her blonde pigtails bounced as she went.

Grams laughed as I recounted my adventures in daycare.

"That little girl is exactly what your little girl would be like." She smiled.

"Bite your tongue, Grams," Teagan said from next to me. "Ember should probably not procreate."

I glared at her. "Are you sure you aren't knocked up, Teagan?"

Grams laughed at the two of us who were now swatting at one another. We were waiting in the activity room of the senior home where Grams and her husband lived. It was arts and crafts night. Edna usually called it arts and farts.

"Hey there, Chamomile."

Speaking of the devil and she appeared. Bucky's grandmother wasn't the person I wanted to deal with after dealing with Lilith all day.

"Who's Chamomile?" Grams asked.

"She is." Edna's finger was an inch from my nose.

"That's Ember. Are you losing it, Edna?" Teagan asked.

Edna looked at me, then to Grams and Teagan. "Am I the only one that knows?"

Clapping from an overly cheerful young woman drew our attention. "Good evening, everyone. We have a very exciting activity planned."

"Is it more cock cozies?" Edna asked.

The young woman's smile strained. "We were never making those, Edna."

"Well, that sucks because I've made a lot of money off those."

The woman ignored her and continued, "Tonight, we get to paint."

"Oh God," I groaned.

"We are painting a real person. No more fruit for us."

"Did we miss fruit painting?" Teagan leaned over and asked me, and I shrugged.

"Will our guest please come out?" She smiled, but something immediately wiped it away. The man who always walked around with his robe wide open was strutting over to an open area. A few of the older women made catcalls and whistled.

"Sweet baby Jesus on a trampoline." Teagan covered her eyes.

"This is what I'm talking about." Edna whistled.

"Mr. Franklin! I told you if you wanted to take part, you had to wear clothes," the blonde hissed.

"I am wearing clothes, sweetheart, but not for long." He dropped the robe and posed.

"Psst. Psst, Ember." Edna tried to get my attention. "Did your tea bags hang low like those?"

"Tea bags?" Grams asked.

Edna patted Grams' head. "Sweet, innocent, Edith. Tea bags are another—"

Grams batted Edna's hand away. "I know the slang term, Edna. What does that have to do with Ember?"

An evil grin curled Edna's lips. "A pair of old man balls slid up Ember's face."

Teagan's and Grams' eyes grew large. "What?"

I looked up at the ceiling and prayed for the tile to fall on either me or Edna. The prayer didn't work. Instead, I put my head down as Edna cackled, drawing glares from all the arts and farts crowd.

19

See You Next Time

"Why are you packing a bag to go to work?" Aunt Beatrice asked as she drank a mimosa and petted Princess. She looked like an evil villain.

"I told you. Bucky is picking me up straight from work. So, you get the apartment for the entire weekend."

Aunt Beatrice shrugged. "Eh...I didn't schedule any of my male friends for this weekend. I'm thinking I will have a 'take care of Beaty' weekend. I've stocked up on batteries, ice cream, lube, and light bulbs."

I stared at her. "Light bulbs?"

She took a sip of her drink. "Yeah. We are out and a few of the lamps are getting dim. Why did you get a strange look on your face when I said light bulbs?"

Shoving my sneakers into the bag, I said, "No reason. Well, I hope you have a great one."

"You know, Ember, you have a fucked-up mind. Did you think I'd shove a light bulb up my ass to see if it would glow?"

"Nope. Didn't cross my mind."

Well, not that scenario at least. I'll never get that out of my head. Thanks, Aunt Beat-Rice.

"I've tried it. It doesn't work."

Without another word, I left. I wasn't about to risk hearing more than I'd like with her.

"Hey!" Bucky said when I jumped into the car.

"Hi. So, what do you have planned?"

"Wouldn't you like to know?" He wiggled his eyebrows.

"Uhm...yeah. That's why I asked you, idiot."

Bucky squinted, looking past me. "What's that?" He pointed toward the daycare.

I looked and sighed. My co-workers were waving along with some children. One was holding a sign with the letters C-U-N-T.

"What are you teaching those children?"

"It doesn't mean what you think."

"Oh, I know what that word means. Every guy knows that word and knows better than to say it in front of a woman."

The evil little girl holding the sign could very well have known what that meant. She was devious. However, I was going to go with how she explained it to me. "It means see you next time."

Bucky looked at me, then back to the daycare, then back to me one more time. "No. That is not what that word means."

"Oh lord. Who gives a shit? Where are we going?"

"We are going hunting." He smiled as he pulled the car out of the parking lot.

"Excuse me? In what world did you actually think it was a good idea to take me hunting?"

"It's not the kind of hunting you're thinking."

"Are we hunting humans?"

He blinked and stared at me. "No. Why would you immediately think that?"

"I've met your grandmother. If anyone is up for hunting humans, it's her."

Bucky reluctantly nodded. "You've got me there. She would definitely do that. This hunting I think you will like. It's a lot of fun."

"I doubt that, but whatever." I crossed my arms and watched the scenery fly by.

"So, are we going to talk about it?" he asked after three seconds went by.

I blew out a breath. It was time to play dumb. "Talk about what? Is there something we need to talk about?"

"Don't play dumb with me. That kiss was electric."

"Ehh...was it?"

"Are you fucking with me right now? I know you felt what I felt."

I went back to looking out the window. The car left the city limits and began winding through the woods. I was so focused on staring out the window, I didn't even realize how much time went by without us talking. Glancing over at him, I noticed a vein throbbing in his forehead.

"Fine."

"Fine? That's all you're going to say?"

"What do you want me to say, Bucky? It was a kiss. It was something we shouldn't have done?"

He furrowed his brow. "Why are you acting like I forced it on you? You were the one who kissed me, remember?"

"I'm not acting any way. I got carried away, and I'm sorry. I shouldn't have done it."

Bucky's knuckles turned white as he gripped the steering wheel tight.

"This conversation was a mistake. Forget I brought it up."

"Look, Bucky, it was—"

"Stop calling me Bucky! I am sick and fucking tired of it!" he shouted.

My teeth dug into my bottom lip. The urge to say something else was burning inside of me because I didn't think that kiss was a mistake. It was the best kiss I'd ever had. Could I tell him that? Hell no.

"Uhm..." Before I could say any more, he snapped his gaze to me and I zipped my trap shut.

Immediately, I turned to look back at the world outside the window. I'm not sure when, but the ride had lulled me to sleep. A hand shoving my shoulder made me jump in my seat.

"We're here," he said.

"Oh." I yawned and wiped the drool off my mouth. Well, wasn't that just a sight? Good thing I didn't want to have sex with him, or that would have been one hell of a turnoff. Peering around, I saw an open space and three men staring at the car with open mouths. It looked like I was going to be spending the weekend with four idiots.

20

SASQUATCH MATING ZONE

A bright fire blazed in the middle of the camping area. I sat there watching the men cook and drink beer. All but one was familiar to me. Xander, Blaze, and Bucky were laughing as Rocco fooled around with some sort of equipment. What the hell had I gotten myself into by agreeing to this trip? I looked over toward the car. Bucky had brought two tents, but the thought of sleeping on the ground made my skin crawl.

A tin foil packet was thrust in front of my face. "What is this?"

"Grub," Xander said with a boyish smile.

"You mean the bugs?"

"For Christ's sakes, Princess, it's chicken and potatoes in a tinfoil packet," Blaze said as he sat down near her. "Bucky, why did you bring her?"

Well, the hotness wore off on him really quickly. "Fuck you very much." I opened the packet.

"She isn't going to talk the whole time we're hunting, is she?" Rocco grumbled.

"I'm quite happy staying at the campsite while the four of you wander off into the woods for some full moon circle jerk. I don't need to see your teeny weeny peenies." I gave them a sweet smile.

The four of them stared at me with their mouths hanging open. I blew on the hot food in the packet, then daintily began eating it. Their gazes were still on me while I ate.

"What?" I asked with a mouthful of food.

Xander shook his head and began laughing. "You really do like the feisty ones, Bucky."

"You don't think Olivia is feisty? Well, you have another think coming if you go after her." Xander blushed. "And from that bright red blush, I'd say she's appeared in your spank bank more than once."

Bucky began, sitting on the other side of me. I slapped him on the back and a piece of food flew out and pegged Rocco in the forehead. It was glorious.

"Fuck, Bucky." Rocco wiped his forehead off.

He coughed, then said, "Sorry, Rocco." Looking at me he continued, "You really have no filter, do you? It doesn't matter who you're around, you will say whatever you want."

I straightened my back. "Yeah. What of it?"

Bucky's eyes twinkled in the firelight. "I find that incredibly sexy in a woman."

Turning away from him, I said, "Well, that sounds like a personal problem. Save it for your circle jerk."

"Why the hell does she think we are going out and jerking each other off?" Blaze asked.

"I don't know. Maybe that's in her spank bank." Rocco smirked.

I curled my lips in disgust. "Look, I know it's almost every guy's fantasy that women pleasure each other. That shit doesn't happen and I'll say it isn't sexy seeing one man jerk off, let alone a bunch of them blowing their loads because they are in the woods doing manly things."

Xander ignored my comment and turned to Bucky. "You didn't tell her?"

"Tell me what?"

Bucky glared at Xander then turned toward me. "Uhm...uh...we're hunting Bigfoot."

A laugh burst from me. I bent over to catch my breath. When I sat up and wiped the tears from my eyes, I noticed I was the only one laughing.

"You aren't serious, are you?" I looked around at the very serious men.

"We aren't just hunting Bigfoot. We're looking for UFOs as well." Xander smiled.

My jaw dropped as I looked at each of the guys. There wasn't a grin among them. Well, fuck a duck. It looked like they were going Bigfoot hunting.

The woods were pitch black. Crunching of leaves and sticks under our booted feet were the only noises around. A random animal scurried away, making me pause. I was not this kind of girl. The kind that went on hikes and slept outdoors. If I was an animal, I would have been an overfed house cat that moved only to find the best place to lie in the sun. I would have never been anything that had to fend for them-selves in the woods.

I sighed as I followed behind Blaze. Bucky made me walk in front of him. He claimed it was so I wouldn't get lost. I think he just wanted to "accidentally" touch my ass.

"Will you stop sighing so loudly?" Blaze hissed.

"How can a sigh be loud?" I said in my normal voice be-cause whispering was bullshit.

Blaze sighed. I snorted. "We are trying to listen for mating calls."

"Mating calls?"

"Yeah. It is well documented that this time of the year, Bigfoot gather to mate," Xander said excitedly.

I stopped walking. "Are any of you on some kind of hallu-cinating drug?"

"No, why?" Bucky stood next to me, making me jump.

"Why? Because all of this is total and complete—" I was cut off by a far-off guttural cry. "What the fuck was that?"

"Bigfoot," Rocco breathed.

"Or aliens," Xander added.

"Nope." I turned around and began walking back the way we came.

"Ember! Where are you going?" Bucky chased after me.

The oversized boots and camouflage clothing I was wear-ing hindered my quick steps. "Whatever that was, I'm not staying out in the middle of nowhere for it to find me."

"You can't walk back on your own. You could get lost."

I stopped. "Then come back with me."

The full moon overhead shone down upon us. I watched as Bucky debated what to do. He looked at me and then back to where the guys were. His shoulders sagged as he looked at me. "Please stick with us longer. I promise nothing will get to you. We are protected."

"Protected. How?" My hands found purchase on my ample hips.

"Rocco and Blaze have guns. Xander has a taser."

"And you. What do you have?"

"I have you to throw at the monster. You'll give me enough time to run away."

"You fucker."

He grinned. "Or we could go back and talk about that kiss? Didn't you say I ruined you for all men?"

"Are you fucking high? I said no such thing."

"Maybe. Maybe not. We can go back to the camp and practice some more."

I let out a frustrated grunt and pushed past him. Marching toward the other guys, I could have sworn I heard the idiot laughing. If he thought he was going to throw me at an animal, he had another think coming. I'd trip his ass and serve him up. An evil grin curled my lips as I met back up with the group with Bucky trailing only a few feet behind me.

21

Negotiations with Bigfoot

I don't have to pee.

I don't have to pee.

I don't have to pee.

Dammit. I have to pee. Warm and cozy in my sleeping bag was where I wanted to stay. The idea of leaving my tent to find a secluded place to drop my drawers and pee was abhorrent. However, nature was calling something fierce. Crawling out of my sleeping bag, I quietly unzipped the tent opening. There were glowing embers of fire which helped guide me where to go and that none of the men were awake. Quickly, I exited the tent and tiptoed toward a large tree across from the tents. I looked around to make sure I was alone and dropped my underwear and squatted to pee.

The relief was nearly orgasmic. In mid-stream, I heard a twig snap. I froze in place and waited. Another twig snapped. Whatever it was, it was coming closer. On a loop in my head, I went through every possible survival thing I knew. Should I play dead? Nah. That was for bears. Should I run? Nah. That just activates their hunting instinct, and I'd be a goner.

Should I stand really still so they can't see me? No again. That was for a T-Rex and I was highly doubtful it was that.

"Please don't kill me, Mr. Bigfoot," I whispered. "I just needed to pee. If you want some juicy morsels, they are sound asleep in their tents."

"Are you selling us out to Bigfoot?" Bucky's voice made me jump. When I jumped, my feet got caught in my panties and I fell forward. My bare ass was in the air. "Hmm...nice full moon tonight."

I hurriedly scrambled up, trying to pull my underwear up while keeping my back to him. "What the fuck are you doing out here?"

"I heard you get up. When you didn't come right back, I worried you'd walked out too far and got lost. But I can see now you didn't. You're just negotiating with Bigfoot while taking a leak."

"Ugh! You're such an asshole. And newsflash, of course, I'm giving you to him. Why would you think I'd sacrifice myself? I don't even want to be out in the outdoors, let alone be eaten by a mythical creature."

Bucky grinned. "You remind me so much of my granny. Now I know why she likes you so much."

"Didn't anyone ever tell you that you shouldn't compare a woman with your mom or grandmother? It's not really flattering. That's especially true since I've met Edna. She's a few ants shy of a picnic."

"And you aren't?"

"Look, I'd love to keep discussing this with you, but I'm cold and would rather not be having a conversation where I just peed." I walked around him, and he grabbed my wrist to stop me.

"Wanna fool around?" He wiggled his eyebrows.

"Uhm...no. I want to sleep. Now if you don't mind." I looked down at where his hand held my wrist.

He lifted a shoulder. "Suit yourself. You know where I am if you want some body heat." He wiggled his eyebrows.

"In your dreams." I marched over to my tent and with a speed I didn't think I had for the middle of the night, I climbed in and zipped up the tent.

My heart beat so loud in my chest, I thought I was going to have a heart attack. I stared up at the ceiling of my tent, contemplating his proposition. He was right about the kiss, though I'd never tell him that. I highly doubted any man could ever compete with him. And I thought we were in a different zip code, so that would be a loophole with us fooling around. My mind ran over the dare/challenge my friends had made me agree to. It was sex. They said nothing about a little finger banging or clam munching. While I contemplated my options, my eyes drifted closed. The last thought I had in my mind was how big Bucky's hands were.

The potent smell of coffee wafted into my tent. My eyes peeled open only to squint them closed when the bright sunshine poured into the tent. Groaning, I ducked back into the sleeping bag, hoping to go right back to sleep.

"Sweet Caroline..." A gruff male voice began singing. It sounded like a cat had its tail stuck in a garbage disposal.

"Bop. Bop. Bah." Another voice sang back.

"Fuck my life." I threw the sleeping bag off and stretched. "At least there is coffee."

"Are you talking to yourself in there, Ember?" Xander asked from outside the tent.

"I'm just plotting your deaths. Spoiler alert...they are going to look like accidents."

Rocco let out a laugh. "Come on, grumpy girl. I've got coffee."

I slid out of the sleeping bag, pulled on a pair of yoga pants, and unzipped the tent. Sun immediately blinded me. "Ack!"

"You'll get used to it. Just follow the sultry sounds of my singing voice," Rocco called to her.

"If I did that, I'd run screaming in the opposite direction." With my hand shading my eyes, I wandered over to the small portable stove where Rocco and Xander were standing holding mugs.

With a huge smile, Rocco handed me a mug. "I didn't know what you liked in it, so it's just black. However, Xander brought some frou-frou creamer, if you'd like some."

"It's caramel mocha almond. I also brought whipped cream for a topping." He opened a cooler to show her the options.

"I'm good with black. I'm going to need it strong to deal with you guys today." I looked around and didn't see Bucky or Blaze. "Where are the other two stooges?

"Apparently, they needed to work out then get firewood." Rocco shrugged.

Before I could comment, a rustling drew our attention. Blaze strode into the campsite. His flannel shirt was open, and he was glistening with sweat. He was a mouthwatering sight. What the hell kind of workout was he doing in jeans and a flannel? In his arms was a bundle of firewood. He walked toward the firepit and dropped the wood next to it. Taking a sip of the hot coffee, I didn't even feel the burn while watching him.

Another noise in the woods came crashing toward us. Bucky wore no shirt, a pair of shorts, and sneakers. He carried an ax and another bundle of wood. His dark hair was damp with sweat. The moisture made his whole body sparkle in the sunshine. My mouth immediately dried up. Blaze looked hot in a lumberjack kind of way. Bucky was on a whole other level. He must have caught me staring because when he walked by, he winked and then placed his bundle of wood next to Blaze's bundle.

"Are you hungry, Ember? I can make some eggs and bacon," Xander offered.

Nodding, I kept my eyes on the sparkling man candy striding around the firepit. Sipping my coffee, I could hide the naughty smirk that curled my lips.

"I don't know if it's eggs she's hungry for, Xander," Rocco teased.

My cheeks flamed as I flipped him off. Turning away from my entertainment, I walked to the edge of the campsite and looked out at the woods. It was pretty in the early morning light.

"Morning, gorgeous." Bucky's voice made me jump, effectively spilling the hot coffee on my shirt.

"Fuck, Bucky. You made me burn my tits."

"I can kiss them and make them feel better."

"If anything, you aren't getting near them now that you hurt them."

"You know I didn't mean to hurt you. Don't you?" Bucky cooed to my breasts.

"Are you baby talking to them?"

"Shh...I'm trying to make it up to them." He leaned closer to her chest, but I slapped my hand against his forehead and pushed him away.

"Back up, Bucky, before I have to do something drastic."

"I'd listen, Bucky. Remember how she was with that ax?" Blaze smiled as he walked by.

"I hate all of you. Why am I here again?"

"Because you need to have platonic experiences with men." Bucky spit my words back at me.

"Yes, platonic, not idiotic."

"We love you, Ember." Rocco, Blaze, and Xander called from where Xander was making breakfast.

"Ugh! It's too early to deal with you morons. I'm going back to bed and hopefully I will wake up and you four won't be so irritating."

"Good luck with that," Rocco called to her.

22

PLEASE BEAM XANDER UP

We were tromping around a field again. When Xander found a place he insisted was a landing zone for aliens, we all stopped and sat in the field. After about twenty minutes, my butt became numb. We were supposed to be staring up at the sky. Every little movement Xander insisted was an alien craft. If it were, I was internally begging for them to beam him the hell up so we could go back to the campsite.

"Look at that. They are responding when I blink the flashlight." Xander turned the light on and off toward the sky.

"It's a fucking plane," I mumbled.

"No. Look." He insisted.

I turned toward Bucky, who sat close to me. "Are you buying this?"

He shrugged. "I'm hoping one day they beam him up."

"He's just going to get his ass probed. He really wants that?" I asked.

"They don't probe your butt. That's just a myth." Xander shook his head.

Bucky and I looked at each other. "What would you do if they did? Would you enjoy it or would you beg to come back?" Bucky asked.

"He'd love it," Blaze said with a yawn.

"He'd ask for more." Rocco laughed.

"Shh...you're scaring them away."

I flopped on my back and stared up at the sky. How had I gotten myself into this mess? Oh yeah, I had to have a non-sexual relationship with men. Well, this was definitely not an activity that turned me on. I felt the grass move next to me. Turning my head, I saw Bucky lying next to me.

"Are you having a good weekend?" he whispered.

"It's definitely not something I thought I'd be doing."

He smiled, folded his arms under his head, and stared at the sky. "It's just a bit of fun. We do stuff like this once a month."

"What, poker isn't fun enough?"

"Oh, we do that too, but sometimes we need to be out in the wilderness." Bucky grinned.

"I guess whatever floats your boat."

He rolled to his side and stared at me. "What floats your boat?"

"You don't want to know."

"Yeah, I do."

"I cosplay."

"You mean like dress up and stuff?"

"Sort of. It's more than Halloween. When I dress up at these conventions, I become that character. People even like taking pictures with me."

"So, what do you dress up as? I'm envisioning a French maid or a sexy witch."

I rolled my eyes at him. "These aren't sex conventions, though that happens pretty often. I've dressed up as quite a few unique characters. This year, the girls and I are dressing up as the Powerpuff girls."

"Teagan, Nomi, and Olivia are into that stuff too?" he asked.

"Well...no but as long as I win this challenge, they have to. We are going to the big comic convention in Las Vegas. I'm hoping to even enter us into the big costume contest." I stared up at the sky, planning out which of us would be which Powerpuff girl.

"Can I come?"

"What?"

"Can I come with you? I'll even dress up. If I can convince either the guys or just Xander, then we could all dress up."

"I'm not sure it would be your scene."

Bucky hooked his fingers under my chin and turned my head to look at him. My eyes found his serious gaze boring into me. "If you're there, it's my scene."

I bit my lip and watched as he slowly leaned toward me. My mind wandered back to the kiss after he defended me to my boss. My lady parts perked up, ready for some action.

"Hey, you two! Look! They're dancing," Xander called over to us.

The moment that was building between us burst. I sat up and moved away from Bucky. He grumbled something under his breath and then sat up. I ignored him and tried to believe that the blinking light in the sky was an alien and not clearly an airplane.

The book I'd brought to read while trying to go to sleep finally ended. I glanced over at my phone and saw it was only ten o'clock. When Xander's expedition to be abducted didn't happen all of us trudged back to the camp. Grabbing a couple of granola bars, I decided it was best for me to hole up in my tent. It seemed everyone had the same idea because even though a fire was lit, there wasn't any chatter. Since I was wide awake, I spent some time staring contemplatively into the fire. I left my tent and looked around. No one was out of their tents. I saw a couple of lights on inside them but it was quiet. Good. I didn't feel like being very sociable.

I shuffled over to a chair in front of the fire. The warmth blasted my face and warmed my body. It was comforting, in a way. As I let my mind wander, a rustling in the woods drew my attention. If a damn alien decided to finally abduct Xander, they were too damn late. My body tensed, waiting for whatever creature was about to appear. A shirtless Bucky holding a few logs stopped and saw me staring at him. Quickly, I turned away because the last thing I needed was to be reminded how damn sexy he was, all sweaty and shirtless.

"Hey. Couldn't sleep?" he asked, placing the logs down.

"Nope. You?"

"Same. I figured I'd get to do some quiet meditation in front of the fire."

I raised an eyebrow at him. "You meditate?"

"Well, maybe not meditate. More like stare blankly into the fire while contemplating my future."

I laughed. "Same."

Bucky pulled a chair next to me. "So, what have you contemplated so far?"

"How not to look at you without a shirt on," I said under my breath.

"Really? Does that bother you?"

"What?"

"Does me not having a shirt on bother you?"

"No. Why?"

"Well, you said you had to contemplate it."

"You heard that?"

He grinned and flexed his biceps. My mouth became dry, and I stood. "I think I should go back to my tent." I managed to walk a few steps away, but he stopped me with a hand on my wrist.

"Please don't leave. I was just teasing."

I sighed. "It's not really that. This is just too difficult."

"What is?"

"Being around you when you're..." I motioned toward his body

"When I'm what?"

"When you're being sweet and sexy and so damn perfect, I want to jump on you and ride you like we're in the rodeo."

His eyes flared. "I was wondering if you felt anything."

"Of course, I feel something but I just can't right now."

He bit his lip. "What exactly can't you do?"

"Have sex."

Bucky grinned. "There is so much more than sex, Ember."

My mind drifted back to the night before, and the dirty thoughts and loopholes I'd come up with just to crawl into Bucky's tent. Every single scenario played in my head. It felt so close I could taste it.

"Wanna make out?" He smiled.

My heart did a funny flip. I'd never had that happen with any man I'd ever been with. What was that? He licked his lips slowly while his eyes flared with lust. That was it for me.

"Absolutely." I grabbed his hand and dragged him over to my tent.

We fell into my tent, all tangled limbs and crushing lips. He broke the kiss to zip the tent just in case the other guys got up. Before he came back to me, I watched as his eyes took in every part of my curvy body. I'd always been self-assured but, at that moment, I questioned whether I was too curvy for him.

"You are so fucking beautiful."

I gave him a tight smile and pulled him down to me. His lips crushed mine. Our tongues tangled, imitating what we really wanted. I broke the kiss, and he immediately began kissing, sucking, and nibbling on my neck. My nipples became so hard and sensitive. The mere brush of his arm across my chest sent shivers of pleasure through my body.

He lifted his head from my neck. "I want to suck your nipples."

"Please..." I begged, as I pulled my pajama top over my head.

A naughty smile curved his lips. His sensual mouth sucked on my pert nipple. Electricity shot through my body with each pull. My hands dug into his hair, pulling him closer to me. Involuntarily, my hips moved against him. I felt his hand flex on my hip as he pulled my body closer to him.

"Fuck, Bucky. Your mouth is amazing." My body felt like a live wire.

"Can I do more, baby?"

"Like what?" I panted.

"I want to taste you."

"No. If we do that, I will want you inside me."

He groaned and buried his head against my breast. "Can I pleasure you? No mouth, just my fingers."

I bit my lip. My body was screaming at me to just do it all. I wanted him more than I'd ever wanted anyone else, but I had something to prove. If I couldn't have his dick, I was going to have those thick fingers fingerbanging me.

"Yes."

The word had hardly left my mouth and his hand was buried inside my pajama pants. His fingers circled my clit, sending erotic shock waves through me. Fuck. I'd had men finger me before. It usually felt like they were in the dark looking for a light switch. I had to manually show them what to do. Not Bucky. The man was a genius when it came to playing a woman's body. I wouldn't let my mind think about how many he'd been with for him to be so good. I simply enjoyed him.

Two fingers dipped inside, then swirled around my clit. When they slipped back in, I shoved my hips, showing that I wanted more. He dutifully added a third finger and curled them inside me. My body bowed off the ground as an orgasm hit me. His fingers continued to pump inside of me while his thumb circled my clit. I tried to hold back any noises but when he bit my neck while performing his finger orchestra-tions, I fell into an abyss. When I opened my eyes, I saw him staring down at me, licking his fingers.

"I got my taste after all."

I furrowed my brow. "Did I black out?"

"Yep, but let me tell you how beautiful you are when you come. I want to see that over and over and over again." He smiled down at me, then leaned forward and kissed me sweetly.

The feelings overwhelmed me. If fooling around made my heart feel this way, what the hell would fucking be like? This was why I did nothing other than fuck a guy. Too many emotions were involved.

"I should probably escape back to my tent." He stared at me with a question in his eyes.

"Yeah, that's probably a good idea." As the words left my mouth, I avoided his hurt gaze.

"Okay. Uhm...this was...uhm...fun."

"Yep." I could have slapped myself for how articulate I was.

"Good night, Ember." Bucky left the tent, and I zipped it behind him.

"Night." My voice was barely above a whisper. Guilt rained down on me as the orgasm high faded. I'd fucked up and had no clue where to go from there.

23

A New Me...Sort Of

Dear Gail,

You feel like a Gail today. Gail seems like a therapist's name. Anyway, so I did a thing with Bucky. We went UFO and Bigfoot hunting with his idiot friends. I swear if Olivia falls for Xander we'll never get them out of our circle. Needless to say, we saw nothing. Well...I wouldn't say I saw nothing. I saw Bucky's glistening body covered in sweat. That was a sight to behold. In fact, it was such a great sight that I may have done something with him. I know. I know. I can hear your shocked sigh now. It was only a bit of making out and some fingerbanging. That man knows his way around a vagina. His large fingers brought my sadly out-of-practice vagina to climax three times before I ran from his tent, leaving my panties behind. He's claiming he doesn't have them, but that makes two pairs of my underwear that he is holding hostage. I've been back two days and all I can think about is doing even more with him. The idiot has invaded my dreams. I'm waking up with soaked panties every morning. I've decided I need to work him out of my system. A new me should do it.

Thanks for nothing,

Ember

Running my hands through my non-existent hair for the tenth time didn't bring it back. In a drastic measure, I decided a haircut would help me get rid of Bucky. I figured a pixie cut would do it. What I hadn't considered was how it would feel emotionally. I cried in the stylist's chair. The poor girl had no idea what to do other than hand me tissues. A half-hour later, I'd left the hair salon with my head held high and a gym bag.

The mirror in the gym really exaggerated how the pixie cut was not a good fit with my curvy body. With a deep breath, I decided it was going to be easier to change my body while my hair grew out. When I'd joined the gym that day, I snapped up an appointment with a personal trainer. They were going to get me in shape in no time. I waited in the free weight area. Muscle-bound men eyed my curves. I'd always been proud of my body but being honest with myself some toning needed to be done. I envisioned the sexy trainer I'd have. Every time the thought popped into my head, it was Bucky. I really needed to get a move on working him out of my system.

"Ember?" a gruff voice asked.

I turned to see a middle-aged woman holding a clipboard. She wasn't exactly what I'd thought a personal trainer would look like.

"That's me."

"Perfect. Let's get started. Come into my office so we can work on your goals."

"What? Aren't we going to workout?" Desperation crept into my voice.

"Well, of course, but if I don't know why you want to workout, then it's difficult to build a program for you. My name is Henry, by the way," she said as she continued toward her office.

I followed behind. "Henry. That's an odd name for a woman."

She shrugged. "It's short for Henrietta. Now, let's talk goals."

For the next half an hour, Henry discussed goals, both physical and psychological. I learned something very important from my trainer. She had zero sense of humor. Apparently, when I said my first physical goal was to leap buildings in a single bound or outrun a speeding train was unrealistic. Another important fact about the stoic Henry was that the more I tried to crack a joke, the harder she made me pay for it when we got to the workout part.

"Come on, Ember. You will not outrun a baby carriage, let alone a speeding train running like that." Her voice bounced off the walls. The other gym rats stared at me as I attempted to not fall off the speeding treadmill.

"I..." heavy breath, "can't..." wheezing breath, "do..." heart attack imminent, "this." I slammed the stop button and flew off the back of the treadmill, landing on my butt.

Henry sighed. "Seriously, Ember? You were only on there for two minutes."

I laid on the ground and stared at the ceiling. Henry stood over me and looked down. "Let's try something slower." I grabbed Henry's hand, letting her help me up.

Another half-hour went by and as I waddled my sore ass out of the gym, I swore to never go back. That was if I could ever leave because I would have bet money my muscles were atrophying. Getting into my car, I slowly eased myself inside. I must have been making strange noises because a few people who were headed into the gym stopped to stare. Without a care, I lifted two middle fingers at the rail-thin women chatting with one another in front of my car. Their shocked faces made me laugh. I immediately regretted it because that hurt too.

My phone rang. Digging through my bag, I retrieved the phone and pressed accept. "Yes."

"Wow...you sound wonderful," Teagan said.

"Uh-huh. What's up?" I relaxed into the seat.

"Come meet us at Midnight Sun."

Looking at my reflection in the review mirror, I winced. Would my friends even recognize the new me? My new/old attitude of not caring reared its head. "Sure. I'll be there in twenty."

"Great. We'll save you a seat." Teagan hung up.

I closed my eyes for a moment. Every muscle in my body cried in pain. This was exactly why I didn't exercise. I was not a 'no pain no gain' kind of girl. Finally, I pulled myself together and pulled out of the gym's parking lot. Midnight Sun was only a few miles away, but it was going to take me a good fifteen minutes to get out of the car.

"Hello, welcome to...Ember?" Nomi's sister Nora squinted at me.

"Aren't I gorgeous?" I fluffed my missing hair.

"Well, of course, but you look different." She looked me up and down. I was still in my gym clothes and my once styled pixie cut was matted against my head.

"Good different?"

"With you, Ember, it's always good." She nodded toward a table where Nomi, Teagan, and Olivia sat. "Go on in."

"Thanks." I winced with every step. It wasn't just my muscles that ached anymore. I'd given myself a wicked case of chub rub, which made me waddle like a penguin.

When I finally made it to the table, Teagan squinted up at me. Her jaw dropped as she took in my new appearance. Nomi was in the middle of a story when she looked up and stared. Olivia was stuck in her phone and had no clue a world outside of it existed.

"Well, what do you think?"

"Fuck me," Teagan breathed.

"Wow," Nomi added.

"What are you two—" Olivia finally looked up and dropped her phone on the table. "You're missing hair."

I furrowed my brow. "I thought you were a writer, Captain Obvious?"

"Yeah, but I had no other words but that at the moment."

"Are you dying?" Teagan asked.

"What? No. Why would you ask such a thing?"

"That looks like a haircut someone who was ill would have."

"I think I look rather cute." I plopped down next to Olivia.

"So, why are you limping?" Nomi asked.

"I tried working out."

Teagan laughed. "How did that go?"

My eyes moved around my friends and I couldn't do it anymore. I couldn't fake the happy new me anymore. My life felt like shit and trying to forget Bucky wasn't working. Tears pooled in my eyes and I looked down at the table, willing them away.

"Oh my God. Ember, what's wrong?" Olivia asked.

I shook my head.

"Come on, Em. We've all been friends too long for you to lie to us. We're here for you."

Taking a deep breath, I let it all out. Everything from my aunt to my dad to the devil children I taught at the daycare. I told them about the gym and how I cried after the lady cut all my hair off. Finally, I broke to them the nail in the coffin. My hot time in the tent with Bucky. When I was finished sharing my word salad, I looked around at them. They all looked the same as when they saw my haircut. Eyes wide and jaws dropped.

"Well?"

"That was a lot, Ember. I'm so sorry you're having a rough go of it. Though I have to say the steamy time with Bucky sounded fucking hot." Teagan gave my hand a squeeze.

"What?"

"Oh, that was definitely the best part of the story." Nomi nodded.

"I agree. I have to say that the devil children and you having to deal with them paints one hell of a picture." Olivia smiled.

"Wait a second. You aren't raking me over the coals about the fingerbang action with Bucky?"

"No, why?"

"The challenge." I threw my hands up in the air.

The three bitches had the nerve to laugh. I was eyeing the knives when Nomi caught me and swiftly moved them out of my reach.

"Ember, we didn't expect you to have no physical contact with men."

"So, this whole time I could have been letting Bucky have his way with me, except for a home run?"

"Well, no, but..."

"Hold on...I am fucking confused. What was this challenge even about?"

"It was to see that you could have a platonic relationship with men without having sex. Have you had sex?" Olivia asked.

"No."

"Okay then. You haven't lost the bet...yet." Teagan smirked.

"You know you're all bitches, right?" I stood and winced.

"I'm honestly impressed that you've spent this much time with Bucky and haven't played cowgirl and well-endowed Indian yet with him." Olivia laughed, but her smile soon fell and she looked away.

"Hi, ladies." Bucky's voice made me freeze. "Have you seen...Ember? Is that you?" He looked down at me.

"Did you cut your hair?" Xander asked.

"No, I washed it and it shrunk." I glared at him and avoided looking at Bucky.

"Sorry, I just asked a question." Xander pouted but soon brightened when he saw Olivia. "Hi, Olivia. I read your last article. It was so good. You're so talented."

We all looked at Olivia, who was back to staring at her phone. I jabbed her with my elbow. "Ow." She grimaced at me.

"Xander said something nice to you," I grumbled to her.

"Thanks," she said without looking at him.

I felt bad for him. Xander was a little weird, but he was a nice guy. I really wished she'd give him a chance.

"Why have you been ignoring my texts?" Bucky asked me.

"I didn't get any texts," I lied.

He grimaced. "It says you read them."

"Yeah, well, I didn't get them. I think the two of you can go now." I shooed them with my hand.

A confused look crossed his face. In a flash, Bucky had covered it up with a tight smile. "It was good seeing you, ladies. We'll see you around."

"Bye," Teagan and Nomi said together.

Olivia and I stared down at the table. A weird silence filled the surrounding space. We were both guilty of being mean to men who didn't deserve it. That guilty feeling that was becoming all too familiar overcame me.

"You two are something else," Teagan admonished.

"Bucky and Xander are good guys. Why do you treat them that way?" Nomi asked.

"I can't be with Bucky right now."

"That doesn't mean you should treat him like trash." Teagan shook her head. "And you..." She pointed at Olivia. "Why are you so mean to Xander? The man is practically in love with you and all you do is hurt him repeatedly. One day you are going to realize that you want him and he won't be around anymore."

"I know," Olivia mumbled with her head ducked.

"Well, this lunch has sucked. Let's order something and talk wedding plans." Nomi used her superpower of redirection.

"Sounds good to me." Teagan waved down a waitress who took our order. For the rest of lunch, there was no more talk of Bucky, Xander, or the challenge. By the end of the lunch, I'd felt better than I had in a while.

24

Psychopath in Training

The colorful alphabet took up the entire top of the dry erase board. Pre-schoolers sat crisscross applesauce on the rug in front of me. I smiled at them and held up my hand. It was a signal for them to close their mouths and lift their hands in unison. When they were all quiet with arms raised, I blinked at the scene in front of me. With their arms raised and outstretched toward me, they looked like little Nazis saluting me. I wanted to break out into hysterical laughter and scream at them to put their hands down. Being the professional I was, I smiled serenely and ordered them to put their hands down.

"Thank you. Now, let's go over our alphabet, shall we?" I pointed to the letter 'a.' "Who can tell me a word that starts with the letter 'a'?"

Little Stuart blinked up at me and asked, "Why did you do that?"

I sighed. "Do what, Stuart?"

"Cut your hair like a boy."

Touching my short hair, I said, "I wanted to try something new. Do you like it?" That was probably the stupidest thing I could have said in front of a group of preschoolers.

All at once they gave a resounding, "No!"

I schooled my features to make sure they didn't know that what they had said had hurt my feelings. "Well, it's a good thing none of you got your haircut."

"You look like Mr. Prickles." Stuart smiled at me.

"Yep. You look like The Prick." The little girl, who looked like Wednesday Addams, grinned.

Mr. Prickles was the classroom's hedgehog. My little weird girl had decided to call him The Prick or Mr. Prick. I was convinced that when she said it the first time and I had changed colors holding back a laugh, she noticed she'd gotten a reaction out of me. Damn my inability to hide my facial expressions.

"Thank you all for your honesty about a topic we weren't talking about. Now, who can tell me a word that begins with the letter 'a'?"

The Wednesday look alike raised her hand. "Yes, Betsy?" I cringed as I said her name. It was the most innocent name for a little psychopath.

"A is for ass."

I sighed. "That isn't a nice word, Betsy. We've talked about this."

She threw her little hands up in the air in frustration. "How is that a bad word? It starts with 'a' and it's another word for donkey."

The kids giggled. I shushed them. "You are correct. I'm sorry. Now, who has a word for the letter 'b'?"

Betsy raised her hand again. "Yes, Betsy?"

"Bitch."

The young kids gasped. "Betsy..." I warned.

"It's the name of a female dog."

Biting my lip, I really began wondering if I could walk out on this job. I plastered a tight smile on my face. "That is correct."

"How about the letter 'c'?" I pointed to the letter on the board.

Betsy raised her hand again.

"Betsy?" I waved my hand toward her since none of the other kids were participating.

"Cunt."

My eyes bugged out. "What?"

"It's what you do with numbers." I sighed, realizing she meant 'count.' When a wicked smile curled her lips, I braced myself. "And a name for a lady."

"What is going on here?" Caroline asked from the doorway.

"We are learning the alphabet," a little boy name Alvin proclaimed.

"Well, it sure looks like you're learning some interesting words. Can I borrow your teacher?" she asked the preschoolers.

"Go ahead. This is boring anyway," the little psychopath Betsy grumbled. What did it say about me that I had an overwhelming urge to punch a kid?

I gave Betsy a dirty look and turned to Caroline. She was trying and failing to hold back a smile.

Once I left the room, Caroline snorted. I crossed my arms. "Mark my words, that little psycho is going to be a serial killer." I tapped my chin. "Well, that or one of those real housewives. What did you need me for?"

"You got a delivery. It's at the front desk." She went back into my classroom to reign in control.

I strolled to the front of the daycare. As I passed rooms, I heard singing and laughing. I was a bit jealous. Thanks to Betsy Wetsy, my classroom always sounded like a hostage negotiation. I was lost in thought when I stopped in front of the desk. Blinking at the gigantic bouquet, I couldn't find any words.

"Are these for me?"

Tammy, our afternoon receptionist, looked around the obnoxious display. "Yep. Someone must really love you. My Dick never does this."

"What?"

"My husband, Dick, he never sends flowers anymore."

"Oh. Who are they from?" I asked.

"I didn't open the card. Though, I was dying to. My curiosity almost got the best of me." She smiled at me.

I dug around the bouquet and finally found it.

Beautiful,

Go out with me tonight. I can't stop thinking about you.

Bucky

P.S. I keep dreaming about having my head between your thighs and your taste on my tongue.

I felt a blush creep up my neck and looked closer at the flowers. They were red calla lilies. He gave me the floral equivalent of vaginas. I guess it could have been worse. He could have given me a bunch of cat o nine tails. They always reminded me of penises.

"Uhm...Tammy...can I keep the flowers up here until I leave tonight?"

"Sure. I can imagine my Dick was the thoughtful one."

"Thanks." I walked away from the desk and stopped down the hallway. Pulling out my phone, I found Bucky's number.

Me: Thanks for the flowers. You didn't have to do that.

Bucky: I wanted to. It seemed like you were having a strenuous day when we ran into each other at Midnight Sun.

Bucky: I wanted to brighten your day. So, what do you say?

Me: About what?

Maybe playing dumb would work.

Bucky: Don't play dumb. How about going out tonight?

Me: Uhm...I don't think that's a good idea.

Bucky: Why?

I bit my lip. I was normally perfectly fine with being mean. In fact, I enjoyed it a little too much. However, the idea of pushing Bucky away with my meanness gave me pause.

Me: Look, I'm just not a go on a date kind of woman.

Bucky: So, me fingering you in a tent is fine then. I'm good for that but not for an actual date.

Me: This has nothing to do with you.

Bucky: It has everything to do with me.

I sighed and debated turning off my phone.

Me: I have to go. Goodbye, Bucky.

My phone began ringing in my hand. Another sigh escaped as I leaned against the wall.

"What, Bucky? I need to get back to my kids."

"I'm not done talking to you."

"Technically, we weren't actually talking."

"Fuck technicalities. I want to know the real reason why you won't go on a date with me. We get along great. We have fun. God knows we almost set the tent on fire with our chemistry. All I'm asking for is one date."

"Bucky...I..." blowing out a breath, I pulled out all the stops, "I just don't want to date you."

Silence filled up the space on the line between us. I looked at my phone and saw we hadn't lost connection. Finally, he broke the silence.

"You've just been using me then."

"I was honest about what I needed you for." I kept my voice flat.

"You're just a bitch who likes to play with men's emotions. You do everything you can to get them to come to you. Fall for you and then you drop them. Let me ask you something. Is that what makes you wet? Does that turn you on? I didn't know you were such a heartless bitch."

I swallowed. "I guess you have me all figured out."

"Fuck you, Ember. You won't be using this schmuck anymore."

The phone went dead. A giant hole formed in my chest. Pain radiated through my body. I'd been called many names in my life. Most from men I'd slept with or who wanted to sleep with me. It never hurt. My mind had a hurricane of emotions swirling around. Why did my normal bitch shield hurt so much when I used it on Bucky? I didn't have the time to analyze it. Turning off my phone, I took another deep breath, centered myself, and entered my classroom.

25

THE BITCH SWITCH IS STUCK

I paced in front of my apartment building. Nomi was on her way to pick me up. We were all supposed to go with Teagan to watch a prospective wedding band. I glanced down at my phone. Nomi was fifteen minutes late, which was strange for her. The ability to be on time, no matter what, was one of Nomi's best traits.

"Hey, Ember." Xander's voice made me jump.

"Oh, hey. What are you doing out here?" I asked as I watched Bucky approach.

"Bucky and I are headed over to work."

"Oh. Over at that sports place you own." My eyes avoided Bucky.

Xander looked between the two of us. "What's going on?"

"Nothing," we said at the same time.

"Uh-huh. I guess we should go. It was good seeing you, Ember."

"See ya later, Xander."

Bucky glared at me. The hatred I saw burning in his eyes cut me deeper than I'd ever been with a man.

"Hey, bitch! You looking for a ride?"

I turned from watching Bucky and Xander and saw Teagan hanging out the side of the car. "Look who's calling who a bitch."

"Yeah, but I'm a bridal bitch. Woot! Woot!" She waved a bottle out of the car.

I got in the back next to Olivia. "She's pretty trashed already."

"Yep. Apparently, some of Grayson's work associates sent them some celebratory champagne. She didn't wait for him to be home to celebrate."

"Woohoo!" Teagan called out of the car again.

"If you don't keep your ass in the car, I am not taking you anywhere but Sunny Pines and dropping you off with Grams," Nomi said.

"I bet those old bitties would love some of this Dom. Ember, you want some?" Teagan swung the bottle back to me.

"Thanks, I'll take that." I grabbed the bottle and set it on the floor between my feet.

"Don't drink all of that," Teagan said.

"Don't worry. I won't." I gave Nomi a nod, telling her I have it under control.

She gave me a slight nod and drove off. We passed Bucky's and Xander's cars waiting to pull out of the parking lot. Teagan gave them big waves while I slid down in my seat.

"Was that Bucky and Xander you were talking to?" Nomi asked.

"Ooooh...this has got to be good." Teagan bounced in the seat in front of me.

"Yes, it was them. Though I only spoke to Xander."

"Oh?" Olivia looked at me.

"Yeah. He's a nice guy. You'd know that if you gave him a try."

Olivia sighed and looked out her own window.

"Why didn't lover boy talk to you?" Nomi looked at me through the rearview mirror.

"I think he's on his cycle."

"Hmm..." Nomi said.

"What's that supposed to mean?" I asked.

"Well, every time I've seen Bucky, he's all about getting your attention. Hell, we could all disappear and he'd only be concerned about you. But from what we saw, he gave you a dirty look and wanted nothing to do with you."

"We may have had a fight."

"About what?" Olivia asked.

"You guys are going to make me talk about it, huh?"

"Yup," the three of them said together.

"Fine. He wanted to date, and I said I didn't think that was a good idea."

"Why isn't it a good idea? We've already told you the challenge isn't that strict," Nomi said.

"I told him that because it's true. I don't do relationships. Even with this platonic friend challenge, I've realized how much messier my life would become if I actually had a genuine relationship. I'd get bored, or he'd get bored and someone would just get hurt. It's best to nip it in the bud now."

A tense silence filled the car. The songs on the radio played on low and felt more like background music to the silence. Even buzzed Teagan was quiet. That was not a good sign.

"What?" I said as we pulled into a parking lot outside a country club.

"Nothing," Nomi said.

"Bullshit. I can practically hear all your judgy thoughts. Just spill it," I spat.

"I think we should all focus on the task at hand," Olivia hedged.

"Oh for fuck's sake. I'll say what we're all thinking." Teagan turned in her seat. "That's the stupidest fucking excuse not to date someone. And I know stupid excuses. I was a virgin until recently."

"It's not—" I began, but Nomi cut me off.

"What Teagan meant was that you may pass up an opportunity for happiness. We have all gotten to know Xander and Bucky. They are good guys." Nomi looked at both Olivia and me.

"I've made up my mind." The words I spoke were a blatant lie. I couldn't tell them the truth that I was scared. That what I feel for Bucky was so intense I'd never recover when it ended.

"I didn't wear boots today, so all this bullshit needs to stop. If Ember wants to keep lying to herself, let her. We have a band to listen to." Teagan opened the car door and fell on her face.

With a sigh, I got out of the car and helped my inebriated friend. "Come on, lush."

"I'm not a lush. It's just that champagne tasted so good," Teagan slurred.

"Uh-huh." I guided her toward the club.

"Good after—" A woman swung open the doors and immediately got a worried look on her face. "Is everyone okay?"

"Yes. This one here is not allowed to sample any drinks today." I laughed.

"Oh, that's okay. You ladies have already been here for that. Now, let's check out our most popular wedding band. They are conveniently playing one today."

Teagan followed the woman. I hung back and looked at Nomi and Olivia. "What was she talking about? I've never been here."

They both shrugged but wouldn't look me in the eye. A pounding headache built behind my eyes. Something was fishy.

"Here they are The Sojourners. They are a Journey tribute band. They also play other songs, but mostly Journey," the country club lady said.

"That's awesome. I love Journey." Teagan rubbed her hands together like an evil villain.

We listened as the band warmed up. The first notes of a popular Journey tune played. When the singer began to sing, it impressed me. He could have passed for the lead singer of Journey any day of the week. The only con this band had were the leisure suits they were wearing. It gave off a real white paneled kidnapper kind of vibe.

"Wow. They're actually pretty good," Nomi said from next to me. "Their outfits suck, though."

"We can change the colors to meet your needs. I believe you said your color scheme is yellow. Isn't that the color of the bridesmaid dresses?" the lady asked Teagan, who was bopping her head.

She stopped and looked at me, then back to the woman. "Yes."

"Wait a minute. Did you pick out the bridesmaid dresses without us?" I asked and looked at Nomi. She was staring intently at the band. It hit me. I was a fucking idiot. They've been doing wedding stuff without me.

"Oh…you didn't just pick them out yourself. You picked them out without me." A knot formed in my stomach.

"Ember, we know you've been having a tough time lately. We didn't want to add more things to your plate," Olivia said.

"Are you fucking kidding me? The three of you planned this huge life event without me. I can't believe you bitches. You know what, fine. Fuck all of you. I'm out of here." I stormed off and grabbed my phone. Thumbing through the apps, I opened the rideshare app and ordered a lift.

"Ember! Wait! Don't go," Nomi yelled.

"Fuck off, Nomi." My voice betrayed the tears I was trying to hide.

"I'm sorry, Ember. We didn't mean to hurt you."

"Well, you fucking did. You're right. My life has been shit lately, but that has never impeded our friendship. We have always been there. Ever since this stupid challenge, you guys have treated me like a pariah. Well, I'm done with that. Go back inside with Teagan. I'm sure there is more shit for you guys to do without me."

"Ember…"

"Go away!" I yelled and turned away from her.

Nomi waited and then began walking away. Before she made it to the door, I yelled again, "Oh and tell Teagan I don't want to be in her fucking wedding anymore."

Pain rolled through me. I'd ask the universe if things could be worse, but the universe always took that as a challenge. Instead, I planned on some serious pity partying when I got back to my apartment.

26

PITY PARTYING WITH BEATY

I stormed into my apartment. My attitude didn't improve during the ride from the country club. All I wanted to do during the ride was sit and stew in my anger. The driver had other plans. He chattered so much that he ended up lost. When he finally pulled over, I demanded he get out and let me drive. He sat there for a few seconds, but when he realized I was serious, he exited the vehicle and let me get behind the wheel.

Another half an hour later, I was slamming the car in park and jumping out. When it looked like he was about to ask me for money I pointed at him. "Don't even think about it. I just did your damn job. You're going to eat this fare."

Slamming the door, I marched to my building. It was uncharacteristically quiet. The security guard wasn't anywhere to be found. It was for the best. I didn't need to exchange small talk with anyone after the train wreck of a day. My anger and hurt simmered just below the surface. If I could make it to my apartment and dive headfirst into a half gallon of ice cream, I may bounce back.

After unlocking the door, I swung it open to find it was dark. Normally, this wouldn't be something to question, but it was a little after noon. The sun should be filling up my apartment, making it seem lighter. I shrugged and realized the dreariness of my apartment fit my mood.

"Shut the door." Aunt Beatrice's voice called from the dark.

"Why are you sitting in the dark?"

"I'm not in the mood for questions," she snapped.

"Okay. Well, I'm going to my room." I started to walk away when I heard a sniffle. Freezing in place, I asked, "Are you upset?"

"Aren't you a fucking rocket scientist?"

I turned on a table lamp and saw her curled up in my chair. Hair mussed, eyes puffy and red, and a look of despair was etched all over her. I walked over to the end of the couch next to the chair. "What happened?"

She dragged her eyes up to meet mine. "Why do you care?"

"If you're going to be a fucker about things, I will just leave you to wallow in your tears." I stood.

"Sorry. I'm not good at these things."

"What things? Acting like a human?" I snipped at her.

"Whatever. You'd never understand."

With a sigh, I sat again. "Just spill it, Aunt Beaty."

"You wouldn't understand. You're so pretty and normal."

"What are you talking about? My life is so fucked up I don't see any way it will ever get better."

Aunt Beaty looked at me, then retrieved a shot glass. I didn't even want to think about where the hell that had been hiding. She picked up the bottle of Jack that was on the floor and poured some into each glass. Looking at me, she said, "A shot for a secret."

I was about to protest until I remembered I was sad, alone, and hated my only friends. Drinking until I blacked out sounded like a viable option. "Okay." I grabbed the shot glass that had been sitting on the table.

After we took our shots, a beeping came from the kitchen. Aunt Beaty got down off the chair and went into the kitchen. I observed her menagerie watch her, then glare at me. She returned with a frozen dinner and placed it on the small table between the chair and couch. I glanced at the meal and grimaced. It looked half burnt.

"I didn't realize you had something cooking in the kitchen."

She shrugged. "I forgot myself."

Peeling back the plastic, Aunt Beaty took a fork and poked at it. "How the fuck can something be both frozen and burnt?"

"The miracles of microwave dinners." I smiled and poured myself another shot.

"Here you go, my lovelies." The menagerie attacked the mess of a meal with gusto. She looked at me and waved her hand to get me to pour her a shot as well. We both downed our shots.

I blew out a breath, enjoying the sting of what I thought was my third shot. "So, are you going to tell me what's going on?"

"Curt."

"One of your many suitors?"

"Yeah, but he was more than just a day of the week."

Taking another shot, I stared at her. It finally hit me. She was brokenhearted. I could relate. My phone vibrated and without looking I hit ignore. It was probably Teagan, Nomi, or Olivia for the millionth time.

"I'm sorry, Aunt Beaty."

She shrugged. "Doesn't matter. I've just got to find me a new one."

I watched her pound another shot.

"What's your problem?" she asked.

Leaning back against the couch, I looked at her. "I have horrible friends and Bucky wants to have an actual relationship." I made a face.

Her brow knitted. "That doesn't sound like genuine problems. You know you're going to make up with your friends and you might as well give up fighting that boy. He's a hunter and you are in his sights."

After pounding another shot, I looked at the two Aunt Beatys sitting in front of me. "Hunter...pfft. That's just a bunch of shit." At least I thought those were the words I said. The two Beatys were becoming three.

"Your ass is drunk. I do not know whose kid you are, but you sure aren't related to me if you can't hold your liquor. You better get to your room before you pass out on the couch. I can't promise that Princess will be nice to you if you do that."

"Puck Mincess." I stood a bit wobbly and grabbed the bottle I'd been taking shots from. Somehow it moved, and I hit the table. Was I magic now? I forced my vision to clear and picked up the bottle. It was really light. I distinctly remembered it being full. Oh well. I found my way to my room and shut the door. I fell onto the bed and held the bottle close like a baby. This was probably the closest I was going to get to being a mother. Irrational anger took over me and I grabbed my phone. I'd give them a piece of my mind telling me I couldn't be a mother. Between texts, I finished the bottle. The last thing I remembered was a blurry porcupine hissing at me.

A horrible chainsaw noise woke me from my deep, dark sleep. I tried to pull my pillow over my head by my hand but hit nothing. Prying my eyes open, I groaned and tried not to vomit. My entire room was upside down. What the hell happened last night? Closing my eyes again, I tried to think, but that didn't work. I took two deep breaths and opened my eyes again. Yep. My room was still upside down. Turning my head, I saw one of the menagerie sleeping next to my head. The god awful noise came from above me. I counted to ten and tried my damnedest to do a sit-up. That shit didn't work. Finally, I was able to roll onto my stomach and promptly fell to the floor.

"Ow. Fuck. Fuckity. Fucker," I spouted as I rubbed the back of my head.

Sitting up, I saw where the horrible noise was coming from. It was the damn porcupine. Cuddles, the porcupine, chuffed, then went back to snoring. My head was throbbing. I gripped the bed to lever myself onto my feet. When I finally managed to get there, I regretted it. My stomach rolled. Despite the dizziness, I leaped over more animals and made it to the bathroom just in time to relive the night before. An eternity later, I was able to stop dry heaving and splashed cold water on my face.

Glancing at my reflection in the mirror, I cringed. "I look like a homeless clown who had a nervous breakdown."

"Yeah, you do," Aunt Beatrice agreed as she passed the bathroom.

"It wasn't a statement that needed reaffirming, Beaty!" I heard her laugh and whistle for her minions. The sound of their paws and claws indicated they were vacating my room.

I collapsed against my pillows. Hangover wasn't the best way to describe how I felt. It was more like drinking so much that I could feel every atom in the world and they were heavy. I couldn't remember the last time I'd been that drunk. My eyes were becoming heavy again when I recalled the last time I'd felt this bad. It was the dating profile incident with Teagan. My body sat up too fast and the world spun. I did really stupid things when I got that drunk. Pulling my laptop from the bedside table, I scanned my emails. Whew. No dating profile confirmation. I relaxed against the pillows, ready to go back to sleep, when my phone vibrated. I grabbed it without looking. My eyes almost popped out of my head. I'd found where I'd fucked up last night. Grimacing, I swiped open my phone. I had twenty text messages.

"Please don't tell me I drunk texted. Please. Please. Please," I chanted.

Me: I would be a great mother.

Well, that didn't start out great.

Dumbass Bucky: Ember?

Me: How dare you think I'd be a shitty lay? I'd be the best you've ever had. In fact, you'd become obsessed.

"Fuck me."

Dumbass Bucky: Uhm...

Me: I hate you.

Dumbass Bucky: Are you ok, Ember?

Me: I miss you and your stupid face.

"Why do I drink?" I groaned.

Dumbass Bucky: Really? I miss you too. I was actually going to call you today.

Me: I'm adopting a platypus. He's going to be my best friend because all of you suck. I'm going to name him Roger.

Dumbass Bucky: Uhm ok. Can I come over or can you come here?

Me: I want your head between my thighs. I bet you could give me multiple orgasms. It's just a shame that I've sworn off people named Bucky.

Dumbass Bucky: You can call me anything if I can do that. I guarantee you at least five orgasms where you're screaming my name.

Me: I have to alsdkjrasdfoeiuaorj

Dumbass Bucky: What?

Dumbass Bucky: Ember? I'm at the door.

Dumbass Bucky: Was this just another one of your games?

Dumbass Bucky: Fine.

I grabbed a pillow and pushed it against my face and screamed. How did I face this? My phone vibrated in my hand.

Grams: Ember, don't forget you promised to come to the service with me today.

Oh hell. I'd promised to go to that church thing for Grams' husband. Fuck me.

Me: Sorry, Grams. I just got up. I'll be there in a few.

Grams: You don't need to go, sweetie.

Me: Getting dressed now. I'll be there in half an hour.

Grams: Great. See you soon.

27

BECOMING A SCENE QUEEN

With a pounding headache, I began running around my room. In fifteen minutes, I was semi-presentable. I speed walked toward the large church that was thankfully only a few blocks away. My thighs rubbed together, reminding me I forgot my Spanx that helped with my chub rub and knowing I'd be paying for that later. I was just glad I had sunglasses on because the sun was obscenely bright.

A block away from the church, I saw Nomi, Teagan, and Olivia standing together. I ducked behind a tree. Talking to my ex-friends wasn't something I wanted to do with a hangover. I peeked around the tree and saw them staring my way. Fuck!

"Ember?" Xander's voice made me jump

"What?" My voice was too loud, and it made my head throb. I looked between Xander and Bucky. Bucky's scowl told me everything I needed to know.

"Uhm..." Xander looked between Bucky and me. "What are you doing?"

"What does it look like? I'm hiding."

Bucky snorted and walked off, leaving Xander and me behind. "Are you okay?"

"Yep. Just hiding from some traitorous wenches." I looked over my shoulder to see Bucky pointing toward me while talking to them. "That dirty, rotten piece of monkey shit," I mumbled and ducked behind the tree.

"Uhm...I don't know if that is a good hiding place."

"Shh...just keep going. If you see Grams, tell her I'll be right there." I looked around the tree to find Teagan, Nomi, and Olivia gone. Breath whooshed from me.

"Why don't you just walk in with us?" Nomi asked.

"Ahh..." I spun and slammed my back against the tree. "What are you doing here?"

Teagan rolled her eyes. "Did you really think we couldn't see you behind this tree?"

"I wasn't hiding. I was...uh...inspecting the bark on this tree." My eyes caressed the tree as I petted the tree.

"Ember, we wanted..." Olivia began.

"Yeah, we better get going." I left the tree and speed walked up to the church.

"Ember! Wait up!" Nomi called.

The hurt from the day before caused tears to well in my eyes. Jogging up the stairs, I found Grams waiting. I gave her a wobbly smile.

"Hey, Grams. I made it." I gave her a hug.

She pulled back and held my face in her hands. "What's wrong, sweetheart?"

"Nothing. So is Vernon looking forward to the ceremony?" I asked hesitantly.

Her brow furrowed. "You're lying, but since we need to get seated, it will have to wait until everything is over. Also, it's not a ceremony. It's more of just honoring those who served."

"Sounds like a ceremony to me." I looked over my shoulder and watched Teagan with her fiancée Grayson, along with Nomi and Olivia, approaching.

"Hey, Grams!" Teagan pulled her grandmother into a hug. I stepped away, letting them have a moment.

Nomi and Olivia did the same as I stepped even further away. I was so busy trying to remove myself from the situation that I almost ran into Edna.

"Watch it!" she snapped, as she and Bucky glared at me when they passed.

"Hey, Ember," Xander said with a small wave as he held the arm of his grandmother, Rachel. He may have waved at me, but his eyes stayed on Olivia behind me. He was hopeless.

"Come on, Ember." Grams entwined her arm with me.

I gave her a small smile. As we strode into the large church, I held my breath and hoped a sinner like myself wouldn't burn upon entry. We walked along the pews, and Grams waved hello and explained to me who each person was to her and Vernon. I couldn't focus on her words because I was still holding my breath. We made it to a reserved row for the family of those being honored. They filled the first row with veterans. Family members filled the next two rows. Grams entered the pew, and I followed. On the other side of her, Teagan, Grayson, Nomi, and Olivia were already seated. When my butt hit the seat, the breath I'd been holding whooshed out. The old man in front of me held onto his hat.

"Ember," Teagan whispered to me around Grams.

I pretended not to hear.

"Ember," she said louder.

I glared over at her past Grams. "Teagan."

"You're just going to keep—" She was cut off when my shoulder was shoved with a hip.

"Move over." Edna stood next to me. Her ass was five inches from my face.

"I believe they reserved this for family," I said.

"I told you, Granny. Let's just go sit with Xander and his—"

"I'm not moving, Bucky. I'm as good as family. Now, move over sinner."

"Sinner? What the—"

Grams' hand on my knee stopped me from possibly getting struck by lightning while cussing out an elderly woman in church. Even if she deserved it.

"It's fine, Ember." Grams looked up at Edna. "Edna, would you like to join us here."

Edna gave me a 'told you so' look. "Of course I would, Esther. I think you need the added support. The bums you brought look like roadkill." She gave me a pointed look. Bucky snorted as he sat down on the end of the pew, effectively putting Edna between us.

"Your company looks like a donkey in a suit," I mumbled.

"Excuse me? Do you have something to say to me?" Bucky snapped.

"I don't talk to barn animals." I looked straight ahead as the pastor walked to the podium.

"A barn animal? A barn animal?" His voice rose, drawing looks.

"Bucky, shut your trap," Edna snapped.

My lips curled into a smirk. His eyes burned with fury.

"Thank you all for coming this morning. God is great." The pastor gave the packed house a toothy smile. "We have a wonderful occasion today. On this Veterans Day, we celebrate those who served in our great military. However, before we go forward, I'd like to speak about today. Psalms 17:9 says, 'Love prospers when a fault is forgiven but dwelling on it separates close friends.'"

"What the hell does that have to do with veterans?" Edna mumbled.

Bucky snorted and said to Edna but looked at me, "I don't believe dwelling on a fault is always what separates close friends. Sometimes that *friend* is just a liar and enjoys playing games."

"Well, I feel that understanding someone's problems is the backbone of a *friendship*. Just because you don't get your way doesn't mean that person is a liar."

"How about when that person kisses the other person in the *friendship* and then wants to just pretend it didn't happen? I'd say that's a liar. A liar and a user."

"A user? You're one to talk. All you want is what's between my thighs." I was panting and realized I was standing and yelling at Bucky.

Embarrassment slammed into me. The eyes of everyone in the church were on me. I needed to leave. Instead of crossing the short distance in front of Edna and Bucky, I shimmied the long way down the pew. My humiliation pushed me to move faster in front of Grams and then Teagan, but I tripped over Grayson's big feet. I fell head first onto Nomi and Olivia. My ass was in the air as I scrambled off them. When I finally got my feet under me, I made it the last few feet and ran my hands down my skirt. I couldn't move fast enough.

"Ember!" Bucky called after me. All pretense of not causing a scene was out the window.

I slammed through the closed double doors and ran to the bathroom. Tears were back in my eyes. I took a long look at myself in the mirror. My short hair stuck out like a brown bush around my head. Jesus, Edna was right. I looked like roadkill.

"Ember." Bucky was standing next to me.

Without looking at him, I said, "What do you want?"

"What is your problem?" He crossed his arms.

"Well, the first thing that comes to mind is that some creep is in the women's bathroom." I lifted an eyebrow at him.

"That's not what I'm talking about, and you know it."

"Just spit it out, Bucky."

"You promised you wouldn't call me that."

"Yeah, well you promised not to be an arrogant asshole. We've both broken our promises."

"Yeah, we did." He stared at me as I stared at myself in the mirror.

My gaze met his. "What?"

"Why did you blow me off last night?"

I turned around and leaned against the counter and shrugged. "I don't know. Guess I just wanted to see if you'd come up."

His eyes narrowed. I'd hit a sore spot. "So, it was just a game."

"Maybe. Maybe not." What the hell was I doing?

"You're a real bitch, you know that?"

My lips curled into a smug grin. "Of course. It's not my fault you didn't realize that."

Bucky spun around to leave but stopped with his hand on the door. "I understand now."

I sighed. "Oh yeah? What is that?"

He looked over his shoulder at me. "You can't have an actual relationship with anyone. That's why you always go after people you can't have. It's easier. You'd rather be a slut and a homewrecker than actually experience something real. Honestly, it's sad and pathetic. You don't even have a genuine relationship with Teagan, Nomi, and Olivia. I'm glad I saw you for what you are before getting my heart involved. Goodbye, Ember."

"You're welcome." I smiled as he stormed out of the bathroom.

Turning back to the mirror, I gave myself a long, hard look. Tears welled in my eyes as I let Bucky's words hit their intended target. I was a dumbass, but it was better for everyone. I'd done this dozens of times. Though, it never hurt this badly.

The door of the bathroom opened. I wiped the tears away and started washing my hands. "Are there more things you need to tell me?"

"Let's go get some ice cream." Grams' voice made me jump.

"Grams? What are you—"

She cut me off. "Dry your hands and let's go." Without another word, she left the bathroom.

I gave myself another glance, dried my hands, and followed her out.

28

Eye Scream Shop

The car ride to the ice cream shop was filled with silence and internal prayers for us to live. Grams wasn't a good driver. Well, that's wrong. She's a superb driver if she were a race car driver. Driving around town, she narrowly missed people, cars, and stray squirrels. I white-knuckled the door. The soundtrack to my likely death was polka music. A thought occurred to me that maybe I was already dead, and this was my own personal hell. Finally, she whipped the car into the parking lot of Eye Scream Shop.

"Here we are," she said cheerfully as she grabbed her purse and left the car.

Prying my fingers off the door, I followed her into the Halloween-themed ice cream shop. We stepped in and "Monster Mash" was playing over the shop's speakers. The dark interior made it difficult to read the menu that hung on the wall behind the counter. The cashier was wearing all black, had some wicked piercings, dark eyeliner, and a sneer.

"Welcome to the Eye Scream Shop. What can I get you?" The counter goth girl said in a bored voice.

"Hello, Sally. I'm going to have the Sunday bloody sundae," Grams said with a smile.

Goth girl sighed. "Is that all?"

"Order something, Ember. It's my treat."

My amped-up senses demanded chocolate. I found the perfect treat for my circumstance. "I'll take a black hole sundae."

"Great. That will be eleven-fifty," the girl said in a very unenthusiastic voice.

Grams handed over her credit card. With a sigh, the girl ran the card, and handed it back. "Your ice cream will be out shortly."

"How will we know it's ours?" I asked.

She pointed to a sign above her head. It said *Pay attention! If you don't claim your ice cream, it will be given away to our resident hell hounds.*

"Hell hounds?" I asked.

She pointed to the two chihuahuas napping behind the counter.

"Aren't those two adorable? Be sure you tell your grandmother I said hello, Sally." Grams linked her arm with mine and dragged me toward a vacant booth. "Here we go." She plopped onto the blue upholstered seat.

I glanced around the gothic-themed ice cream parlor. It was quite different from the cheery place of my youth. A smile curled my lips when I realized some of my happiest memories of my teenage years were in this ice cream parlor with the woman sitting across from me.

"Thank you for bringing me, Grams."

She gave my hand a squeeze. "Of course, sweetheart. Now, we need to get straight to it. What the hell is going on with you?"

"Uhm...what?"

Before she could answer the question, our order was called. "I'll go get that." She sprang from the seat and grabbed our sundaes.

A text disturbed my brief reprieve. It was my dad.

Daddy-O: Hello, Peanut.

Me: Hey, Dad. How's it going?

Daddy-O: Not good, sweetie.

I furrowed my brow. Fear and panic flooded my veins. He was the last of my immediate family. I couldn't lose him.

Me: Are you ok? What's wrong?

Daddy-O: Well...you see...I have a problem.

"Here you are, sweetie. Ember, is everything okay?" Grams' forehead was lined with worry as she placed the sundae in front of me.

"I'm not sure. It's my dad." I went back to typing on my phone.

Me: Dad just spit it out, please.

Daddy-O: Starshine and I broke up.

Internally, I was cheering. With a smile on my face, I typed my very empathetic response.

Me: Oh no. I'm so sorry, Dad. What happened?

Daddy-O: I found out Starshine was sleeping with the guru, Moonrise.

I rolled my eyes at the stupid names this hippie cult had.

Me: That's horrible. At least you can come home now. Aunt Beaty misses you.

Daddy-O: Ha. Ha. Ha. You forget I know exactly how my sister is. That gets to my other point. Can I stay with you?

Me: Can you...what?

Daddy-O: Stay with you.

Me: What about the house? I guarantee you'd be more comfortable at your house.

Daddy-O: I'm no longer allowed there.

Me: Dad, I'm really confused.

Daddy-O: A few weeks ago, Moonrise came to me about a vision he had. It was about the house. He said keeping the house was preventing me from ascending. I turned it over to them.

"What the actual fuck?" I mumbled under my breath.

"Ember?"

I met Grams' concerned gaze. "Sorry, Grams. I'm almost done."

Quickly, I typed the last message.

Me: Of course, Dad. Come on over.

Daddy-O: Thank you, Peanut. I love you.

Me: Love you too. I'll see you soon.

Shoving my phone into my purse, I didn't even want to think about what my father had just told me. He had given my childhood home away to some guru. I hated everything in that moment. My gaze landed on my poor sundae. It was a melted mess.

"Dammit." I picked up my spoon and slurped up some of the soupy mess.

"What is going on?" Grams asked.

I blew out a breath. "My dad broke up with his hippie girlfriend."

"Oh no. Is he okay?"

"Yeah. He's fine. She screwed around on him with the guru of that cult she'd conned him into joining. But that isn't the worst part."

"It isn't?"

"Nope. Apparently, that derpy guru convinced my very educated father he would only become enlightened if he gave the cult his house." Grams sucked in a breath. "Yep. My childhood home. For all I know, they are performing human sacrifices or other ungodly things in my childhood bedroom where I had at least one participation trophy."

Grams slid her hand over to mine. Tears welled in my eyes. How was I upset over a stupid house that was being defiled by a weird group of people? I looked into Grams' eyes and the dam broke. Sobs tore from me. Grams moved to my side of the booth and held me as I ugly cried. Loud, obnoxious sobs tore from my body. After an eternity, I finally calmed down. Grams was stroking my short hair as I pulled myself together.

"Feel better?" She wiped the tears from my face.

I nodded. "Yeah. I'm sorry."

"Don't be sorry. You were holding too much inside, Ember. What do I always tell you and Teagan?"

"That our virginity was a limited edition and shouldn't be taken out and played with?" I gave her a smirk.

She smacked my shoulder. "I can't believe you remembered that because you sure didn't follow it."

I shrugged. "It's more fun to play with it."

"I don't know what we are going to do with you, Ember."

"I'm sure Bucky has some ideas. Most of those would probably entail taking me out back and shooting me."

Grams nodded. "What is happening there? Clearly, you two love each other."

The soupy ice cream got sucked in and I choked. "What?"

"Ember. Everyone in that church watched the two of you. Quite honestly, it was arousing."

"Uhm...I'd rather not have that kind of talk with you, Grams."

"Oh pish. This isn't about me. What is going on with the two of you?"

"I pushed him away like I do with everyone else."

"I noticed you and the girls weren't talking either."

"No. We had a fight."

"What happened?"

I took a deep breath and laid everything out for Grams. Everything from the bet to Bucky's kiss in the Mexican restaurant to my fight with Nomi, Teagan, and Olivia and finally to what I said to Bucky in the church's bathroom. When the last word left me, I felt wrung out. Between the crying jag and the confession, I wasn't sure I had anything left in me.

Grams sat quietly. My gaze found hers. "Well, it looks like I need to have some words with my granddaughter. But that can wait. Let's tackle the Bucky issue."

"Grams, I don't think—"

"Yeah, I'm pretty sure we established that. I think you need to forget everything that led up to this sham of a friends-only relationship with Bucky. You need to be honest with him, but most importantly, you need to be honest with yourself."

"I'm not—"

"Let me finish. I've known you most of your life. You haven't had an easy go and you have always used sex as a weapon. It was something you could control. If you focused on purely physical pleasure, then you'd never have to worry about getting hurt. You protected your heart by not letting any man closer than his condom-covered penis. Only this time you messed up, Ember. Everything with Bucky was emotion. You couldn't hide behind sex. I think if you take a moment to look inside you will find you care for him more than you'd like to admit. That's why you needed to sabotage anything with him."

I bit my lip. Her words pointed out everything I refused to see.

"It's too late."

Grams gave my hand a squeeze. "It's never too late, sweetie. You just have to get off your ass, swallow your pride, and talk to the man. If he's stupid enough to continue being mad, then he was never good enough for you to begin with."

I looked at the horror show of a sundae in front of me as her words rolled through my head. "You're a wise woman, Grams."

She laughed. "I don't know about wise but I'd say experienced. Now, why don't we get out of here since you're expecting another guest at your apartment?"

"Sounds like a plan. Thanks so much, Grams. I love you."

"I love you too, sweetie." She grabbed our ice cream trash and dumped them in the trash can. I looked at the goth girl, who was still sitting at the counter with an ambivalent look on her face. Kids these days. They did not know how easy their life was. I followed Grams out the door before I could be that near middle-aged woman giving a teenager a lecture about how easy they had it. I was getting older by the second, but I wasn't that old yet.

29

THE MESS GETS MESSIER

Trudging into the apartment building, all I could think about was how good it would be to lie down and take a nap. The lobby was empty, and the elevator came quickly. My conversation with Grams played over and over in my head. When the elevator stopped on my floor, I was still in my head but got off the elevator. The autopilot stopped three doors down from my apartment. I could hear a booming argument echoing through the corridor.

"I'm not fucking going anywhere," Aunt Beaty's voice yelled.

"Beatrice, you knew this wasn't permanent. You need to take your creatures and go." Dad attempted a civil tone.

"It's not my fucking fault your whore of a girlfriend slept with that charlatan and now you are out on your ass."

"Ember already said I can stay here. Dad trumps crazy aunt any day."

I heard a glass bottle settle onto a counter. Fuck me. If I didn't get in there and settle this who knew what would happen? I'm more worried about my dad's safety. Aunt Beaty wouldn't hesitate to bust a bottle over someone's head, even if that meant she'd need her step stool.

Jiggling the door handle as loud as possible, I entered my apartment. My eyes grew large at the sight in front of me. Boxes and bags were piled everywhere. What in the hoarder's hell did I walk into?

"Hello, Peanut. I'm glad you're home. Now you can tell your aunt that she can pack up her stuff."

"I told you, Dennis. She knows who she should keep, and it's not the father who sold her childhood home for a handful of magic beans." Aunt Beaty stepped off the stool she'd been using to get a glass.

"What is going on in here?" I shut the door behind me.

"I brought some of my things with me." Dad gave me a big smile.

"He's cramping our style, Ember. Tell him." Aunt Beaty took a swig from the bottle, ignoring her filled glass.

"This is a lot, Dad."

He blinked up at me like a cute little farm animal. It was a form of torture for a parent to guilt their grown children into doing things they didn't want to do.

"Stay strong, Ember," Aunt Beaty said.

"Beatrice, do not manipulate my daughter. My dear daughter that I sacrificed a lot for."

"Now who's manipulating who, Dennis."

"This is between—" Dad countered.

"That's enough, you two. I'm too exhausted to deal with this right now. You two need to figure out something. I don't care who sleeps where, but there is not enough room in here to store all this crap." I looked at my dad. "We will need to talk about the house, but not right now." Moving toward my bedroom, I stopped in the hallway and turned back to them. "Don't disturb my nap or both of you are out of this apartment."

I dragged myself into my room. The patter of paws behind me echoed. Cuddles and Princess wandered into my room and then made themselves comfortable on the end of my bed before I could shut the door. Placing my phone on my nightstand, I let the wise words Grams drummed into my head float through my mind. My last thought was of Bucky and the hurt on his face.

"Shh...she's going to be pissed if we wake her up."

Voices broke into my blissful sleep. The voice was right. I grabbed the pillow and covered my head.

"Now look what you did," another voice said.

Muffled under the pillow, I said, "If you value your life, I'd suggest getting the hell out of my room. I told you not to disturb my nap."

"I don't believe we got that message." My sleepy brain finally caught up, and I knew who was in my room: Nomi, Teagan, and Olivia.

Throwing the pillow, I sat up. The pillow nearly hit Cuddles and Princess. A hiss and chuff were directed at me. My gaze saw my three ex-best friends.

"What do you three want and how did you get in here unnoticed? Where are my aunt and Dad? Did you have to step over dead bodies to get in here?"

"There were no dead bodies, but it looked like your aunt and Dad were splitting a fifth of vodka," Olivia said.

"Yeah, they were thrilled and told us to wake you up. They said you'd been sleeping for a while." Teagan walked toward the bed.

"I have?" I grabbed my phone off the nightstand and let out a frustrated breath.

"What's wrong?" Nomi asked.

"I'd only been sleeping for half an hour. Those lushes." Shaking my head, I looked back at the trio. "Now, back to why you're here."

Teagan cleared her throat. "We need to talk."

"You have me cornered in my room. Spit it out." I pulled a pillow into my lap and began nervously pulling at a loose thread.

"You know it wasn't long ago that we would have called you a lush." Teagan let out an anxious laugh.

"Uh-huh. Is that really what you want to talk about? What you three used to call me? I used to call you friends. How about that?"

Nomi moved to stand next to Teagan. "That isn't what we came here to talk about. We're sorry, Ember. We didn't mean to hurt you."

"Too late. You did."

Teagan sat on the bed near my feet. "Look, I fucked up. I just thought with everything that was going on with you, the last thing you needed was wedding crap."

"You're right. You fucked up. Instead of assuming, maybe you should have asked me. When have I not told you a straight answer?"

"We know, Ember. Please believe us when we say our intentions may have been misguided, but they came from a place of love." Olivia's soft voice was barely audible.

My gaze rose from the pillow to Olivia, Nomi, and Teagan. "It may have been out of love but it was fucked up. Doing wedding stuff with you guys was the lone bright spot in my world right now. I mean come on. You saw part of the mess when you came in here. Two drunk siblings are on my couch. I am a preschool teacher for what I can only describe as up-and-coming serial killers. I've fallen for the one man I should never want and I pushed away said man because I'm an idiot and expect everything to fall apart no matter what I do. So...yeah it wasn't just wedding planning to me. It was something happy to look forward to instead of the mess that is my constant."

Teagan took my hand in hers. "I'm sorry. We really didn't mean to hurt you."

I shrugged. "Okay."

"Do you think you can forgive us?" Nomi asked.

"I don't know."

Olivia sucked in a breath. "What if we say we are all in on that convention and you can pick out whatever costume you want?"

I perked up. "Seriously?"

Teagan nodded. "Yep."

"Sweet. I was thinking body paint and pasties."

Their eyes bugged out. "Uhm...seriously?" Nomi asked.

I grinned. "Maybe. It depends on how much I want to punish you."

Teagan laughed. "Grams said you'd say that."

"What?"

"She tore into us. I'm surprised I'm not walking with a limp." Teagan pretended to rub her butt.

I laughed. "I always loved that woman."

We all laughed, then they sobered and Teagan looked at me. "Are we good?"

"Yeah. We're good. Just don't leave me out anymore. Well, if you're going to be a lush, you can just invite Olivia and Nomi. I don't need to pick your drunk ass off the ground." I smiled.

"Hell no. You're coming to everything now." Teagan pulled me into a hug. I felt Olivia's and Nomi's arms encircle all of us.

Nomi pulled back and looked at me. "Now, what's this about you falling for Bucky?"

I swallowed. "What?"

Olivia cocked her head. "You thought we'd miss that part in your little rant."

"Uhm...I don't remember saying that."

"Bullshit. Grams told us we need to get you to move on Bucky too," Teagan said.

I cocked up my eyebrow. "Those are the words she used?"

She shrugged. "I may have changed it up a bit, but the idea is the same. So spill it."

"Fine. There really isn't anything to spill. He wanted something more, and I did what I do. I pushed him away."

"Why?" Olivia asked.

I shrugged. "It would end eventually. Better to get ahead of everything."

Nomi grimaced. "Seriously? You are an educated woman. So, I know you're not this dumb."

"Excuse me?"

"I think what Nomi is saying is that you are thinking with your head instead of your heart. You've convinced yourself that love doesn't last or even exist. But if you don't give Bucky a chance, you could miss out on one of the best things in your life," Olivia said earnestly.

I huffed. "You're one to talk, Olivia. You won't even give Xander the time of day."

"She's right." Nomi nodded.

Olivia sighed. "Fine. If you make things right with Bucky, I will give Xander a chance the next time I see him. I will only give him a chance if you finally resolve this sexual tension you and Bucky have had for ages."

A grin curled my lips. "Challenge accepted."

30

LOVE IN A STAIRWELL

*D*ear Karen,

Things have changed. In a matter of two days, my best friends became ex-friends and then back to best friends. My father dropped the news he gave my childhood home to some cult, and he's now living with me. I made a deal with my devil of a friend that I would finally straighten things out with Bucky. That one is the most painful. How am I supposed to do that? I've never chased men. When I broke it off, I never went back. This is new to me. What the fuck am I supposed to do?

Why am I asking you these questions? You are totally a lady with long hair on top with the rest cut short and you're constantly asking for the manager. I guess when I figure things out, I'll let you know.

Later Karen,

Ember

The elevator let me out on Bucky's floor. I almost chickened out and pushed the up button to take it back to my floor. My reflection taunted me when I reached for the button. To escape it, I exited. I moved toward Bucky's apartment but stopped a few doors away. I had no idea what I was going to say. It was close to nine at night and I could hear the din of activity in the surrounding apartments.

After Teagan, Nomi, and Olivia left, I'd tried to convince myself that I'd go to Bucky right away. Rip it off like a Band-Aid. Unfortunately, my room was a mess that needed to be cleaned in that moment. Then I had to wash my hair. By the time all the chores and preparation were done for the week, I had to peel my drunk father and aunt off the floor. It was too late to do anything. At least that was what I told myself. The same thing happened on Monday when I came home from work. It was amazing that when I wanted to avoid something, I could find a love for cleaning.

When Tuesday rolled around, I'd gotten texts from the girls asking how things went with Bucky. I had to finally stop procrastinating and do it. Fear was making my palms sweat more than a teenager waiting for a date.

"Come on, Ember. You got this." With a deep breath, I finally approached his door. I glanced over my shoulder at Xander's door. Everything was quiet. Perfect. The last thing I needed was an audience for my humiliation. I raised my hand and knocked. There was a faint noise in response, but the door didn't open. I knocked again a bit louder. Approaching feet made me step back from the door.

When it opened, I said, "Bucky, I know—" My words caught in my throat when I saw it wasn't Bucky at the door. A beautiful, curvaceous blonde wearing only a skimpy tank and short shorts stood there. I glanced at the apartment number and then back at her.

"Can I help you?" her sultry voice asked.

"Uh...uhm...I thought Bucky lived here." Words stumbled off my tongue.

"He does. He's in the shower." She cocked her head. "Are you Ember?"

"Yeah. I just—" My words were cut off when I saw a half-naked Bucky come into view. A towel hung low on his hips while he used another to dry his hair.

"Who was at the door, Kins?" He paused when his eyes met mine. "Ember? What are you doing here?"

I looked between Bucky and the Kins chick. "This was a mistake." Taking off on a dead sprint, I ran to the elevator and manically pressed the up button.

"Ember!" Bucky called.

Panic made me do stupid things. Things like running to the stairs instead of waiting for the elevator. Without looking at him, I made a mad dash to the stairs and burst through the door. My legs carried me up the stairs two at a time. After only one flight, they dropped to one at a time. A pain in the back of my thigh crumpled me on the next landing. Fuck me. I had at least three more floors to go. Frustrated tears burned my eyes.

"Ember." Bucky's voice echoed through the stairwell.

I stood with the help of the railing. A hop step took me a few more steps.

"What are you doing?" The nearness of his voice made me scream.

"Jesus Christ." I sat on the step, giving up my journey to my apartment.

"Are you okay?" He squatted in front of me.

"Yeah. I'm perfect. Just decided to move into the stairwell. It's much more comfortable."

"Uh-huh. You really are a shit liar." He gave me a crooked grin.

"I have to excel at something. It might as well be a shit liar." I tried to stand and winced.

Bucky's arm wrapped around my waist. "I've got you."

"I'm okay." I tried to move away from him.

He held me tighter to his side. "Just lean into me."

Reluctantly, I let him help me up the stairs to the next floor. His barely clothed damp body pressed against mine. My mind wandered to what was under that towel. With every bit of will, I had pushed those thoughts down. Instead of thinking about his hidden treasure, I focused on my thighs which were about to combust. There was no way I could make it any further up the stairs. I pulled away from him.

"I'm just going to catch the elevator from this floor." I averted my eyes from his very tempting body. "Thanks for the assistance."

When I moved to open the door to the floor, he closed it with his hand over my head. "That's it? You show up at my door, run away from me and then just want to disappear after I help you?"

I took a deep breath. "It was a mistake. I'm sorry I disturbed you." With a tug, I attempted to open the door. It wouldn't budge. Damn him and his glistening muscles.

"Turn around, Ember." His deep voice caressed my ear.

Slowly, I did as he asked. I focused my eyes on his collarbone. Every cell in my body urged me to glance down. It was an epic struggle. Bucky curled his finger under my chin, tilting my head up to meet his gaze.

"Now tell me, what was a mistake?"

"Nothing. It was stupid."

He shrugged. "Humor me. It's the least you can do."

A snarky comment was on the tip of my tongue. I pushed that impulse down and took a deep breath. "I came down to apologize, but I didn't expect you to have...uhm...company. I'm sorry."

His lips pursed. "I'd like to hear what you had to say."

"Seriously?"

"Yes, seriously."

"It doesn't matter. You've clearly moved on."

"Just tell me, Ember."

"Fine. I was going to tell you I was sorry I lied."

"What did you lie about?"

"I lied..."

"Yes."

"I lied about not having feelings for you. Despite myself, I care more for you than I have any other man with whom I've been involved. You're a good guy with a body I'd like to climb, but it doesn't matter now. You've moved on. I was too late." My voice ended in a whisper.

Bucky inched closer. "You have feelings for me."

"It doesn't matter—" He cut off my words with his lips when they captured mine. His body pressed against me. The cold of the door seeped through my shirt, but I could barely feel it. Fire and passion flowed through my veins. I could think of nothing but his lips on mine.

Way too soon, he broke the kiss by pulling back and looking at me. His hand left my hip and caressed my cheek. "You're so fucking gorgeous."

I snorted. "Not compared to the woman in your apartment."

It was his time to snort. "I'm sure my sister would love to hear that."

"Your sister?"

"Yeah. Do you really think I'd be here kissing you if I had a woman in my apartment?"

"Well..."

"Look, I know what it looked like when we met. I was open about sleeping around. Once you gave me a chance, I haven't been with another woman. In your eyes, I see my future." He kissed my nose.

"But I pushed you away."

Bucky's lips curled into a grin. "I told you. You're a shit liar."

My jaw dropped. "Are you telling me you knew I had feelings for you and you let me believe I pushed you away?"

One of his shoulders lifted. "You needed to figure it out on your own."

"You're a lot smarter than I thought you were."

"I'm not sure how I should take that, but I should probably get back home before I get arrested for indecent exposure." He stepped back, and I could take in all his barely covered glory. "You need to stop looking at me like that."

"Or what?" I smirked.

He moved back into my space. "Or I'm going to have to take you right here."

My chest was rising and falling. The fire in his eyes made me wet. "What if that's what I want?"

A primal growl left him, and his lips slammed against mine. I held onto his muscular shoulders. His hands wandered over my curves, and he pulled me hard against the impressive tool he was packing. My hands roamed down his chest and landed on the top of the towel around his waist. Before I could whip it off him, he stilled my hands.

"Stop. We can't," he breathed out.

"Why not? You want it and I want it."

He leaned his forehead against mine as I ran my hands up his chest to his shoulders. "I do, but not here. It needs to be special. You deserve special."

I huffed out a laugh. "I'm no virgin, Bucky."

"It has nothing to do with being a virgin. It has everything to do with you being someone who deserves to be treated with respect and care."

"So we'll never have hot stairwell sex?"

Bucky's deep laugh echoed around us. "Oh, we can definitely do that. I just don't want that for our first time."

I leaned my head against the door. "All right."

"All right. Come over for dinner tomorrow?" He gave me a strained smile.

"Sounds like a date."

I watched as he visibly relaxed. "Perfect. I'll see you tomorrow at six."

"Okay."

He turned to leave but came back and kissed me on the spot where my neck met my shoulder. A chill ran through my body. Who knew that was an erogenous zone?

"See you tomorrow, Ember."

"See ya."

His towel-covered ass jogged down the stairs. He turned back and gave me a panty-melting smile. I sighed, then left to get the elevator. The pain in my hamstring came back with a vengeance. I may have been limping, but the memory of Bucky's kisses still made me tingle all over.

31

A Spot Welded Lego

The little devils wrecked the room. A preschool room was expected to be messy, but this was out of hand. I was teaching each of the children to be organized. It wasn't going well.

"Wow. They did a number in here," Corrine said from the door.

"Yeah. I don't know what got into them today," I said as I picked up a headless doll and a three-wheeled car.

"It's probably the upcoming holiday."

I turned toward her with a furrowed brow. "Holiday?"

Corrine laughed. "Thanksgiving is in a week. Don't tell me you forgot."

"Oh my God. I can't believe I forgot."

She smiled. "It's understandable, but I'm surprised you didn't notice all the turkeys." Corrine pointed around the room at the construction paper turkeys. "From what you've told me, your life has been crazy. So, what has you distracted lately?"

Turning my back on her, I bent to pick up a Lego that was apparently spot welded to the floor. "What the hell?"

"You okay, Ember?"

I was pulling with both hands to remove the block of death from the floor. "How did the kids manage to get this damn thing welded to the floor?"

"It's probably a glorious mix of candy, dirt, glue, and fairy dust." Corrine laughed.

"Ha. Ha. I need to get this off." I tugged harder, but the damn thing didn't budge an inch.

"Leave that be." I looked up at her. She was leaning against the wall with her arms crossed. Standing, I stretched the crick I had in my back.

"All right. I'm leaving it alone."

"Good. Now, spill it."

"Seriously? You wanted me to stop what I was doing just to tell you about my love life?"

She nodded. "Absolutely. I have been married for twenty years. Don't get me wrong. I love my husband. He still surprises me with his tricks. In fact, he did this—"

"Whoa! I have to see your husband when he comes in here. I can't know those kinds of things about him."

"I'm just saying. I'm happy, but I like to relive that excitement when things were new."

I collapsed into one of the small chairs at a table. She joined me and leaned in. I couldn't hold back the laugh. "I can't believe I'm going to tell you about this."

"Think of me as a really interested therapist."

"Fine. You remember—" My words were cut off with the cacophony of children coming in from their outdoor playtime.

"Miss Ember!" A little boy dressed in a mix of Spider-man and Batman ran toward me.

"What's up, Howie?" I knelt in front of him.

He looked from side to side. "Miss Ember..." Howie leaned close.

"Yes, Howie?" I whispered back.

"Kathy kissed me."

"Oh." I was not prepared for that. With a glance, I looked over at the caramel-colored skin girl dressed in a pretty pink dress and her hair in braids.

"Should I be upset?" His big brown eyes looked up at me.

"Well...uhm..." This conversation told me I was nowhere prepared to have children.

"I mean, she asked me if I could kiss her, but she only likes Batman and not Spider-man. She had the nerve to..." He looked over his shoulder at Kathy, who was watching us with a smile. "She said she liked Bruce Wayne instead of Peter Parker."

"Oh well, that is a problem."

He threw his little hands in the air. "How can I possibly be in love with a woman who disagrees with me?"

"Uhm..."

"Howie?" Corrine joined us.

"Hi, Miss Corrine," he said shyly.

"I think Mr. Axel could help you better than Miss Ember." The three of us looked at the very bookish Axel. His parents had high hopes for him and I don't think that included being a preschool teacher. I held back a giggle when I realized all the girls in the class surrounded Axel.

"Do you really think?" Howie looked at Corrine skeptically.

"I think he's perfect for the job." Corrine stood. "Mr. Axel?"

Axel turned toward us and smiled. "Yes, Miss Corrine?"

"I'm going to borrow Miss Ember for a bit, but I think Howie has a very important question to ask you."

Axel furrowed his brow and extricated himself from the little girls. I watched as he bent down to Howie and some colorful patterns were peeking out from under his sweater. Hmm...maybe I underestimated Axel.

"Come on, Ember." Corrine linked her arm with mine and practically dragged me out of the room.

When the door shut behind us, I pulled away from Corrine. "What was that all about?"

She raised her eyebrow at me. "I'll talk to you about that in my office." Corrine proceeded to walk down to her office.

I followed behind, a bit confused as to what exactly was going on. When we arrived at her office, I closed the door and sat in a chair in front of her desk.

"So..." Corrine leaned back in her chair.

"Did you just bring me in to get the gossip about my non-existent love life?"

"Yes and no. That was my original thought for having Axel take over your class, but when I saw you checking out his tattoos, I knew I had to get you out of there."

I chuckled. "I was just admiring the work."

"Not the way you were looking. I'm glad poor Axel didn't see you. He would have gone up in flames from embarrassment."

"Please. Any guy that has sleeve tattoos doesn't embarrass that easily."

Corrine leaned forward. "Stop stalling and tell me what happened."

With a sigh, I opened my mouth to spill the entire story, but a man in a fitted three-piece suit barging through the door interrupted us. I blinked up at him in amazement. He was a stunning specimen of a man. Not as built as Bucky, but he could wear the hell out of a suit.

"Hey, babe." Corrine stood from her desk and planted a kiss on his cheek.

Mr. Hotness, who I assumed was Corrine's husband, looked at me with a very discerning look. I felt like a bug under a microscope.

Corrine nudged him with her elbow. "Cole, be nice to Ember." She looked at me and smiled. "This is my husband, Cole."

I stood and put my hand out. "Nice to meet you, Mr. Lavender."

He grimaced. "It's Cole Wolf. Lavender is Corrine's maiden name. I still don't understand why she insists on using it."

"You know darn well it's because I run a preschool." She beamed up at him.

Cole gave her a warm smile and then looked back at me. "So, you're Ember. I've heard many things about you."

A strained smile curled my lips. "Oh really? I hope it was all good."

His blank look told me it wasn't.

Corrine smacked his chest. "Knock it off, Cole. Stop giving Ember your lawyer look. She was just telling me about her night."

He looked at me longer, his lips curled, and he started laughing. "Did you and Bucky finally do it?"

"What?"

"Corrine has been telling me all about your escapades. So, did you two finally scratch that itch?" He smiled and sat in the chair I had vacated.

"Uhm...I'm not quite sure what's going on?" I looked between my boss and her now jovial husband.

Corrine sighed and returned to her desk. "You see my husband is an asshole just like the rest of them."

"Hey! I was just having fun," Cole defended.

"Uh-huh." Corrine raised an eyebrow.

"What?"

"Why are you still here, Cole? Ember was just getting to the good stuff."

"That's why I'm staying. I want to hear the story."

My jaw was hanging open between the two of them. A vibration in my pocket notified me of a text. It was the perfect excuse to escape whatever was happening in the office.

Digging my phone out, I held it up. "I've got to check this. I'll be right back."

Without letting them say a word, I popped out of the office and closed the door behind me. Relief flooded every cell in my body. A hysterical laugh bubbled up when I saw the text.

Teagan: So is he a push pop or a long john?

I decided to play dumb.

Me: Did you have a stroke? What the hell are you talking about?

Nomi: You're the one who came up with those terms, Ember.

Dammit. Group chat.

Me: I plead the fifth.

Teagan: Sounds like it's a push pop.

Me: Don't you guys have anything better to do than bug me at work?

Nomi: Nope.

Teagan: Absolutely nothing.

Olivia: I do but they told me I need to be on this chat.

Me: Well, I'm glad you're on Olivia because guess who has a date tonight?

Olivia: Fuck my life.

Me: If you finally hook up with Xander you'll finally get some fucking in your life.

Nomi: There she is.

Teagan: Glad to have you back.

Me: I have no idea what you guys are talking about but I have to get back to shaping young minds for the future.

Olivia: Our future is doomed.

I really hated my friends sometimes, but that small text exchange felt like my life was finally getting back on track. Now, if only I can survive a date with Bucky without doing all the kinky shit that would totally get me pregnant with a litter of his babies.

32

An Edibles Education

The apartment was suspiciously quiet when I got home. No crazy sex acts were going on in the middle of the living room. The menagerie was absent as well. As I glanced around, I noticed all my dad's things were piled nicely in the corner. The normality of everything made me slightly scared. If I found dead bodies in the hallway, I was out. I knew enough about true crime to know I'd get blamed.

"Hello?" I called into the silence.

A cavernous silence I hadn't experienced since Aunt Beatrice moved in surrounded me. It was comforting and a bit unnerving. Dropping my purse on the table, I headed to my bedroom. I glanced at my reflection in the mirror and winced. A sticky substance had strands of my hair clumped together. My chin had a dark substance smudged on it, and the mascara I'd applied this morning found its way under my eyes, making me look like a demented raccoon.

"Well, shower it is." The clock on my nightstand made me cringe. I had forty-five minutes to get ready and find my way down to Bucky's apartment. I needed to be quick, but thorough in that short amount of time.

Rushing over to the bathroom, I turned the hot water on high and the radio on some classic rock station. As the water beat on my shoulders, I relaxed. The stress from my day and anxiety about my upcoming date with Bucky melted away. The lyrics to a song seemed pertinent to my situation, and I sang. My hips swayed with the music while I used my shampoo bottle as a microphone. I forced myself to stop dancing while I shaved some of my intimate parts. The last thing I needed was a wayward swipe of the razor to continue the self-imposed dry spell.

When everything was hairless, clean, and ready for action, I shut off the water and wrapped myself in a big fluffy towel. My reflection in the bathroom mirror looked ten times better. With the song from the shower still in my mind, I bopped over to my room, humming the song that played on repeat in my head.

"What should I wear? Oh...oh...oh...what should I wear?" I sang as I sifted through my closet. I pulled out a blue sweater dress. It was perfect. The stretchy fabric hugged all my curves just right. Flinging the dress on the bed, I pulled out a sexy matching bra and panties.

A matching garter belt went with the set, and I held it up. "Do I want to blow his mind this time around or should I wait till next time? Nope, it will be next time. I use this and I'll end up getting knocked up."

Slipping on the bra and panties, I did a little sexy dance. This was the first time in a while that I felt confident, sexy, and nervous. "I'm getting laid. I'm getting laid. He's definitely got a bomb pop instead of a push pop." I danced around my room.

My phone rang with Nomi's distinct ringtone.

"What's up, bitch?" I answered.

"Just calling to see if you were nervous, but it sounds like the cockaholic is back in charge."

I laughed. "I wouldn't say that, but I'm feeling good."

"That's great. So, I've been thinking about your dad's problem."

"Aunt Beaty?"

Nomi snorted. "No. The house."

I sat on the bed. "What about it?"

"Well, I don't want to go too much into it, but I have one of our paralegals looking into the legalities of the cult taking ownership of the property."

"You think we can get it back?"

"Maybe. I don't want to get your hopes up, but I'm working on it."

"Fuck me. Thanks, Nomi. Is this going to cost us an arm and a leg? Because if it is, you know I'm only working at a daycare right now."

"Are you fucking serious? Do you really think I'm going to charge one of my best friends? Did you hit your head recently?"

"Sorry. The way my life has been lately, I have to ask those kinds of questions."

"I know. Just remember, I have your back and so do Olivia and Teagan."

"Thanks, Nomi."

"Well, I'm going to let you finish getting ready for your hot date. Before I let you go, what are you wearing?"

"Blue sweater dress and my stiletto boots."

"Oooh...someone is looking to get her some push pop."

"You're such a bitch."

"Love you too, Ember. Have fun and remember, it's not the size that matters but the motion of the ocean."

"Holy shit, did you fuck that up. I'm hanging up now. Love you, Nomi."

"Love you too, bitch."

"Oh, and Nomi?"

"Yeah?"

"If you manage to get my dad's house back, you'll get your pick of which Powerpuff girl you want to be at Comic Universal."

"Oh joy."

I laughed as I disconnected the call. Tossing the phone on the bed, I grabbed my dress and started wiggling it over my head.

"What the fuck is going on?" Beatrice's voice made me freeze.

The dress was barely over my head and I spun around. My foot kicked something pointy. An angry chittering told me what, or should I say, who it was. "Sorry, Cuddles." I finished pulling the dress down and looked at her. "Where did you come from?"

"Your father and I took the animals for a walk." Right on cue, my father poked his head into my room.

"Hi, pumpkin."

"Hey, Dad. You took them on a walk? How did that work?" I walked over to my closet and pulled out my knee-high stiletto boots. My feet were going to pay for wearing these, but hopefully I wouldn't have them on long.

"We pulled them along in a cart."

Midway up my calf, I stopped zipping and looked up. "You put them in a cart. Like a shopping cart?"

Beatrice rolled her eyes. "No, you idiot. It's more of a wagon than a cart and you know damn well I didn't pull a damn thing. Your father did all that work."

I finished zipping the boots and looked at my dad. "Lucky you."

"It was actually pretty nice." He smiled.

Beatrice walked over to me. "I gave him one of my edibles. I wouldn't doubt he's seeing purple elephants right now."

"What?" I screeched.

"Keep it down. You know your father. It doesn't hurt him to loosen up."

I looked over at my dad, and he had a funny look on his face. "You think he needed to loosen up? He just got out of a damn cult. How much looser should he be?"

"Oh yeah. I forgot about that." Beaty waved her hand dismissively. "Doesn't matter, it should wear off soon...ish."

Before I could say a word, my dad walked over to me and started petting my hair. "I can hear your hair growing. It sounds like pop rocks."

I grabbed his hand and held it in mine. "Dad, why don't you go sit on the couch? I bet you could hear my hair growing from there."

He caressed my short hair and said, "My beautiful fire."

My eyes misted over, and I guided him to the door. He turned and walked toward the living room. I spun to Aunt Beaty. "You are responsible for him. Which as those words leave my mouth, I realize it's like I'm leaving a toddler in charge."

She slapped her hands on her hips. "Is that a short joke?"

I gave her a flat stare. "No. It's a commentary on how mature I think you are. Now, will you let me finish getting ready?"

She stared at me a moment, then turned to go. Of course, she had to have the last word. "Good luck. You're gonna need it." She shot over her shoulder.

My pinchy heels clicked on the floor as I marched over to the door and slammed it shut. Glancing at the clock, I was going to be late. "Fuck my life." A chittering from my bed made me jump. Cuddles was laying there watching me. "Well, Cuddles, it looks like it's going to be a minimal make-up night. What do you think?"

She huffed and turned her back to me. That wasn't a good omen.

33

Rice Isn't Supposed to Be Crunchy

When I stepped off the elevator on Bucky's floor, a wonderful smell floated toward me. My stomach grumbled, reminding me I only had a handful of chocolate-covered peanuts for lunch. Inhaling deeply, I forced myself to walk slowly to his door. I raised my hand to knock, but the door swung open, making me freeze with my hand in the air.

The pretty woman from the other day was dressed in a short pink sequined dress and holding a matching clutch. I was instantly jealous that she could look so perfect. Her long blonde hair was curled and styled perfectly. My hand involuntarily went to my short hair. I missed my long hair at that moment.

"You're back." Her voice tinkled like a bell.

"Uh..."

"Kinsley! You better leave before Ember gets here," Bucky called from somewhere in the apartment.

Her painted red lips curled up on one side, and she leaned toward me. "Should we tell him you're here?"

"Uhm..." Jesus. My language skills needed work.

"What are you doing—" Bucky's words cut off when he saw me. "Ember. You're here. Uhm...it looks like you've finally met Kinsley."

"Yep. We are best pals now, Robbie." Kinsley winked at me. "Well, my ride will be here soon. You two have fun. Do everything I would do." She moved past me and wiggled her fingers at me.

I watched her get on the elevator and finally brought my gaze back to Bucky. My eyes bugged out as I took him in. He wore a button-down shirt untucked with the sleeves rolled up to show off his muscular forearms. Holy shit! That was some intense forearm porn right there. The dark jeans fit comfortably over his athletic frame. I'd be panting if my mouth wasn't dryer than the Sahara.

A sexy grin curled his lips as his eyes wandered over me. "Did you want to come in?"

"Oh uhm...sure." All at once, I was nervous and regretted agreeing to this date.

As I stepped past him, his cologne wafted around me and made my mouth water. My wobbly knees somehow took me further into the apartment. Glancing around, I recalled the short time I'd been here before. It was a pretty typical bachelor pad until I turned toward the kitchen. The previously pristine kitchen had dirty pots and pans cluttering every surface.

"Whoa," I muttered.

"Sorry, I didn't have time to clean up yet. I didn't mean for you to see that. You were supposed to see that." He pointed toward the table I hadn't noticed thanks to the cologne/Bucky haze that had consumed my brain the moment I stepped into the apartment.

"Oh my." I walked toward the candlelit table. Two place settings with mismatching plates and a napkin animal. Or at least an attempt at one. A lone rose sat next to the napkin origami. Buck walked over and picked it up.

"This is for you."

Heat flooded my cheeks. "Thank you. This is really nice."

He looked a bit embarrassed. "I didn't have a chance to run to the store to get matching plates, but we do have wine glasses. Would you like some?"

Bucky walked toward the mess of a kitchen.

"That would be great. Though I shouldn't drink much before we eat."

He stopped opening the wine. "Oh my God. Sit down. Let me get you some food." Bucky rushed over to the table and grabbed my plate, causing the napkin to flutter to the ground. I picked it up and sat down. My leg bounced nervously as I heard him banging around in the kitchen. What the hell was he doing?

"Here you go." He set the plate in front of me.

I took a deep breath, expecting the wonderful smell from the hallway. The food smelled nothing like that. It looked presentable, but it didn't smell great. I gave him a small smile as he poured me a glass of wine, then retreated to get his own food. With a fork in hand, I pushed it around on the plate. It sounded hard. I thought it was supposed to be Chinese food.

"Go ahead and dig in," he said as he sat across from me.

I piled food on the fork and took the leap. An overpowering taste of garlic and peppers made my eyes water. When I started chewing, everything was crunchy. Rice was definitely not supposed to be crunchy. I continued to chew with a strained smile on my face.

"It was my first time making Chinese. I hope it's okay." He watched me intently.

I swallowed and immediately shoved another spoonful into my mouth. Oh God! The second spoonful was worse. How could it get worse? Did he even cook the rice? My eyes met his as he finally took his first bite of the meal. He immediately grimaced as he chomped on the crunchy rice.

"This is awful." He spit his food into his napkin. "Do you like it?" He raised an eyebrow in question.

Grabbing my wine, I took a swig to help me swallow the food. "No. It's utterly horrible. I didn't want to seem unappreciative, especially when it looks like you worked so hard on it."

His lips curled. "You were trying to protect my feelings?"

"Yes. Why are you smiling at that?"

"Because in all the time I've known you, you've never held back your opinion to save someone's feelings. It's one of my favorite things about you."

"All right then, here's some truth. Your cooking sucks and the state of your kitchen is making my skin crawl. I need to wash and organize everything in it. How do you live like that? Why the hell did you need to use every damn dish in the house to make that concoction?" Ember breathed out.

Bucky brought the wine to his lips. "There you are."

"There I am what? I'm serious. I'm about to clean your kitchen."

"What the hell kind of date is that if I let you clean and organize my kitchen?"

"It would be a much better one once I can relax. Please let me do it. It won't take long."

He sighed. "Fine." I jumped up and started walking toward the kitchen. "On one condition," he said as he leaned back in the chair.

I turned back toward him. "What's that?"

"You have one hour. I'm going to order us a pizza. You have until that gets here."

Glancing toward the mess, then back to him, I grinned. "You have a deal."

Thirty minutes into cleaning Bucky's kitchen, I was feeling infinitely more relaxed. The dishes were almost finished. All I needed to do was put the food away and take a look at his cabinets to see what the ideal setup would be for the next time I came over. In mid scrub, I stopped and realized I was planning even more time with him.

"What's wrong?" Bucky asked from the stool he was perched on.

"Oh...uhm...nothing. I was just plotting out how to organize your entire apartment."

He glanced around, then back at her. "Have at it."

"Really?" I perked up.

"Yes...just not tonight."

"Oh."

"Don't look so sad. As much as I'm enjoying watching you in your element, I want to spend some date time with you. I promise next time you can organize or wash something else. You could even do my laundry."

I scrunched up my face in disgust. "Ew...I'm not touching your skid-marked underoos."

A mischievous glint in his eyes made me pause. "Don't worry. I don't wear underwear."

I rolled my eyes. "All right, pervert."

"What? I'm serious. I only wear underwear on special occasions."

"You realize you should wear them every day."

"You don't understand how great it feels to free ball it?"

"Oh God!"

Bucky was laughing when the doorbell rang. He hopped off the stool and approached the door. Before opening it, he turned to me. "Looks like your time's up. Put that sponge down."

I grumbled but saw him tense. "What are you doing back here?"

Kinsley marched into the apartment. "It was lame."

"Kins, I told you not to come home tonight," Bucky gritted between his teeth.

"I know, but the girls all hooked up and left me at the club. Only weirdos were there, so I called a taxi and here I am. By the way, you really should give me a key to your place. This ringing the doorbell to my own apartment is getting old."

Bucky rubbed his forehead. "Well, you need to stay in your room."

She glared at him with a look that could wither a person. "Robbie. I will do as I please and considering you have your girlfriend washing the dishes, I can't imagine anything too hot and heavy is going on. I'm going to get changed and be right back."

We both watched as Kinsley sashayed toward a hallway. Bucky was mumbling to himself as he joined me back in the kitchen. "I'm sorry about that."

I shrugged. "It's all right."

"No, it's not. I was trying to make it a special night and instead my twin sister has to crash our date."

"Look, it's fine. We can eat the pizza and watch a movie. I'll even let you sit next to me."

His eyes sparkled when the doorbell rang again. "You bet your sweet ass I'm sitting next to you."

Opening the door, he let out another sigh. "What are you doing here?"

Xander bounced on his toes. "I saw Kinsley came back. Does that mean Ember left? Do you want to watch the game?"

"Ember hasn't left and no, we aren't watching the game."

Xander blushed and looked over at me in the kitchen. I gave him a small wave. "Hi, Xander."

"Hey, Ember," he called to me before looking back at Bucky. "So...what are you two up to?"

"It's none—" Bucky began.

"We ordered pizza and are going to watch a movie," I shared.

Bucky slowly turned to me with wide eyes. I bit my lip to hide the laugh bubbling up inside me. Xander brightened. "That's great to hear. I've been dying to watch that new superhero flick." He bounded into the apartment.

More grumbles from Bucky as he walked over to me while Xander made himself at home on the couch.

"Why the fuck did you do that?"

I shrugged. "To fuck with you."

His gaze narrowed. "I may need to spank you for that."

My body tingled with anticipation. "Promises. Promises."

"Ember..." Bucky growled but stopped when the doorbell rang again. "I swear, if this isn't the fucking pizza." He whipped open the door and standing in a popular pizza joint's uniform was a gangly-looking teenager.

"Mr. Aptforbee."

"What?" Bucky asked.

"Are you Mr. Aptforbee?" The teenager looked at the receipt.

"I have no fucking clue what you're saying."

The teen balanced the pizza and shoved the receipt in his face. Bucky let out a long-suffering sigh. "That's the address, you idiot. Can you just get me my pizzas?"

"Oh sorry, man. Here you go."

Bucky snatched the pizzas from the kid and slammed the door. He looked at me, Xander, and Kinsley, who had joined just in time to see the show. "Don't say a word."

A beat of silence fell around us, only to be broken when we all started laughing uncontrollably. Bucky dropped the pizzas on the table and retreated down the hallway. Our laughs only grew with his little tantrum.

34

WTF? No Seduction?

Kinsley, Xander, and I watched the opening credits of some comic book movie. We munched on pizza as we gazed at the television. The three of us used paper plates as we were crammed on the couch together. It was quite the impressive set up of speakers and television. It actually felt like you were traveling back in time with the main character.

"Shh...I think I hear something," Kinsley stage whispered.

I looked over my shoulder to see Bucky leaning against the wall with his arms crossed.

"Do we want to know what you've been doing back there?" I asked.

He gave a small smile. "I'll show you later."

"He was probably just dropping a stink pickle," Kinsley said casually.

"A what?" I asked.

"You know...dropping the kids off at the pool," she said.

I shook my head.

Kinsley sighed. "Dropping a deuce."

My eyes grew wide. "Oh." I looked back at him. Bucky was beet red.

"I did not. How's the pizza?" He walked toward the table.

"It's gweat," Xander said with a mouthful of pizza.

"Nice, Xander. So, why are the two of you in my house ruining my date?" Bucky gave them a pointed look.

"I'm staying with you, duh," Kinsley said, flipping her long blonde ponytail over her shoulder.

Xander looked at me, then at Bucky. "I thought Ember invited me."

I bit my lip as Bucky let out a defeated sigh. "I'm getting some wine. Ember, do you want some?"

"That would be great, Robbie." Kinsley held up an empty wine glass from where'd she'd set it.

"I'll take a porter if you don't mind," Xander added.

"Let me help you." I stood from the couch.

We met in the kitchen. "I'm sorry," he mumbled to me as he grabbed a glass for me while his was still on the bar from earlier.

"What for?" I handed him the wine and grabbed Xander's beer from the fridge.

"I feel like this is a high school date with two chaperones. We are adults." He filled the three wine glasses.

"Well, I know I am. The jury's out about you." I grinned and grabbed my wine and Xander's beer.

"Hey!" He popped my hip with his.

I giggled and went back to the couch. Kinsley was now taking up three-quarters of the couch and Xander was clinging to the available corner. After I handed Xander his beer, I took a seat in the chair closest to the door.

"Seriously, Kinsley?" Bucky looked irritated.

"What? I'm exhausted. It's been a hell of a night for me. Just relax."

He sighed heavily and sat in the chair on the other side of the room. We sat quietly for two hours watching the superhero movie. Kinsley and I sat up a little straighter when the extremely muscular superhero had his obligatory shirtless scene. My eyes dragged from the television to Bucky and my mind conjured up all kinds of ideas that could get him shirtless. While I was checking him out, our gazes locked and heat filled my cheeks. More than one time throughout the movie, I could feel his eyes on me more than the film.

"That ending never gets old." Xander sighed.

"You've seen that before?" I asked.

"Of course. I saw it three times in the theater, own it on Blu-ray, watched it with the director's commentary and have it pre-ordered with the special collector's edition cover." Xander bounced in his seat.

"Wow. If you've seen it so much, how could you look so enthralled?"

He blinked at me and continued to blink at me. I actually looked over my shoulder to see if something was behind me. Xander was clearly malfunctioning.

"Xan, chill out, okay?" Bucky said.

"She doesn't understand," he breathed and looked at Bucky.

I glanced over at Kinsley, who yawned. She curled back on her side. "Are we watching the next movie?"

Exhaustion weighed on me. "I don't know if I can do another movie. It's been a long day."

"You aren't leaving yet, are you?" Bucky asked.

"I'm not really up for another movie."

He nodded and stood from the chair. Walking over to me, he held out his hand. "Will you come with me for a minute?"

My eyes flicked from his outstretched hand to his warm smile. I placed my hand in his and he pulled me to my feet.

He looked at Xander and Kinsley. "We'll be back. Start the movie without us." Bucky yanked me toward the hallway he'd come from earlier.

"Don't forget to wrap it up," Kinsley called.

"You're about to be homeless, Kinsley," Bucky called back.

I giggled as he dragged me further into the darkness. The door at the end of the hall was cracked open with a soft glow emanating from the crack. He pushed it open and led me inside. Three large candles flickered.

A smile curved my lips when I looked around the room. It was a testament to his athleticism. Trophies and ribbons covered every shelf. I wandered over to his dresser where the candles sat. A photo of two little boys in little league uniforms was in a wooden frame. I picked it up and turned toward him.

"You and Xander?"

He nodded. "We were probably about seven in that picture."

I snorted. "I didn't realize the two of you knew each other for so long."

"Yeah. Our grandmothers are friends and then so are our parents. It was practically preordained for us to be buds." He took the picture from me and smiled.

"So, what was your plan?"

Bucky placed the picture back on the dresser. "What do you mean?"

"Well, you got me back here. You set up a romantic setting. Clearly, you had a plan."

"Uhm…"

I furrowed my brow. "Don't tell me you didn't have one specific plan in mind."

He shrugged. "Actually, I didn't. I also hadn't planned on being chaperoned on our first date."

"What about the candles?"

"The light bulb in the lamp is busted. I keep forgetting to replace it."

"You really didn't plan to seduce me?" I crossed my arms across my chest. Irrational anger and disappointment flooded through me. Why was I pissed that he didn't want to get in my pants?

"What's that look for?"

I turned away from him. "What look?"

Bucky chuckled and pulled on my arm to spin me back toward him. His hand came up and caressed the crease between my eyebrows. "This look. If I didn't know any better, I'd think it pissed you off I hadn't planned to seduce you."

A crazy, high-pitched laugh burst out of me. "Why would you think that? That's ridiculous."

His hand drew down the side of my face. Something wild and sensual swirled in his eyes. He dragged his thumb across my bottom lip. My tongue darted out to wet my lips but glided against his thumb by accident. Fire lit in his eyes and it wasn't from the candles. Before I could say a word, Bucky's lips crashed with mine. It was an all-encompassing kiss. He tried to pull away, but my fingers gripped his short hair and held him against me.

I felt his lips curl. "Now who's seducing who?"

"Fuck you," I said with no fire behind it.

"Gladly," he growled.

35

FUCKING CHARMER

Bucky shut the door that was still ajar and picked me up and carried me to his bed. Our lips met with an urgency that seemed out of character for two people with the level of experience we had. I know for me his kisses made me drunk. I couldn't get enough and wanted all of it now. Teagan, Olivia, and Nomi used to refer to me as a cockaholic. That might have been true, but with Bucky, if his bedroom skills were anything like his kissing, I could become addicted to this man.

"You are so fucking sexy," he said as he laid me down on the bed.

I felt a blush creep up my neck. "Uh-huh. Just get over here already."

He'd begun unbuttoning his shirt but stopped and cocked his head. "You don't believe me."

"Does it matter? I want what you have and you want what I have. That's all that matters. Now, take off those pants. I've been dying to see what you're packing." I grabbed for the top button on his jeans.

His hands stilled mine, and he sat on the bed next to me. "You know, this isn't about sex for me."

I sighed. "Bucky, can't we just have fun? Does this have to be a thing?"

"I thought I told you what I want last night in the stairwell."

My eyes closed, and I tried to recall what he said, but all I could remember was his abs and that low-slung towel. It had only been a day and I couldn't even remember his words. This man knocked all sense out of me with just his kisses. "Sorry I don't remember your words from last night."

He grinned. "I told you I think you're gorgeous and you're my future. That means this is not a short-term thing. I'm in this for the long haul. Are you okay with that?"

I leaned back on my elbows. "Bucky, I've never been in a long-term relationship. Hell, I don't even think I've been out with the same guy over three times."

"That's fine. I don't mind being your first." He smiled and kissed my nose.

"Why do you have to be so fucking charming?"

"Why did it take you so long to realize that?"

"You're such a fucker." I smiled and leaned up to kiss him. Pulling back, I looked him in the eyes and said, "I'm willing to give this a real chance, but just so you know, I'm probably going to fuck this up."

Bucky shrugged. "I probably will have my own set of fuck-ups. I'm sure the makeup sex is going to be worth it."

"Why don't we get on with trying it out in the first place?" I grabbed for his pants again and he stopped me. "What now?"

"I want something from you first." He held my hands in his lap.

"What?"

He licked his lips and gazed down at me. "You need to start believing me."

I furrowed my brow. "What the hell are you talking about?"

"You need to learn to believe me when I say you're beautiful or you're gorgeous or you're a hot mama."

"A hot mama? Really?"

"Yep. Can you do that?"

"I will try."

"Good. That's all I'm asking." He let go of my hands and gave me a sinful smile. "Now, where were we?"

I gave him a smile and reached for the button on his pants. "I was right here."

"Hold on, baby. I want to see you first." He stood from the bed.

Biting my lip, I smoothed my hands over my sweater dress down to the hem. Sitting up, I continued further and unzipped each of my boots. Giving him a coy smile, I laid back on my elbows and nodded toward him. "Your turn."

His sexy smile made my body tingle. "You're going to pay for that little tease." Bucky unbuttoned his shirt, revealing the sculpted chest that kept me up last night. I licked my lips ready to trace every contour of his body. "I see what you're thinking, but it's your turn again."

With a huff, I reached to the bottom of my dress and pulled it over my head. It fell to the floor with his shirt. His eyes roamed my body, making it heat with each passing glance. I leaned back to put myself in the sexiest position possible. Boy was I happy I put on my sexy underwear.

"You are so fucking hot." Bucky leaned over to kiss me but I put my hand to his lips.

"I think you're forgetting something." I eyed the offending pants he was still wearing.

He unbuttoned his pants for a view of the happy trail that led to the one place I was dying to go. My eyes watched as he slid the zipper down painfully slow. Just as he was getting to the good stuff, he stopped.

"What are you doing?"

Bucky's grin told me I was going to be both the winner and loser of this little game we were playing.

"I'll be right back." He ran out of the room.

What the fuck was going on? Shaking my head, I laid against the pillows and stared up at the ceiling. He had some suspiciously placed hooks. Hmmm...Bucky had secrets I was dying to figure out.

"Okay. Do you trust me, Ember?" Bucky shut the door and kept his hands behind his back.

"Why?"

"Do you trust me?"

"With what?"

"With giving you pleasure that you'll never forget and beg me for every day after this one."

I raised an eyebrow. "Hmm...that seems like a hell of a guarantee."

"One hundred percent guarantee, but you have to trust me."

I pretended to think about it. Did I want Bucky giving me mind-blowing orgasms? Yes, please. Was he going to know how absolutely hot I was for him? No. Well, at least not right away.

"If you think you're up for it, sure, I trust you to give me pleasure."

"I'm so glad you said that. Now, lay back and arms up."

"What?"

"You said you'd trust me, Ember. I promise this won't hurt. Now, arms up." He waved his hand for me to follow his instructions.

I laid back and raised my arms. Bucky pulled something from around his back. He leaned over me and tied my wrists together with a piece of cloth. When they were tied, he hooked them on a hook I didn't see on his headboard.

"Good, now let's begin."

My eyes widened as I watched him walk over to the dresser. He picked up a cup and came back to the bed. He sat next to me and placed the cup on the nightstand. Every nerve in my body was tight with anticipation.

"What are you doing?" I asked.

Bucky drew his finger over my lips. "Shh...I'm in charge. The only things I want to hear from you are my name, more, please, and oh God."

A giggle escaped. His eyes flashed. He reached over and pulled the cup of my bra down and pinched my nipple. The pain zinged through my body but quickly became pleasure.

"Don't do that again or I will have to punish you again."

I rubbed my thighs together, trying to ease the need I felt. This side of Bucky was so fucking hot. If I'd known he was like this, we would have been fucking this whole time.

"Keep still. Don't make me tie down your legs." He took something out of the cup and popped it into his mouth.

Leaning over, he took my nipple in his mouth. The coldness of an ice cube made me shiver and contract my nipples. A moan threatened to escape. It was too early to give it to him. He then put the ice cube in his hand, went back to my nipple, and bit it. An electric shock wave flowed through me.

"Fuck!" I cried out.

Bucky sucked my nipple and swirled the hardened nub with his tongue. Every swipe of his tongue was driving my body more and more into a frenzy. The nipple popped out of his mouth and he had a satisfied look on his face.

"We'll get to that soon." He pulled down the other cup of my bra and popped the ice back in his mouth. My body was going into overdrive as my untouched nipple was getting the ice cube treatment. The blissful torture was driving me crazy.

Bucky continued alternating the cold ice with the swipe of his hot tongue. When the ice was all but melted, he finally moved lower. I was on the edge, barely clinging to my sanity.

"You taste so damn good," he mumbled against my rounded stomach.

"You are torturing me."

I felt his lips curve against my lips. "Now you know how it feels."

"What?" I squeaked as his tongue delved into my belly button.

"You've been torturing me since the day we met." His lips moved down to the top of my panties. There was no way he couldn't smell how aroused I was. My panties were soaked.

His teeth nipped at my hipbones, sending a shiver through me. This man knew all the spots. It was no wonder why women crawled all over him. My panties slid down my legs. Our eyes met as he meticulously divested me of my soaked panties.

"You're so fucking wet. Is it for me?"

His roughened hands moved up and down my thighs. With each pass, his thumbs got closer to my pussy. Ecstasy was building with each pass. I tried to open my thighs, but he held them together.

"Stop that or I'm going to have to spank you." Bucky reached around and grabbed my ass.

"You're killing me."

A sexy grin curled his lips. "You should see yourself right now. You're the one killing me. The beauty and perfection are almost too much to handle. Tied up for me like a present is threatening my restraint."

It was my turn to grin. I shimmied a little to entice him to finally lose control. In response, he growled, pulled my hip over, and swatted my backside.

"Ow. Why'd you do that?"

"I warned you. Now let me taste you."

Licking my lips, I spread my legs wide. His hands caressed my thighs as he took all of me in. Settling between my legs, he slung them over his shoulders. My body quivered in anticipation. I watched as his face lowered to my dripping wet pussy. He breathed in and placed a small kiss on the outside of my lips. I relaxed against the pillows. My arms were a little sore, but it didn't matter when his tongue licked from bottom to top.

"Oh God..." I moaned.

I felt his lips curl into a smile as he targeted my clit. Flicking his tongue back and forth drove me back to the edge of an orgasm. My body begged to feel the ecstasy crash over me. He held my hips down with his arm over them. His free hand drove three fingers inside of my drenched pussy.

"Bucky, please," I begged.

Instead of speeding up, he slowed down. His tongue lazily laved over the tight bundle of nerves. The fingers that felt so full inside me were only shallowly pumping. I could feel myself retreating from the edge of that blissful place I wanted to be.

"What the fuck are you doing?" I yelled.

"Trust me," he mumbled against my clit.

"If you don't get back down to business and make me come, I swear I will smother you with my thighs. If that gives me that fucking orgasm, then all the better."

The fucker had the nerve to chuckle. Who fucking chuckles when you're going down on someone? Apparently, Bucky did. I swear if it wasn't completely weird, I'd tell his freak of a grandmother about her grandson. If this ever happened again, I'd be the one tying him up.

Just when I thought I was going to have to use my killer thighs, he bit down on my clit and shoved his fingers in and curled them. Sensation shot me back to the brink of orgasm. His sucking and ministrations of my clit while he pumped against my g-spot. All at once, a tidal wave of orgasm overcame me. My back bowed off the bed, and I saw stars.

"Fuck! Yes!" I screamed.

After what felt like an eternity, I collapsed back onto the bed. Bucky was back to the slow pumps and licks. My body was covered with a sheen of sweat, which was cooling rapidly. My nipples pebbled and were ready for another round. I froze at that thought. How was I ready for more when I was pretty sure I blacked out for a few minutes?

"Ready for more?" he asked.

"I'm ready for your cock inside me." I was never shy about saying what I wanted but saying those words to Bucky made me blush.

"I don't know if I'm done feasting."

"Feast later. Fuck me now. While you're at it, you can untie me."

He chuckled again. "You're so cute when you think you're in charge."

I bit my lip to stop the words I wanted to say from escaping. Gently, he took my legs from his shoulders and put them on the bed. Moving to where my hands were tied, I waited to finally feel them free. That's not what happened.

Bucky unhooked the belt and gently eased me onto my stomach. An unfamiliar fear of vulnerability made me panic.

"Uhm...Bucky. I'm not—"

"Relax. I'm not done. I promise you're going to enjoy this. Now get up on your knees."

"Do I look like a fucking trick pony? I'm stuck on my stomach with my fucking hands tied. You're going to have to do that work, bucko."

His breath tickled the shell of my ear. "I can't wait to use that mouth for something much more productive."

Thoughts of all the naughty things we could do floated through my head. While I was thinking of that, Bucky pulled up my hips so my knees were bent, but my hands were still attached to the hook. My body was becoming tense with anticipation. I heard the telltale signs of him finally getting rid of those pants. My curiosity was too much to take. I glanced over my shoulder to finally see him in all his glory. The sight before me made my mouth dry and my pussy wetter. He saw me looking and swatted my ass. I didn't care. Everything he did to me turned me on. Bucky walked to his nightstand next to his bed and grabbed a foil packet. He disappeared behind me and I could hear the crinkle of the packet being opened.

"Are you ready for me, baby?" His hand caressed my ass.

"Fuck yeah I am."

"Oh, how I love that mouth of yours." He pulled my hips toward him and slammed into me.

Stars burst into my vision. He waited for a moment while I adjusted to his girth. A slight pinch of pain reminded me it had been a while since I had anything more than a push pop penis. It felt good.

"Sit back." He pulled my hips.

"What?"

"Sit back so your fabulous ass is touching my thighs."

"Uhm...I'm not sure—" I began as he pulled me down, filling me even deeper.

I blinked. My ass was on his thighs, and my back was against his sculpted chest.

"Move, Ember," he growled in my ear.

I started bouncing on his lap. His fingers dug into my hips pushing me up and down his cock. Fuck me but his cock found my g-spot, and I was racing back to another orgasm.

"What are you doing to me?" I whispered as my body grew tighter and tighter.

"Anything and everything to give you pleasure, baby."

Words eluded me as I rode him faster and faster. Sweat was covering our bodies. The image of a slip and slide wormed its way into my mind.

"I'm gonna come," I breathed out as my pussy contracted around his velvet-wrapped steel inside me.

"Fuck, Ember. You're everything." He pushed my hips up a bit more, so he was fucking me harder and harder in a modified doggie style, slamming into me so hard the headboard creaked. I didn't care. That magic cock was riding me right back to orgasmland.

"Are you going to come again?"

"Yes. Keep going. Don't stop."

"Good."

A few moments later, I was back on the merry-go-round in orgasmland, and Bucky had joined me with his own shouting climax. He held my hips to him. I wasn't completely sure how he was holding onto me with how sweaty we both were.

"Hold still." Bucky reached up and unhooked my hands. We both tumbled to the bed. Neither one of us had the muscles to hold us up. Somehow, he was still inside me.

"Fuck. Why didn't we do that sooner?" I asked.

"If it had been up to me, I would have taken you out behind the laser tag dome and fucked you fifteen minutes after meeting you."

I snorted. "Such a gentleman."

He untied my hands and pushed my short sweat-soaked hair out of my face. "I would have at least given you two orgasms before I came."

I smacked his flat stomach. "You're such a fucker."

He rubbed his nose against my neck. "Yes, but I'm your fucker."

My body froze. I never had someone say something like that. There were plenty of men who wanted to own me, but none ever wanted me to own them. It kinda freaked me out.

How was one supposed to react? Just say "Sure and I'm your fucker too?" Those words would never leave my lips.

"Want some water?" he asked as he nibbled on my earlobe.

"Hmmm...." was the only thing I could say because his mouth just felt too damn good.

He chuckled. "Let me get rid of this, get you hydrated, then I will show you more of the tricks in my bag."

Bucky detached from me. I rolled onto my back and watched him walk over to his bathroom that I didn't remember seeing in his room. His tight ass begged for my nails to dig into it.

"Hey, Ember?" he called from the bathroom.

"Yeah?"

"What are you doing next Thursday?"

Geez. Give a guy access to your pussy and he's already addicted. "Probably just working. Why?"

He left the bathroom with a cup of water and a warm washcloth. He furrowed his brow in confusion, and he sat next to me on the bed. "Here you go. I also brought the washcloth in case you wanted to wash up."

I took the cup and the cloth from him. "Thanks. What's wrong?"

"Huh?"

"You have a confused look on your face."

"Oh. Uhm...well, I was just confused why the daycare would need you to work on Thanksgiving."

"Fuck me."

"In a minute."

"Shut up. I can't believe I forgot again."

His furrow deepened. "Forgot again?"

"Yeah, earlier today my boss reminded me that Thanksgiving is coming up."

He chuckled. "Well, that doesn't sound like you have any plans."

"Actually, I do. I'm cooking for my dad and aunt. Would you like to come?"

What the fuck just popped out of my mouth?

"Really?" His intense eyes burned into me.

I could have just said sike or just kidding, but something stopped me. "Of course."

A bright smile reached his eyes and made them glitter. What the hell was wrong with me? I was waxing poetically about a man's eyes. I wondered if I had some sort of head trauma I didn't know about.

"I'd love to, but I have a slight problem."

"What's that?"

"My sister and grandmother."

Kinsley, I didn't mind. Edna was a whole other issue.

"Bring them."

Who the hell was controlling my mouth? It had to be my vagina because my brain was clearly still on the merry-go-round in orgasmland.

Bucky kissed my nose. "Sounds great. Let me know what we should bring." The only thing I could do was nod. I'd never made Thanksgiving dinner and had no real clue what I needed or needed someone else to do.

"I'll get back to you about that after I talk to Beat-Rice."

"Perfect. Now, are you ready for another round?" He took the cup and washcloth away from me. For the rest of the night, we didn't say much that wasn't punctuated with moans and praying to every deity that existed.

My body shot straight up to a sitting position. I glanced around and didn't recognize where the hell I was. The barest slivers of sunlight shone through a break in the curtains. My body ached, and it all came back. Laying on his stomach, Bucky was gloriously naked. I blushed as I unabashedly checked him out. While doing so, I saw the time.

"Fuck," I mumbled.

I looked around and couldn't find my clothes. Out of panic, I grabbed Bucky's shirt from the previous night and my shoes. Underwear, bra, and dress were lost in the dim room. I tiptoed to the door and froze when I heard Bucky move. I watched him grumble, grab the pillow I'd slept on, and moan. Fuck if that wasn't just as sexy as his bare ass. Giving myself a mental shake, I crept out of the room. It was almost six in the morning. I was banking on everyone staying asleep.

My bare feet moved over the lush carpet. Bucky really did have a fantastic apartment. I was thinking so much about the damn carpet that I didn't smell the coffee or see the gorgeous blonde leaning against the counter.

"Morning," Kinsley chirped.

I yipped like a little dog. "What?"

"I said good morning. Did you sleep well?" She hid her knowing smile behind a mug that said *Not Today Satan*.

"Uhm..." I was fucking inarticulate when I was trying to sneak out of a hookup's apartment.

"Am I interrupting your walk of shame? Don't worry I've been there. I just didn't expect you to do it to my brother. After all the ruckus Xander and I heard last night, I would have bet money he'd be making you breakfast in bed."

"Uhm...I have somewhere I need to be."

Kinsley raised a perfectly plucked eyebrow. "Really?"

"Uhm...yep." I inched closer to the door.

She looked at me a bit longer but soon broke out into giggles. "I get it, Ember. Go on and get outta here before Don Juan wakes up."

"Thanks."

She raised her cup to me. "Sister walks of shamers need to stick together. Is there anything you want me to tell him?"

I stopped at the door and gave it some thought. Did I want him to contact me? If I did, did that mean I wanted more from him? If I didn't, did that mean I was using him again? Fuck, it was too early for an existential crisis. Way too early and not nearly enough coffee. I decided I needed to go with my gut.

"Yeah. Tell him to text me later."

Kinsley smiled again. "Will do."

I nodded and escaped out the door. Giddy anticipation of talking to Bucky later that day pebbled my skin and made me smile.

36

STAN DOWN

*H*ello wenchy Wanda,

    It's the night before Thanksgiving and I think I've made a terrible mistake. In my defense, I was under the influence of a mind-controlling drug. It just so happens a magic penis administered it. How could I agree to cook Thanksgiving dinner when I could barely boil water? When I finally got down off my high from M.P aka magic penis, I set about researching exactly what I needed. It was then I discovered I had almost nothing that I needed. I panicked and called Grams. Without calling me a dumbass, she gave me a list of everything I needed and sent me an email with all the ingredients that were essential for cooking Thanksgiving dinner.

    You would have thought that was the simple part. Make a list and stick to it. That's not how my life goes, Wanda. That's just not how it goes.

"Come on, Grams. Come on, Grams. Pick up the phone," I mumbled as I pushed a limping shopping cart through the produce aisle at the grocery store.

"Thank you for calling. I can't take—"

"Dammit." I shoved the phone in my purse and pulled out the list. "Okay. This is something I can do. I'm a grown-ass adult. I can find yams."

The crippled cart fought me with every push. The store was so crowded I couldn't think. I grabbed a bag of potatoes, a bag of salad, celery, and an onion. I knew those things. As a woman, I wasn't completely useless.

"Here yammy, yammy, yammy," I muttered.

People stopped and stared as I wandered around. As I drove by one aisle, I grabbed the garlic I'd almost forgotten. By the third pass, I was ready to say fuck yams. They sounded like a bogus vegetable, anyway. My defunct cart chose that moment to turn right when I was headed left and I slammed into another cart.

"Oh, I'm—" I began but stopped. Ten-second Stan was there.

"Hello, Ember. You're looking lovely." He gave me a toothy smile.

I grimaced. "You're looking slimy as ever." With some effort I yanked the cart sideways, making a screeching sound. I felt heat rise in my cheeks as people stopped in their tracks to stare.

"Wait, Ember. I wanted to talk to you." Stan grabbed my cart while abandoning his.

"Why the fuck would I want to listen to anything you had to say?"

He had the sense to look ashamed. "I know what I did was wrong and I regret it. I've been meaning to call you." I tried to pull the cart away again. His grip wouldn't allow it. "I want to offer you a job."

"What? Wouldn't the wifey have an issue with that?"

Stan shrugged. "She doesn't need to know."

"How wouldn't she know? I'm the best professional organizer in the business."

I watched his Adam's apple bob. "It wouldn't be a job like that. It would utilize your..." he cleared his throat, then continued, "uhm...your other considerable talents."

"What in the—" I stopped as realization hit. He wanted me to be his whore. What fucking world had I just teleported into? That would be the only rational excuse for this push pop dick to proposition me to be his whore in the middle of the fucking produce aisle.

"I can make it worth your while. I can get your car back, a nice apartment, and a generous weekly allowance. What do you say?" He dragged his hand up my arm.

I didn't know whether I was going to vomit or rip off his fucking arm and beat him with it. Before I could give into my impulse to tear off his appendage, another hand removed his from my body. I had to blink twice at what I saw. Bucky was squeezing Stan's wrist, and a look that said "I'm not afraid to go to jail," painted his features.

Stan winced in pain and tried to pull from his grip. Bucky let him go by shoving his own hand back at him. Why was Bucky's murder face making me hot? Clearly, I was twisted, but I knew he liked my twisted. I couldn't hide my grin.

"Hey, baby. I finally found the green beans." He placed two cans in my cart while continuing to glare at Stan.

"Thanks, hunny bunny," I cooed and leaned into him.

Bucky shot me a heated look that made me shiver.

"What's next on the list?" He took the piece of paper from me. "Oh yams. Here they are." He placed a sweet potato in the cart. How did I not know yams and sweet potatoes were the same thing? I wanted to slap myself, but it wasn't the time with Bucky about to murder my old boss.

"Who's this?" Bucky asked.

I raised an eyebrow at him. He knew who Stan was. He'd met him when Bucky and I had our first kiss. But with the ridiculous look on Stan's face, I was eager to play along.

"This is my old boss, Stan. Stan, this is my boyfriend, Robbie." I caressed Bucky's forearm. It flexed under my ministrations immediately, making my lady bits pant.

Stan smirked. "This guy again? I remember him from the Mexican restaurant. I didn't buy the boyfriend thing then and I'm not buying it now. Someone like him will never be into you. Now, let's go back to our discussion."

A twitch in my eye made it difficult to focus on Stan. It didn't help a red haze also covered my vision. However, before I could unleash a torrent of profanities accompanied by a swift kick in his tiny marbles, he was on the ground holding his face.

"What the—" My vision sharpened, and I saw Bucky standing over Stan.

"You fucking piece of shit. How dare you talk to her that way? I should kill you for what you just said. Instead, I'm just going to fuck up that face, so you have to come up with something to tell that bitch wife of yours. But if I hear you bothering Ember ever again, I will..." He bent close to Stan and spoke, so only the two of them heard his words. It must have been something graphic because Stan paled while holding his bleeding nose.

"Let's go, baby." Bucky placed his hand on my back and guided me away from Stan, who was still laying on the floor.

"What just happened?" I mumbled as we passed people staring.

He gave me a sweet smile. "I have no idea what you're talking about."

"The fuck you do. What did you say to him?" I stopped pushing the cart and crossed my arms.

Bucky leaned in and kissed my nose. "Don't worry about it. It's between us. Now, let's go. I still have to find something to bring tomorrow since a certain person won't tell me what she needs."

My eyes narrowed. "Don't try to distract me."

"If I wanted to distract you, I'd do this." He pulled me flush to his body and claimed my lips, making me moan.

The kiss ended way too soon. My head was spinning as he let me go. I leaned on the cart to make sure my weak knees didn't let me fall on my ass. My eyes focused on his cocky grin. The fucker was trying to distract me. But for the life of me, I couldn't remember one thing about what we were talking about.

"You play dirty," I mumbled, as I could finally move down the aisle.

"Damn straight. I'm ready to use every weapon in my arsenal. Now, get that sweet ass moving." He slapped my ass, which made me yelp.

I glanced at my watch and grimaced. "Fuck."

"What's wrong?"

"It's going to be tight with the bus. I really didn't want to pay for a rideshare."

He furrowed his brow. "Why are you taking the bus?"

"I don't have a car, remember?"

"Yes, but I'm here. I'll take you home."

"You don't need to do that. I'm perfectly fine taking the bus."

He spun me around and cupped my face. "You are going to do your shopping, and I'm going to drive you home and carry the groceries to your apartment."

"But—" I began.

"Listen to me. There is no need for you to take the bus. We live in the same damn apartment building, Ember. Not to mention these are the things a man does for a woman when he cares about her. And don't get it twisted. I care about you." He turned from me, and barely above a whisper, I could have sworn he said, "More than you're ready to know about."

I wasn't sure I'd heard that correctly with the grocery store music drowning out the soft-spoken words. "All right, and if you want to bring something tomorrow, I'm going to need something important."

"Tell me."

"Wine. Lots and lots of wine."

His loud, boisterous laugh echoed through the store. I felt my nipples pebble. How could this man turn me on with just a laugh? Instead of jumping him in the middle of aisle two, I kept moving and forced myself to go back to the task at hand.

I felt his hand on my lower back and he whispered into my ear, "You can count on me, baby."

Something about the way he said those words made me think it wasn't the wine he was talking about.

37

Fisting Turkey Day

This fucking holiday was the worst. Whose brilliant idea was it to have a whole holiday centered around food? Especially stupid food that no one ate on a regular basis. I glanced at the alarm clock blaring. The piece of crap was screaming at me to get my ass up at the god awful time of six o'clock in the morning. I slapped the shit out of my alarm, causing it to unceremoniously dive off the nightstand.

"Great." I fell back against the pillows.

The memory of inviting Bucky, Kinsley, and Edna propelled me to my feet. I needed to be my best today. I'd make the best turkey and grin while Edna choked on all her snide comments. With a grin, I threw on my favorite pair of sweatpants and a tee that proclaimed I was a sasshole. I shuffled out to the kitchen and started my coffee. I needed to be locked and loaded with caffeine to be kick-ass today.

Glancing at the couch, a chainsaw was going crazy. Dad was dead to the world with half of Aunt Beaty's menagerie curled up with him. While the coffee brewed, I went back to my room and grabbed my earbuds. Nothing like some hard rock to get me ready to kick a turkey's ass. After choosing the perfect rock song, I popped in the earbuds and jammed. While the opening chords blared, I grabbed Grams' detailed list for the perfect Thanksgiving. I looked at the list and wilted. I'd be lucky if I could do half of the shit. Oh well, time to pull up my big girl panties and get to work.

Her instructions were so detailed even a moron could follow them. I'd just finished the stuffing when I saw movement out of the corner of my eye. Aunt Beaty was awake and getting coffee. I continued listening to my music while getting the stuffing ready to put in the bird. Aunt Beaty took a seat at the counter and watched me. Her gaze unnerved me. I knew she had comments but tried to ignore her with my loud music. It didn't work.

Pulling out an earbud, I turned around. "What?"

She took a sip of her coffee and said, "What? I'm just watching my niece make Thanksgiving dinner."

"Uh-huh. I know you. You have commentary on what I'm doing. Just lay it on me so I can focus on this."

"Jesus, Ember. You get laid one time and you're a crabby bitch when you don't get the dick again."

My jaw dropped. "What the fuck are you talking about?"

"Oh puhlease. You may have fooled your father, but I could tell by the way you walked that you got fucked good. I'm assuming it was that fine ass Bucky. I can't say I blame you. If I was a year younger, I'd jump on that like a fucking bounce house."

"There were so many things you just said that I want to wipe from my memory. I'm getting back to stuffing the bird. Now, if you'll excuse me, I need to begin fisting the bird." I popped my earbuds back in, but before I could press play, I heard Aunt Beaty clear her throat. I sighed. "Comments?"

She drummed her fingers against the mug. "Are you forgetting anything?"

"No. I'm following Grams' directions to the tee." I held up the wilted paper. I'd managed to spill both coffee and egg jizz on it, but it was still legible...sort of.

Beaty grinned. "All right, I'm going to take a shower. If you need help with anything on the list, I can help when I'm done."

"Uh...sure. I'm pretty sure I've got this but thanks."

"Okay then. I hope your father is up when I'm done because I need to watch the parade. He's going to get a face full of ice water if he's not." She hopped off the stool while leaving her dirty coffee mug on the counter.

I waited until I knew she was in the shower to finish up stuffing the bird. When I heard the water running, I relaxed. The stupid turkey needed to get moving. It had a good eight hours to bake. The house was going to smell amazing by the time Bucky arrived.

"Fuck. Fuck. Fuck," I muttered as I peeled the sweet potato.

"Are you okay, sweetie?" Dad asked.

"Yep. I've just realized how much I hate sweet potatoes."

"Why?"

"They are a nightmare. Not to mention I completely forgot to make them and our guests will be here in twenty minutes." The peeler mangled the potato.

Dad placed his hand on my arm. "Relax. No one comes to Thanksgiving thinking everything is ready. It never works that way. Now, what can I help with?"

I glanced around the kitchen and took stock. Turkey finishing...check. Leftover stuffing baking...check. Green bean casserole baking...check. Potatoes boiling...check. Having a single fucking clue what to do next...hell no.

"Uhm..."

He gave me a soft smile. "How about I put out the appetizers? I can put the cheese, crackers, pickles, and olives on a platter. That way people can nibble a bit while you finish up."

I smiled and leaned over and gave him a peck on the cheek. "You are the best dad. Thank you."

"Anything for you, sweetie." He moved about the kitchen, gathering everything he needed, then moved to the other side of the counter to assemble the charcuterie board.

I let out a breath, letting my shoulders relax a fraction. Closing my eyes, I centered myself. The sweet potatoes were about to become my bitch. I grabbed my largest knife and took my anger out on the first potato. It didn't work. The knife wouldn't cut through the fucking rock posing as an ugly vegetable.

"What the fuck?" I tried pulling the knife free, but the potato stuck to it. "What is with this cunt of a vegetable?"

"Ember!" my dad admonished.

"Sorry, Dad, but this stupid potato won't let me butcher it." I started banging the potato on the counter, trying to dislodge the knife.

Dad stopped my wild flailing by putting his hand on the one holding the knife. "Let me cut them up and you can do the board. It won't take me long."

I let out a long sigh. "Fine, but I don't think—" My words cut off as he sliced through it like it was butter.

He gave me a smile and then nodded toward the counter. Trudging over to the counter, I shabbily dumped everything into different bowls.

"Well, doesn't that look like a shit sandwich?" Beaty looked at my poor excuse of a charcuterie board.

"Beatrice," Dad growled.

"Look, I call it like it is, Denny. You should know that by now and that…" she pointed toward the bowls, "that is a piss poor example of a charcuterie board."

"Then don't eat it, you evil Oompa Loompa." I walked away from the counter and rejoined my father, who was finished with the sweet potato.

"Ember…" Dad turned toward me.

"No. You don't understand what I've been through with her." Scooping up the potatoes, I dropped them into the empty pot.

"Oh really? Are you saying I don't know what it's like to live with my sister? Do you forget so easily that she was living with me before she came here?"

"I know." I turned toward my aunt. "Sorry, Beaty."

She walked away, threw her hand in the air, and flipped me the bird. Before I could respond, a knock echoed through the apartment. My nerves went into overdrive. I wiped my hands on the apron I was wearing and marched over to the door. Swinging it open, it surprised me to see Edna there. It wasn't so much that she was there, it was that she was holding a large tinfoil-covered pan.

"Um...Happy Thanksgiving?" I looked around Edna to Bucky and Kinsley. Bucky mouthed "sorry."

"Move it or lose it." Edna shoved me out of the way. My heels caught on the leg of the table by the door and I began falling backward. Before I could land on my ass, Bucky was pulling me up.

"I'm so sorry, Ember."

"It's fine. Really, it's my fault. I should have expected her bowling me over as if she were a professional football player."

He snorted, then sighed. "I'm also sorry about all of this." He held up what he was carrying.

"What is all this?"

He bit his lip and shuffled his feet. My mind immediately shot to an image of a little boy who looked like him but had my eyes. What in the fuck was that? Did I just imagine having Bucky's baby? That convinced me right there that my twat was in charge of my brain and she needed to get her act together.

"Granny brought Thanksgiving with her." Kinsley filled in the silence that was left when my mind decided to lose it and Bucky was trying to figure out any way not to tell me.

"What do you mean she brought Thanksgiving?" I shut the door behind them.

"I brought all the essentials. Figured your shit would be fucked up since you've never done this before. I'm actually the hero of the day." Edna opened the oven, took out my turkey, and replaced it with hers.

"Granny! This is not your house. Put that back." Bucky dropped what he was carrying on the table and marched over to the kitchen.

As Bucky fought with Edna, my dad walked over to me. He looked shell-shocked. Dad had been hanging around that hippie commune for too long. He'd forgotten how bat shit crazy people were.

"You really want to be part of that family?" he asked.

"What? They are just here for Thanksgiving. You're acting like Bucky and I are a step away from the altar."

"You should be," Beaty said.

"Screw you," I mumbled.

"I'm serious. You're getting older by the minute and those ovaries are shriveling up as we speak."

"First things first, keep your mind off my lady bits. Second, I work with snotty kids all day long. Do you really think I need to have some of my own?"

Dad turned to me with big puppy dog eyes. "I'm never going to be a grandpa."

I glared at Beaty. "Look what you did." She shrugged and walked back to her menagerie. I turned to Dad. "You had to have realized the closer I get to forty, the less likely I was going to pop out any kids."

"Not to mention you can't gain any more weight," Edna said with a smirk.

"Granny!" Bucky glowered at her, wrapped an arm around my waist and gave me a peck on the cheek.

The look of disgust on Edna's face was priceless. A wicked idea burned into my mind. I turned toward Bucky, grabbed his face, and pulled him into an overly passionate kiss. Unfortunately, I didn't think the plan through. Bucky got into it and pulled my leg to his hip. I could feel his trouser snake getting excited, which in turn made my clam happy.

"All right, you two." Kinsley walked over holding Cuddles, the emotional support porcupine.

"What?" Bucky asked.

My dad cleared his throat and held his hand out. "I'm Dennis, Ember's father."

Bucky blushed and shook his outstretched hand. "I'm Robbie."

"You can call him Bucky," Edna interjected. "I'm Edna. I'm sure you've heard of me."

"Uhm…" Dad looked at me confused.

"She's one of the ladies who lives at the same place as Grams."

The dots connected, and Dad nodded. "It's nice to meet you."

"I'm Beatrice. Robbie knows who I am." She winked at him.

"Fuck! You have a damn Keebler elf." Edna sneered.

Beaty glared at Edna. "Well, I may be magically delicious, but at least I don't look like a shriveled prune with a mullet."

"Oh shit," Bucky mumbled.

"What did you say, lawn gnome?" Edna stepped toward Beaty.

"Bring it, crypt keeper." Beaty crossed her arms, waiting for Edna to swing.

I stepped between them. "I don't have time for this shit. Go sit somewhere just don't touch each other."

The two in question turned their pissed-off looks toward me but I couldn't have cared less. Passing by them, I marched over to the boiling sweet potatoes. Bucky could handle them since he brought the main instigator.

38

Magic Peen Strikes Again

A half an hour later, dinner was finally ready. I set everything on the counter. Tension filled the apartment. Beaty and Edna had kept their fight banked, but like any fire, it could burst into flames at any moment.

"Don't forget to put out what I brought. Let the people pick if they want to eat good food or mediocre," Edna bellowed.

"Granny," Bucky said for the hundredth time.

I closed my eyes and counted to ten.

"Are you okay, Peanut?" Dad asked.

My lips curled into a fake smile. "Of course, Dad."

He gave me a side squeeze and a peck on the cheek. When he turned to go, I followed. "Where are you going, Dad?"

"I'm sitting down at the table. Why?"

I held up the electric carving knife and fork. "Uhm..."

"Oh, honey, I can't do that. I've got carpal tunnel from working at the commune." He held up his wrists as if I had X-ray vision and could immediately see the problem.

"Okay. Sorry about that."

"Don't forget to take the stuffing out first, Peanut. It makes carving easier." Dad nodded enthusiastically.

"Thanks." I grabbed the dish of extra stuffing and scooped the stuffing in the bird into the bowl. When I thought I was done, there was something more in there. "What is that?" I went elbow deep and pulled out a bag. "Did this thing come with its own spices?"

Beaty laughed. "Nope. That's the gizzards, dumbass. I was trying to tell you that earlier, but you were Miss Know-it-all."

"Fuck me, that's great," Edna cawed.

A blush colored my cheeks. I ignored them and grabbed the knife to begin carving.

"I can do it," Bucky offered.

"Bucky! This is Ember's Thanksgiving. Carving the turkey is part of it." Edna sat with a smug look on her face.

I narrowed my gaze at Edna and then turned toward Bucky. "It's fine. I've got this." Before Bucky could say anything more, I started up the electric knife. The sound of it gave me a sense of power. It was like I was holding a mini chainsaw made for destroying a turkey.

With the power in my hand, I began carving. Fierceness flowed in my veins as slice after slice fell from the bone. Just when I felt like everything was going perfectly, the stupid knife got stuck on something.

"What the fuck?" I tried to dislodge the thing, but it wouldn't work.

"Let me help." Bucky tried to take the mini chainsaw away.

"I've got it. Let it go."

"Why can't you let someone help you?" He tugged on my hand.

"I'm fi—" As I pulled the knife, everything went sideways. The knife lodged on a bone and the whole bird flew at me. The damn bird landed on my chest and slowly slid down. I froze and couldn't do a thing except let the bird slide down. Thankfully, Bucky was Johnny on the spot. He caught it before it could do anything other than ruin my outfit. Bucky deftly placed the bird back on the plate and silence filled the apartment. That only lasted for a few moments. Edna and Beaty's loud, obnoxious laughs filled it up.

"Are you okay, Ember?" Bucky put his arm around me.

My face flamed with embarrassment. Turkey juices covered me. So much for me trying to look cute. Tears burned my eyes, and I refused to let them see me cry. I pulled away from Bucky and ran to the bathroom.

Sitting on the toilet, I cried. I may have smelled delicious, but the grease and juice that covered me made me cringe.

"Ember..." Bucky's voice floated through the door.

"Go away, Bucky." My words were muffled by the hands over my face.

"Let me in."

"I said go away." Tears and snot mingled with the turkey juice all over me.

The door creaked open and then shut.

"Oh my God! What the fuck are you doing, Bucky?" My eyes were still covering my face.

Bucky pulled my hands from my face. "I came in here to make sure you were okay."

"I am. Now you can go away. I don't need you in here while I stew in turkey juices." I pulled my hands out of his grasp and swiped away the snot that was dripping out of my nose.

He stood from squatting in front of me and went to the sink. I didn't pay attention to what he was doing. I just assumed he was washing his hands because he touched me and the turkey grossness. Defeatist thoughts plagued me as I stared at the towel rack across from the toilet. I was spiraling so quickly that I didn't realize Bucky hadn't left until he squatted back in front of me.

"Hold still." He swiped the warm washcloth over my face. I probably should have protested, but I was so shocked I couldn't move.

"Unbutton your blouse," he said.

"What?"

Bucky cocked up one eyebrow. "Unbutton your blouse."

My teeth dug into my bottom lip as I contemplated listening to him. Finally, I realized I was going to have to remove the shirt at some point. It might as well be with him. Slowly, I pushed each button through the opening. His gaze was locked on each piece of skin that was revealed. As I slowly opened my blouse, he slid the warm washcloth over my exposed breasts. I bit my lip, trying to hold back a moan. Bucky's warm washcloth ministrations were turning me on. What the hell was wrong with me?

"How is it I'm covered in turkey juices and all I can think about is you fucking me?"

"Oh thank God." His lips crashed onto mine.

I fumbled for his zipper while he picked me up and set me on the counter next to the sink. Our frantic kisses were getting more and more desperate. I hear a rip just as I got his zipper down. All at once, he thrust into me. Memories of our passionate night together flooded my thoughts.

"Damn you're tight. Ever since I had you, I've been unable to think of nothing else." Bucky's pants echoed through the small bathroom.

"Shh...do you want them to hear us?" I moaned as he adjusted his thrust to hit my g-spot.

Bucky pulled my ass closer as he pounded into me. "Can you be quiet when you come?" His hand reached between us and strummed my clit.

"Fuck!" I said way too loud.

He bit my earlobe, making me shudder. "I think I have my answer."

"Who cares? Just fuck me so I can forget this whole damn holiday." My climax was getting closer and closer.

"As you wish." Bucky picked up speed. His hips pistoned into me. A banging sound was getting louder and louder. I didn't care. I needed a Bucky orgasm, and I needed it now.

My big O was just on the brink. I was getting desperate and reached between us to give my clit a few quick flicks. I'd forgotten that Bucky's hand was still there, and he smacked my hand away.

"Your orgasms are mine, Ember. I don't even want you pleasuring yourself."

"Well, then get on it."

A devilish grin curved his lips. As his hips ground into me harder, I felt a pinch on my clit. Not just a pinch but a pinch then a twist. That shot of pain threw me over the edge. I came so hard I thought I blacked out. When I came back from the O high, Bucky was frozen coming inside me. Every muscle was taut. I gazed up at his face and inwardly cringed. His O face was hilarious. It was a strange mix of a toddler with a full diaper and a toddler who had just had a taste of lemon.

Quickly, I looked away before I could start laughing. How did I not see that the last time we did the mattress mambo? I thought about it and smiled. I didn't have time to notice his face, too enamored by his magic penis. As it slid out of me, I realized that was still true. Magic penis trumped disturbing O face any day.

"Well, shit." I leaned against the wall.

"That isn't the normal reaction I get after having mind-blowing bathroom sex." He cocked his head to the side like a puppy.

"Do this often, huh?"

"Really want to talk numbers?" He lifted his eyebrow in question.

"Well, not while the magic peen is around. I don't need him getting upset with me." I grinned. "We should probably at some point."

"Magic peen?"

"It figures you'd hear one thing."

Before Bucky could come back with a witty retort, a banging on the bathroom door cut through our post-sex bubble. We both froze, holding our breaths.

"We all know you're in there. When you're done stuffin' the muffin, you may want to join us for Thanksgiving dinner." Kinsley's voice was like a bucket of cold water.

"Well, fuck me," I grumbled.

Bucky's lips curled into the sexy grin I was beginning to love. "I believe I already fulfilled that wish, my lady."

"Fuck you, you idiot. Now get off me so I can clean up and do a quick change."

"I could always lick you clean." He leaned over and slid his tongue up my neck.

I shivered. "I fucking hate you."

He placed a light kiss under my earlobe. "I don't think that's true, but I can wait." Bucky pulled away from me, allowing my feet to hit the tiled floor. My jaw hung open at his words. While I stood there staring at the complex idiot, he managed to get himself back in order.

With a hard kiss on my lips, he said, "Get yourself cleaned up. You look like you just got fucked by a magic penis." He smacked my ass and left the bathroom.

After I stood there for a hot minute, my brain finally kicked into gear and I moved to the sink. The reflection in the mirror gave away the magic of that peen. Damn that irritating, pain in the ass, sex on a stick moron and his magic penis that I was slowly getting addicted to.

"That fucker," I muttered as I splashed cold water on my face.

39

THE DYNAMIC ASSHOLES

It was a rainy Black Friday. Nomi, Teagan, Olivia, and I always went out shopping on the most important of holidays. Actually, we didn't really shop. We enjoyed drinking wine from thermoses while narrating people going crazy for televisions and toys. However, this year we were looking for items for our costumes for the Comic Universal being held in Las Vegas. It was in the middle of a crowded Target that my dear friends grilled me about Bucky.

"Hold on, hold on, hold on. You actually fucked in your bathroom while the family was waiting for you to come back to Thanksgiving dinner?" Teagan asked as she looked through the racks of clothes.

"Yep."

"All right! The cockaholic is back." Nomi looped her arm around my shoulder.

"I wouldn't say she's back. I'd say I'm getting to be a cockaholic for one magical peen." As I pulled the perfect shirt from the rack, I grinned. "Ah ha. I found something we can use."

Teagan and Nomi groaned. Olivia was furiously typing on her phone. I shook my head. "Liv, who the hell are you texting?"

"Huh? What?" Olivia blinked up and looked around, confused.

"Jesus, Olivia. Can't you unplug for a few hours to spend with your friends?" Teagan shook her head.

"I'm sorry." She blushed and shoved her phone into her purse. "There it's gone. So, what were we doing?"

"I found the perfect shirts that would work."

It was Olivia's turn to groan.

"Hey! Enough groaning. You guys owe me, remember."

"We know. We were just hoping you wouldn't torture us too much."

A devious grin curled my lips. "Well, you all thought wrong. Don't worry, I've got other things planned too."

The three of them froze. "What do you mean?"

"Well, I figured we'd do two things at once. We'd go to the con and party like we are in our twenties for Teagan's bachelorette party."

"Are you fucking kidding me right now?" Teagan bounced on the balls of her feet.

"Nope. Look what I got for us." I pulled out my phone and scrolled to the tickets.

The three of them gathered around. "Holy fucking shit. You got us tickets to Mount Olympus Gods?"

"Yep. It's the hottest strip show in Las Vegas right now."

Teagan squealed. "I can't wait to tell Grayson."

"Why?" Nomi asked.

"Yeah, why? Isn't he going to freak?" Olivia chimed in.

Teagan shrugged. "We share everything and I sure as hell won't be able to hold back from telling him about this." She pulled me toward more racks. "Come on. Let's get this done because I need to tell Grayson."

"You two have a strange relationship," I muttered.

"Maybe, but at least we didn't screw while our family was in the next room." She winked as I felt heat flood my cheeks.

Bucky's deep laugh echoed through the room. "Seriously? Teagan is telling Grayson? They are a weird pair."

Lifting my head off his bare chest, I looked at him. "Right? That's what I said. So very weird."

With a contented sigh, I nestled back on his chest. "So what's your reaction?"

"What do you mean?"

"Well, I told you I'm going to see a bunch of hot sweaty men dancing for me. Do you have any opinions?"

Bucky shifted onto his side, making me look up at him. "No. I trust that you seeing those guys are going to make you want to come straight back here." He bit his lip and continued, "However, I had a thought. I was wondering...you know what, never mind." He shook his head and laid back down, slinging his arm over his eyes.

"Come on. What is it?" I poked his side.

He shook his head. "It's nothing."

"The least you could do is tell me since you just blew my back out." I lifted his arm from his eyes and grinned.

In a lightning-quick move, Bucky had me on my back with my arms pinned over my head. "Blew your back out? You know what I do to dirty girls, don't you?"

"Hmm…do you tame me by using that magical peen?"

He let out a laugh, then leaned down and captured my lips in a sweet kiss. It didn't last long enough. I could feel him getting hard again. Wrapping my legs around him, I used my heels to nudge him closer to my entrance.

"You're going to be the death of me, Ember."

"You will die happy."

"Yes, I will." He leaned down to kiss me again when my brain kicked in and the magic from his peen wore off.

"Dammit. You almost did it."

Bucky cocked his head to the side and blinked. "Did what?"

Instead of pulling his hips closer with my heels, I dug them in, making him wince. "Tell me, asshole. How dare you use MP against me?

He let my hands go and fell away from me and back onto his side of the bed. "What if I came to Vegas too?"

"What do you mean?"

"I mean, I'd like to come to Vegas with you and the girls."

"It's a bachelorette getaway."

"You're also going to the con. I wouldn't interrupt the bachelorette stuff. I'd just join you at the con. What do you think?"

That fear of getting too serious came rushing back. It felt like it was moving too fast. I enjoyed our more and more frequent trysts, but what was really going on with us? Were we at the point of going to Las Vegas together? What would it mean if I said yes? More importantly, what would happen if I said no? My head pounded with all the thoughts racing through my head.

"I think I have my answer. It's okay, Ember. It was just an idea."

"It's not that I wouldn't enjoy you coming. It's just...I..." The bed sheet twisted in my hand.

Bucky placed his large hands over mine. "It's okay, Ember."

"Okay. Now, can we go back to what we were doing?"

"Yes, ma'am." Bucky pulled me on top of him and kissed me hard. MP was stirring on my thigh and making me wet. I moaned into his mouth, but before we could get to the good stuff, his bedroom door crashed open.

I screamed and moved off him, pulling the sheet to my chest.

"Are we going?" Xander asked.

"What the fuck is going on here?" I looked between Bucky and Xander.

"Did he ask you?" Xander came to the foot of the bed.

"Get out, Xander!" Bucky growled.

"Come on, you agreed. I've been waiting out there for an eternity."

"What in the actual fuck is going on? One of you assholes better explain before I get into a murderous rage."

"Bucky said he was going to convince you to let us tag along to Vegas so I could get closer to Olivia. She won't return my calls. I just need to talk to her."

I glared at Bucky. "So, you lied."

"Ember..."

"Fuck you." I pointed to Bucky, then turned toward Xander. "And fuck you."

I pulled the sheet off the bed leaving Bucky without a way to cover himself and marched out of the bedroom. Kinsley was in the kitchen and she looked at me with a raised eyebrow.

"Your brother is a prick."

"I told those two idiots to skip the game and just ask you outright. I'm guessing they didn't take my advice. Dumbasses."

I grunted and left the apartment. Anger and humiliation burned through me. Just when I thought I'd found someone who cared about me, all he wanted to do was get his friend laid. If I could come up with a better word than fucker, I would have had that tattooed on his forehead.

40

Unwanted Upgrade

Dear Fucking Francine,

We are on a plane on our way to Vegas. It's been three weeks since I spoke to that manipulative prick Bucky. Yeah. Yeah. I know. I'm being stupid probably, but it really pissed me off. It's a bachelorette party for Christ's sake. The only men who are allowed are the scantily clad ones. But, it's not just that he shouldn't be there, it's more like he's inserting himself into my life. He and Xander had a whole plan that involved Bucky screwing me until I'd agree for those morons to come along. Honestly, I think what I'm the most upset about is they didn't outright ask me or the girls. They had to be sneaky. The one time I was contemplating a real future with someone I was possibly ready to more than like, and he proves all men are the same. He had to go and be a dumbass.

Now I'm on the plane hoping it doesn't crash into the side of the mountain before I get to have great makeup sex with him. Yes, I know I'm crazy. I was just saying how much he pissed me off. Well, that doesn't mean my stupid girly emotions don't still really like him and his magic peen. That definitely is an incentive. I guess the girls are right. I'm back to being a cockaholic. Only this time it's one prick I'm after. Damn Bucky and his magic peen.

Stop judging me, Francine.

Ember

"Are you still doing that journal?" Nomi asked from the seat in front of me.

"Yeah. It's gotten to be a bit of a habit. Now turn around and sit down. I'd like for this plane to take off at some point. I still don't understand how our seats got messed up." A mom was holding a baby and a little girl sitting next to me.

"Ma'am, are you sure you don't want to switch?"

She smiled as she cooed to the baby. "That's okay. Thank you, though."

The little girl glanced at her mom and then at me. "You're too old to have babies."

"Ouch. Why would you say that?"

The little demon next to me raised her hand and pointed toward my face. "You have a lot of lines on your face. You remind me of my grandma."

"What?" A laugh in front of me made me glare at the seat as it shook. "Well, one day you will have these wrinkles too. It means you had a hell of a time."

"No," she said, shaking her head.

"Yes."

"No."

"Yes."

"No."

I sucked in a frustrated breath. "Why don't you look out the window?"

"There is nothing to see. We haven't moved yet."

"Fine." I pulled my phone out and began playing a game.

"That was the wrong move." She pointed to my screen.

"How would you know? You're only like five."

She shrugged. "I still know my colors and it looks like you don't."

That damn seat in front of me shook again. I smacked it and turned to the little girl. "Here. You think you can do better, go right ahead." I handed the phone to her.

Another shrug and she began playing the game. While Satan's offspring played on my phone, I leaned my head back against the headrest. The captain finally came on the speaker to instruct the flight crew to begin their spiel. I watched as they demonstrated how to buckle a seatbelt, where the emergency exits were, and how to inflate a life preserver in case of a water landing. All the while, the plane made its way toward the runway...finally.

"Here." The little girl shoved my phone at me.

I grinned. "Not so ea—" My words caught in my throat as I saw the high score. She'd managed a score ten times higher than mine. My gaze moved from the phone to the little girl. A shit-eating grin curved her lips.

"You're something else."

"It's okay. Most old people can't keep up with me."

"Ember. Leave the nice lady alone. We've talked about showing off." The mother admonished the child just as the plane took off.

"What did you call her?" I asked.

The mother could barely hear me over the screaming of the infant in her lap. "Ember. I know it's an unconventional name, but I think it fits her personality. She's quite the spitfire."

The damn seat in front of me shook again. I gave it a kick. "It is quite a lovely name."

Unfortunately, the mother didn't hear me due to the screaming child. This moment in my life solidified the exact reason I am not and never will be a mother. Before Beelzebub Jr could say anything else, I popped in my earbuds to drown out the world with some hard metal. The plane ride was only the beginning of our fun times. I couldn't wait.

Three hours later...

"I slept like a baby." Nomi yawned, sitting next to me in the cab.

"Shut up, asshole." I shoved her with my shoulder.

"What?" She bit her lip, holding back a laugh.

"What is going on with you two?" Teagan asked from the front seat next to the driver.

"Are you going to tell her, or shall I?" Nomi crossed her arms.

"I fucking hate you."

"No, you don't. Go ahead. Share with the group."

An aggrieved sigh burst from me. In as few words as possible, I explained the little antichrist and the baby that didn't stop crying for the entire plane ride. My head pounded in time with the music that played in the lone earbud I still had in my ear.

"You left out the best part," Nomi said.

"Oh for fuck's sake," I mumbled.

"What was the best part?" Olivia turned toward me.

My glare only made Nomi grin more. "The little girl's name was Ember."

"No fucking way. Didn't you call her little devil?" Teagan scoffed.

Before I could answer, the taxi pulled up in front of a glittering palace of a casino. The four of us spilled out of the taxi and into the Nevada heat. A smile curled my lips as I saw person after person already dressed in their favorite characters. It was glorious.

"Oh Jesus." Teagan stared at a scantily clad version of a children's cartoon character.

Olivia giggled. "This reminds me of—"

"Shut up, Olivia." I cut her off. "Let's just go check in."

We rolled our suitcases through a crowded lobby. I'd been able to book our room with only a few left. The long line in front of us moved at a snail's pace. I was exhausted and wanted to take a nap fifteen minutes ago.

"Excuse me." A man in a really nice suit with a name tag gave me a bright smile.

"Can I help you?" I dropped my bags and crossed my arms. My irritability was ready for a fight.

"I think I'm the one who can help you. Are you Ember Tyler?"

"Yeah."

"Oh God. What did you do, Ember?" Teagan looked at me with a nervous look on her face.

"I didn't do a damn thing." I turned my attention back to the suit. "Now, what do you want, buddy?"

His smile faltered. "May I speak with you over here?"

"Just me?"

"You all may come."

"I swear if we step out of this line to follow you and then have to get back into line, I'm warning you...I will murder you." I picked up my bags and moved out of line.

"She's not lying. She watches murder documentaries and takes notes," Olivia added.

Mr. Suit swallowed but kept his strained smile on his face. "Just over here, please, Ms. Tyler."

"Do you know what this is about?" Nomi asked me quietly.

"No. I bought and paid for the rooms through Groupon."

We followed the man past the line of guests waiting to check in. He led us through an area that proclaimed VIPs only. Thoroughly confused, I followed him up to the desk.

"I hope this is a pleasant surprise." He slid a packet and room keycards over to me.

"What is all this?"

"You have been upgraded." He smiled.

"Uhm...what?"

"You have been upgraded to the presidential suite."

"Fuck me sideways." I looked from him to the packet in front of me.

He cleared his throat. "I'm going to have to pass, ma'am." He tapped the packet. "Inside, you will find your spa appointments for tomorrow and your restaurant reservations for your entire stay. Someone has comped them."

So many things jangled in my head. I was never this lucky. We had a secret benefactor and I could have bet my life's wages on who that was. I swiped the keycards and packet off the desk and walked over to the girls who were standing a short distance away.

I held up the packet and keycards. "Grayson."

Teagan blanched and looked around. "What? Where?"

"Not here, Teagan. He paid for all this stuff."

"What do you mean?" Nomi and Olivia went through the packet as Teagan pulled out her phone.

"Grayson upgraded us to the presidential suite, got us spa appointments, and even paid for all our dinners." I crossed my arms over my chest.

"Holy shit. He went crazy." Nomi whistled as she went through the spa items.

"Yeah," I grumbled.

"What's wrong?" Olivia asked.

"I wanted to do this. I had everything planned...now Grayson had to butt in and throw his money around. It just fucking pisses me off."

"Ember, why can't you just enjoy that we're getting a presidential suite?" Nomi asked.

I looked down at my shoes and then back to Olivia and Nomi. "As you guys know the last few months have been difficult for me. I'd saved up to be able to give Teagan a kick-ass bachelorette party and now, Grayson has to swoop in with all his fanciness and shit on what I did. I can't afford a presidential suite."

Nomi put her arm around me. "You didn't need to do any of this for us to appreciate you. We know it's been tough. Why don't we all just enjoy Grayson throwing around his cash and have a great time?"

"Fine." My voice was barely above a whisper.

While Nomi and Olivia cooed over the spa options, I heard Teagan on the phone. "Oh, baby. That was so sweet. You didn't have to do that."

"I wanted to, love. I know Ember is going to kick my ass, but I wanted you ladies to have a hell of a Vegas trip."

"Why do I hear Grayson's voice?" I asked Nomi and Olivia.

They stopped and listened. "I don't hear anything. There are a lot of people here."

"I love you, baby," Teagan cooed into the phone.

"I love you more." Grayson's voice got louder.

"Oh, I heard that now." Nomi looked around.

"Would he really just show up?" Olivia joined Nomi and me as we scanned the lobby.

"What are you three looking for?"

"Your fiancé," I grumbled.

"Grayson isn't here. Why would he be here? Can we go up to our room? I need a nap." Teagan grabbed her suitcase.

"Maybe it was a coincidence. Another guy that sounds like him."

I squinted toward a particular group of men. There was something familiar about the one with his back to us. He had one hell of an ass.

"Come on, Ember." Nomi nudged me.

"Fine." I grabbed my suitcase and begrudgingly trudged to the special presidential suite elevator. "This is obnoxious."

"What is? The elevator?" Olivia asked as we entered.

"Among other things."

"Can you let it go? I think we all need a nap and then we can go wander the strip."

Something set off alarm bells. "We can't tonight."

"Why?"

"We have the Mount Olympus Gods tickets tonight." I smiled.

"Oh, hell yeah! Let's nap it up so I have energy for those hot men!" Teagan pushed the elevator button fifteen times, willing it to move faster.

I laughed but couldn't get the feeling of being watched. The tingle between my shoulder blades told me so. When we entered the elevator, I glanced out the door but didn't see anyone. Something was up and I would punish anyone who came between us and a good time this weekend.

41

CHICKEN DANCING STRIPPER

The surrounding crowd was electric. Women talked loudly with eager anticipation. Waiters brought drinks to all the tables as we waited for the show to begin. Jetlag still weighed on me. I attempted to nap, but irritation kept me awake.

"This place is crazy!" Teagan said excitedly. "How did you manage to get us seats in the front?"

I took a sip of the strong drink the handsome waiter set in front of me. "I'm magic."

Nomi snorted. "Sure. I'm sure you paid top dollar for this."

"Nope. I've still got connections."

"You've got stripper connections?" Olivia asked.

"What? No. I have connections who can get me the tickets I want." I didn't tell them that I offered to organize my boss's house if her husband, who had connections to the hotel where Mount Olympus Gods were performing, could get us kick-ass seats. Honestly, it was a win-win situation.

"I don't care how you got them. This is the best thing ever." Teagan bounced in her seat. I couldn't help but smile at my friend. I didn't have the means to have an extravagant to do for my best friends, but I could still make them smile.

The house lights lowered, and the energy pulsed through the room. Women and men whistled and hooted.

"Ladies and gentlemen, welcome to the Golden Lion hotel and casino. It is home to the best damn show on the strip. Now, we have a few rules. We want you to scream and yell for your favorite god. But that is all you can do. No touching. We may choose some of you lucky ladies to come up on stage. That is the only time you are allowed to come on stage. Other than that, have a blast and let these gods make your dreams come true." The cheering erupted as music pounded.

"What does having dreams come true have to do with gods? Isn't that genies?" Olivia asked.

"Liv, stop being so literal and just enjoy the half-naked men we are about to behold," I spoke loudly to be heard over the music.

Olivia's cheeks flushed, and she turned her focus back to the stage. The curtains opened to show a large throne. The music faded while thunder and flashes of lightning took over. A large man with long blond hair strode onto the stage. His muscles moved with every movement of his body. He was shirtless except for a white leather kilt.

"I am Zeus, King of the Gods. My fellow gods and I will show you what gods can do that mere mortal men lack. Your world will change forever. Now, let's start off with my brother Poseidon."

Three drinks, many gods, and an hour later, the show was still going strong. My voice was rough from screaming at all the hot strippers. This was the best thing ever. All the hot gods were definitely going to be housed in my spank bank.

"We have a special treat. We will bring four lovely ladies up on stage," Zeus declared.

I looked around to see who was being picked. No ladies moved. Men and women waved their arms and screamed their willingness to join the dancers on stage. Four masked men came up to our table.

"Those four." Zeus's voice pointed at our table.

"What's going on?" I looked around.

Teagan and Nomi jumped up. "We've been picked."

"Wait...uhm..."

Teagan's eyes met mine. "Come on, Ember."

"I don't—"

"The old Ember would have been up there already," Nomi challenged.

"Ugh! Fine." I let the masked men behind us escort me on stage where four chairs lined the stage. The bright spotlight did two things perfectly. First, it blinded me, making me see floating dots. Second, it shaded the masked men who stepped in front of us.

"These four lucky ladies get a treat. Some demigods have joined us tonight. We have Perseus." Zeus pointed to the guy standing in front of Teagan. "Hercules." The one in front of me waved. "Achilles." The masked man in front of Nomi waved. "Orpheus." Olivia's masked dancer gave a small wave. "Are you ladies ready?"

The crowd cheered. I just shrugged. Hercules in front of me was pretty hot. Actually, his abs were definitely lickable. The minute that thought came into my head, Bucky's annoying face blocked out that thought. I could still feel the ripple of his abs as I ran my tongue up them. Damn him. I had a sexy as sin guy dancing in front of me and all I could think about was his dumb ass. I missed him. My mind flashed to the present and the incredible dancer in front of me. He moved like he would give you the fuck of your life. I could appreciate him, but it did nothing for me. What was wrong with me? A little voice in my head answered.

You love him.

"What the fuck?" I mumbled. That wasn't possible. How could I actually love that asshole? I was pissed off at him. The voice gave me my answer.

You love him. You miss him. You can still be pissed at him, dumbass.

My voice was a bit of an asshole. I liked it. The masked demigod gyrated on my lap. He really was good. I looked over at Nomi, and hers was equally good. Glancing over at Teagan, she was having a hell of a time, but her dancer seemed less experienced compared to mine and Nomis. As Mr. *Magic Mike* continued to dance, I peeked over at Olivia and almost laughed. Her dancer was doing the chicken dance. Something was off with these guys. When I looked back over at Teagan, I realized I didn't care what was up. This was what it was about.

The music ended, and the crowd of rowdy onlookers cheered and hooted. We clapped as well. Each demigod helped us out of the chair and back to our seats. As quickly as we were seated, the masked dancers were gone. The show continued, but I was no longer focused on it. I pulled out my phone.

Me: I miss you.

Annoying Dumbass: I miss you too. Does this mean you've forgiven me?

Me: No. It means I must have hit my head or something.

Annoying Dumbass: Or my magical penis has you under its spell.

Me: It's funny when I say that. It's creepy when you do.

Me: I have something to tell you when I get home.

I bit my lip. My fingers itched to type it out, but even my cowardly self realized that was a stupid idea.

Annoying Dumbass: I can't wait to see you. Have you enjoyed the strip show?

I looked at the phone. How did he know we were at the strip show? Did I tell him when we were going? I couldn't remember. But something about the way he said it made me suspicious.

Me: What do you mean?

Annoying Dumbass: Didn't you say you were going to that famous strip show tonight?

Me: I don't remember telling you that but yeah. We're having a great time. We even got pulled up on stage.

Annoying Dumbass: You didn't strip, did you? I'm not the jealous type but I am not a fan of those oiled-up guys seeing your rack. They're for my eyes only.

I snorted.

Me: You realize I wasn't a virgin before you right?

Annoying Dumbass: Neither was I but that doesn't mean I want other men or women looking at your goods while you're with me.

I blinked.

Me: We're together?

Annoying Dumbass: That's something I want us to discuss when you get home.

Butterflies went into overdrive. Bucky's the only man to do that to me. That idea would have made me cringe only a few weeks ago. Now, it made me want to catch the next flight back to him.

Me: I have to get back to the show. We'll talk when I get home.

Annoying Dumbass: I'll be dreaming of you until then.

Me: You're such a corn dog.

Annoying Dumbass: Yeah but you like my stick.

Me: I just rolled my eyes so hard I have a headache.

Annoying Dumbass: It's cause you know I'm right.

Me: I'm done here. I'll see you when I get back.

I shoved my phone back into my purse. When I finally looked back at the stage, the dancers were taking a bow. Everyone around me was standing. I jumped up and clapped along with everyone else. The curtain closed and the house lights illuminated the audience.

Teagan spun around with a huge smile on her face. "Thank you so much, Ember. That was the best thing ever." She pulled me into a tight hug.

"I'm glad you enjoyed it. I did not plan the going on stage thing, but I guess it was a bonus."

As we gathered our things, a throat cleared behind us. "Excuse me, ladies, the demigods would like to meet you personally."

"What?" I crossed my arms over my chest.

"I'm an engaged lady." Teagan waved her giant rock at the guy.

"We completely understand. They just want to thank you for being good sports."

The four of us looked at each other. Nomi shrugged. "What can it hurt?"

I turned back to the butler-looking guy and said, "Lead the way, Jeeves."

He grinned and led us backstage. Women who stood around hoping to take a stripper for a little private ride made catty remarks to our backs. That was the best incentive to walk with my bad bitch attitude.

Jeeves held open the door that said staff only. We walked through to see half-naked men milling about and talking. Jeeves moved us through the crowded hallway. The familiar men smiled and winked at us.

"I'm an engaged woman, Ember." Teagan had a death grip on my arm.

"Let go, you're hurting me. They aren't going to do anything, Teagan. Relax."

"Here we are, ladies." Jeeves knocked. A muffled reply came from the other side. "The ladies you requested are here." Another muffled reply followed. Jeeves gave us a smile. "Have a good evening."

The hair on the back of my neck stood up. Something felt off with this. I took a deep breath, looked at my friends, and turned the doorknob. "Might as well rip the Band-Aid off."

The door swung open, and I froze. The sight before me immediately boiled my blood. Murder was on my mind and these three men were going to be the ones in the hole.

"What's wrong—" Teagan's words died on her lips.

Only one word escaped mine. "Bucky."

42

LOVE ON A GONDOLA

"That dirty, low-down, good for nothing asshat. He lied to me. He blatantly lied to me. And to think I was going to tell him I loved him. Well, that shit is gone. How could I love someone who is conniving?" I turned to the man in gold who was frozen in a pose. "You're right. I can't."

"Ember!" Bucky's voice called out.

"There's the scum now. Thanks for listening." I began speed walking to get away.

"Ember, stop!" Bucky was gaining on me.

I glanced over my shoulder and immediately ran into someone. "Oh my goodness. I'm so sorry."

"Do you like monkeys?" the guy asked.

"Uhm sure. I gotta go."

"I like monkeys too. Would you put me in a cage?"

"What? No."

"But I like it." He smiled at me.

"Ember!" Bucky was only a few feet away.

"You know what, buddy? That guy right there loves putting people in cages and loves monkeys. I think he's your guy."

The strange guy's eyes lit up, and he intercepted Bucky. I couldn't help but laugh as I heard Bucky trying to fight off the guy who wanted to be in a cage. The crowd opened before me and I walked quickly to blend in. I walked past a casino that proclaimed to have gondola rides. There wasn't any place better to lose someone than in a casino, but a casino with boats in it was even better.

A group of people hustled in. The expensive-looking casino opened up before me. It didn't look like a casino at all. There were shops and fish tanks everywhere. I heard water close by. That had to be where I could get on a gondola. Arrows pointed my way. A wry grin curled my lips at the thought of Bucky being accosted by monkey guy. Luck was with me and the gondola ride line was free and clear. I walked right up, paid, and waited patiently for a gondola.

After a few minutes, one pulled up and deposited a couple who were mauling each other.

"Next." Gondola guy gave me a dimpled grin.

I stepped onto the boat and jolted when someone followed me. My whole body slumped when I realized who had followed me.

"How did you find me?" I asked.

"Oh, you mean after your lovely trick of sicking monkey guy on me?"

"Are we ready?" Gondola guy asked.

"Uhm..." I began.

"Absolutely," Bucky said at the same time.

"Okay then." The boat pushed off from the little dock.

"It wasn't a trick. I really thought the two of you would hit it off. He likes to be locked in a cage and you are a controlling, egotistical ass monkey."

His brow furrowed. "What?"

"Just shut up so I can enjoy the boat ride in silence."

"Nope."

"Why are you so insufferable?"

"I want to know why you're nuclear level pissed off at me?"

"If I tell you the obvious answer, will you shut the fuck up so I can enjoy the ride?"

He shrugged.

If I didn't know I'd get wet as well, I'd push him out of the boat. "You came to Vegas."

"Yeah. So?"

"I told you not to come. It pissed me off when you and Xander tried to sexipulate me."

"What the fuck is that word you just said?"

"Sexipulate. It's manipulating me by using sex."

"I don't think that's a word."

"Doesn't matter if it's true."

"I didn't use sex to manipulate you. It was bad timing by Xander. I hadn't had a chance to really talk to you about the idea before he burst into the room."

"Look, it doesn't matter. You guys came even when I said not to. Not to mention the whole texting thing."

Bucky had the sense to look ashamed. "I'm sorry for that. I wanted our big reveal to be a surprise and if I acted like I was there, then it would have been ruined."

My stupid resolve was crumbling. The anger that had been boiling only a few minutes ago was getting to be a simmer. Damn him and being charming.

"It still doesn't explain why you're here."

He bit his lip. "Grayson."

"Grayson felt the need to spy on Teagan." The simmer became volcanic.

"No. He thought a bachelor party in Vegas sounded fun. Then I think he got carried away."

"You mean all the crap he did?"

"Yeah. So, he's the one that set up the dancing on stage?" Red colored his cheeks. "No."

"Then how did you guys get to be special dancers?"

"I know some of the guys and the manager."

"What? How?"

He blew out a breath. "I don't have any student debt."

"Uhm…okay. That's not remotely an answer."

"I don't have any college debt because I was a stripper in college. It's how I paid my way."

I slowly turned to him. My eyes bulged out of my skull. "You're fucking with me."

"Nope."

"Well, you were suspiciously good at the dancing."

"Thanks, babe."

"And Xander was terrible."

Bucky let out a loud laugh that echoed around us. "Yeah. I tried to give him pointers but when I saw him doing the damn chicken dance, it took all of me not to bust up laughing."

"It looked like the ladies in the audience dug it, though." I smiled.

"He didn't give a damn about those ladies. He wanted to impress Olivia."

I snorted. "Liv can't dance either. The only dance she knows how to do is the chicken dance."

"Sounds like a match made in chicken dance heaven."

"Yeah, if she gave it a chance."

Silence settled around us. It felt a bit like they were talking about me as well. I half expected the gondola driver to begin singing in the silence. Wasn't that what the Italian ones did?

"So..." Bucky burst the silence.

"What?"

"Are you still mad at me?"

"Yes. No. I don't know. Probably."

Bucky laughed. "You sound pretty certain about your feelings."

I stuck my tongue out and crossed my arms over my chest. He nudged me, making the gondola sway.

"Watch it! You could have tipped us."

"Just by doing this." He nudged me again, making my hand go in the water.

"Please stop that," the gondola driver asked.

Unfortunately, I was too focused on plotting my revenge to hear him. Bucky's smirk irked me to no end. So, when I threw all my weight into my revenge nudge, I didn't anticipate his dodge. My considerable weight's momentum carried me directly over Bucky and into the water. I panicked for a moment, thinking I was going to drown, when I realized I could stand and the water came up to my chest. I looked down to find my white shirt plastered to my curvy body. My hair was stuck to my face and the jeans I wore were waterlogged. Murmuring brought my attention to the crowd behind me. Phones were out videoing my humiliation. I looked at Bucky, who was trying and failing not to laugh.

"Give me your hand. I'll pull you onto the boat." Bucky stuck his hand out.

"Fuck you very much." I began walking against the current of the indoor canal.

"Come on, Ember. Let me help you." Bucky continued to hold out his hand.

Seeing as my attempt to escape him in the water didn't work, I let him help me.

"Fine." I grabbed onto his hand.

"You should know by now you aren't going to win like that." He grinned as he attempted to pull me.

His little comment really pissed me off. So, instead of letting him pull me up, I yanked and pulled him into the water with me. The poor gondola driver joined us because the whole thing ended upside down. Bucky popped up from the water, smiling.

"What are you so happy about? You're wet now."

"Now I can do this." He pulled me to him and crashed his lips onto mine.

I gripped his shirt, holding him to me. Oohs and ahhs pulled me out of my lust haze his kisses always put me in.

We looked around and grinned. People clapped for us, and Bucky waved to the crowd.

"Glad you two are happy. I have to work the rest of my shift in wet clothes." The gondola driver tipped the boat right-side up and got in.

"Sorry, man. Help us in and we promise to tip you big."

He glared at us. "No, thanks." He pushed the gondola down the canal away from us.

"That fucker," I mumbled.

"No worries. I got this." Bucky climbed out of the canal. He reached down to help me up. "Try not to pull me in this time."

"Fuck you." I let him help me out of the water. The air-conditioned air immediately made my nipples hard as diamonds. They really could cut glass if needed.

"Oh look." Bucky pointed to something over my shoulder.

"What?" My hair was in my face again.

"A gift shop. We can get dry clothes."

"I can't waste money on that shit."

He shrugged. "My treat. Come on, let's get you out of those wet clothes." He pulled me to my feet and my wet feet slapped against the marble floor.

"Fuck me."

"In a bit, love." Bucky smirked.

"Not that, you pervert. I lost my damn sandals in the canal. How did I not notice that?"

"We'll get you all set in here. Come on." He pulled me into the shop.

"Oh boy," I muttered as I took in all the Las Vegas themed items.

43

A Proposal

The chintzy Las Vegas flip flops slapped against the shiny marble flooring. My sopping wet clothes were in a bag I carried. I stopped in front of another boutique and stared at my reflection in the window. My hair was a mess and my makeup was gone, except for the waterproof mascara. That was smudged under my eyes, making me look like a raccoon. That wasn't the worst part. Velour neon pink pants with the words *Las Vegas* across the butt covered my legs and my shirt was a size too small and proclaimed my job was better than yours with a picture of a stripper. I was just glad the make-shift paparazzi weren't around to see my new duds.

"You ready?" Bucky joined me.

"How the fuck do you look hot and I look like someone's demented racist aunt?"

He snorted. "I think you look hot."

I lifted an eyebrow and seriously contemplated his sanity.

"Are you hungry?" he asked.

"I don't—" My stomach protested before I could get the words out of my mouth.

"Let's go." He took the bags from me and wrapped an arm around my waist. "While you were getting changed, Grayson texted. Everyone is at a bar in here and asked for us to meet up."

"Sure. Why not? We can just add to my humiliation." The snark was strong with me.

"Good. I told him we'd be there."

"You really are a pushy asshole."

He leaned down and pressed a kiss where my neck and shoulder met. "Yes, but I can't wait to get those clothes off you. I can tell you aren't wearing anything else and it's making me hard."

I gulped. My eyes immediately went down to his crotch. Yep. He was hard and fucking impressive in gray sweatpants.

"Do we really have to meet up with them? If they're out, then we'd be alone." I batted my eyes at him.

"Ember! There you are." Teagan waved from the entrance of a bar.

"Sorry, babe. We're already here."

"What in the holy hell are you wearing?" she asked.

"I had a minor incident."

"What kind of incident would make you wear something out of Edna's closet?"

I glared at Bucky when he laughed. "I fell out of a boat." We were walking in to the restaurant and Teagan froze.

"Hold up. That was you two?"

"What do you mean 'us' two?" I asked.

"The whole place is buzzing about a couple who fell into the canal, then practically had sex against the canal wall." Teagan stopped in front of a high-top table. "I found them."

"What in the hell are you wearing?" Olivia slurred.

"How many drinks have you had?"

"Pfft...not many. I just had two Long Island teas. "

"Uhm...Olivia..." Bucky began, but I put my hand on his arm and shook my head.

"Just take it easy, Liv," I said and sat down in one of the open seats. All the ladies were seated with Grayson, Xander, and Bucky standing around us.

Nomi took a sip of her drink and stared at me. "I'm going to go out on a limb and say you're the couple everyone has been buzzing about."

"Oh, for fuck's sake," I mumbled, while Bucky nodded his head vehemently.

Before I could say anything, I heard, "Hey look! It's the canal couple. You guys are hot!" a girl shouted.

"Wha—"

"Yeah, you are. Can I get your autograph?" A drunk guy ripped open his shirt.

"Uhm..." My mouth hung open.

"You sure can, buddy." Bucky popped off the cap of a permanent marker and signed his name. Where the hell did he get a permanent marker?

"Here, Ember." He handed it to me.

Captain Slosh-faced stumbled toward me. I lightly scribbled something that was definitely not my signature or even words. I placed the cap back on the marker and the guy hooted.

"Yes! I'm going right now and getting this tattooed." He brushed through the crowd, making people spill their drinks.

I looked at my friends. "Do you really think he's going to get that tattooed?"

"People do really stupid things in Vegas. I'd say you two are going to have your signatures on some randos chest for all of eternity." Nomi smirked.

"That's both cool and creepy." Bucky smiled.

"I'll agree with creepy, but that is all."

"Oh my God, you're giving out autographs? I want one. How much do they cost?"

"Oh they—" Bucky began, but I cut him off.

"Fifty bucks," I said.

"Sweet. Here you go." She dropped two twenties and a ten on the tabletop. A line formed behind the girl.

"Why are you charging them?" Bucky said out of the corner of his mouth as he signed a napkin.

"Why not?" I handed the napkin to the girl.

She smiled and read the name. "Thank you so much, Velma." Then she skipped off.

"Velma?" Teagan asked.

I shrugged and signed the next napkin. Each napkin had a different name etched on the napkin for posterity. Bucky was still dumb enough to continue signing his own name. Sucker.

"How much did you fleece those people of?" Bucky tutted as we walked away from the Venetian.

"Thirty-five hundred." I grinned.

"Holy shit! I can't believe we made that much."

"What is this 'we' shit? You wanted to just give it away."

"Come on, Ember. What are you going to do with that kind of money?"

"Oh I don't know, pay off credit cards. Save some for a rainy day. Pay rent so Beaty can get the hell out."

Bucky nodded. "Good point."

We walked in silence and then stopped in front of the Mirage to watch the volcano erupt. He linked our fingers together. I leaned close and realized I was entirely happy to be with this man at that moment. No other man ever made me feel that way.

"I have a proposition."

My eyebrows lifted to my hairline. "Is it to have sex on all this money? Because I was just thinking that."

"Uhm...no. Though that does sound enticing except for that change. I don't want to find dimes in places they don't belong."

"Party pooper. What is your proposition?"

Bucky flashed me a sexy smile. "Let's get married."

I blinked at him and wondered if he was serious. When he didn't immediately say "Just kidding," I started laughing uncontrollably. People walked by and gave me strange looks. After a few minutes, I pulled myself together.

"That was a good one."

"I wasn't joking, Ember. Will you marry me?"

"This has to be a joke. I mean, we barely know each other." I started walking away from the exploding volcano.

Bucky pulled me to a stop. "There is only one person I know better than you."

"Oh really?"

"Yeah. Ask me anything."

I crossed my arms over my chest. "You really want to do this?"

"Come on."

"Fine. What is my favorite color?"

"You like to say it's black because of your soul, but in reality it's blue."

"Lucky guess."

"Try me again."

"What was my hobby growing up?"

He grinned. "You collected rocks because you went to a cavern on a school trip and fell in love with rock formations. You would have become a spelunker if it weren't for your fear of bats. The only thing you fear more than bats is sharks."

"How in the fuck did you know all that?"

"I pay attention."

"I never told you that."

"You didn't. Your dad did."

"Fuck me."

"Later. So, what do you say?"

"Are you really serious right now?" I bit my lip.

"Serious as a heart attack." He held both of my hands in his. "I'm in love with you, Ember. I can't see my life without you."

"I love you too," I breathed.

By the look on Bucky's face, he and I were equally shocked those words came out of my mouth. Was I truly ready to say I loved him? Hell if I really knew. Was I scared as hell? Hell yes. Am I just going to jump into the deep end of the love pool? That's the only way I do things.

Bucky pulled me to him and kissed me with all the passion we both felt. He stepped back and went down on one knee. "Ember Tyler, will you marry me?"

I looked around and saw that we drew another crowd. It was the third of the night. My eyes met his. All the emotions he felt were right there. I was looking at the man I wanted to spend the rest of my life with.

"Yes."

"Woohoo!" Bucky hooted, pulled me close, and dipped me while planting a bone-melting kiss on me. Clapping and cheering from the surrounding crowd made me blush.

"Come on. Let's get married." I pulled him toward a taxi stop.

He gave me one last kiss as the taxi stopped in front of us. We hopped in and as one we said, "Take us to the nearest chapel." The taxi driver nodded and zoomed back into traffic.

44

I Don't But They Do

The Best Little Chapel in Vegas wasn't flashy. It was gaudy. It was cheesy. The only thing flashy about it was the sign that flickered above the doorway. The neon buzzed like a bug zapper. Was this place really going to be the place I got married? All my dreams when I was a little girl flashed through my mind. The days I spent playing with my Barbies, pretending to have a lavish wedding on a Greek island.

"You okay?" Bucky rubbed my lower back.

I blinked and gave him a tight nod. "Let's get this done." Walking through the door, a drag queen dressed as Dolly Parton manned the desk.

"Hey, ya'll! How are ya'll doing tonight?"

"Great. We want to get married." The words came out on a shout, making Dolly blanch.

"Okay...here are our packages. Go ahead and pick one. We have a couple in the chapel right now, but you'll be next." She handed us a sheet with their different packages.

"These all look great. What do you think?" I looked up at Bucky. A strange look crossed his face. He took the paper from me.

"You don't want to do this."

"What? Of course, I do. Look at these great options. We could have Elvis and Marilyn Monroe officiate the wedding." I pointed toward the paper as I tried not to throw up.

"Remember when I told you about how horrible of a liar you are?"

"Yeah."

"Well, you haven't gotten any better since I said that."

I sighed and moved to a small seating area. A framed picture of a happy couple kissing was above the chairs. The reflection in the picture showed Bucky's approach. He wrapped his arms around me.

"You don't want to get married," he whispered in my ear.

"It's not that."

"Then what is it? Is this too fast? Is it me?" Bucky rested his chin on my shoulder.

"No. It's none of that." I turned in his arms and wrapped mine around his neck. "It just occurred to me that this isn't what I want."

"Okay...what do you want, Ember?"

"I want the Barbie wedding."

He blinked at me. "You've lost me."

"When I was little, I used to sit and play with Barbies. I'd put on little weddings in elegant dresses and then tuck her and Ken in a tissue box for them to make babies."

"So, you want to have sex in a tissue box?" He grinned.

I smacked the back of his head. "You're an idiot. Why do I like you?"

He squeezed me closer. "You don't like me. You love me and I hear what you're saying. It's not this you want. You want a big wedding with a big dress and the entire menagerie of Beatrice's proceeding you."

"Something like that. I'm sorry. It's not that I don't love the idea of marrying you. It's that I just realized I wanted it to be special. I never thought I'd get married, but the idea of marrying you in a place like this..." I looked over at Dolly. She was giving me a knowing look. "Sorry." She shrugged, and I looked back at Bucky. "A place like this doesn't feel right."

He gave me a long, thoughtful look and dragged his hands from my waist up to cup my face. "Ember, I don't care where or when we get married. It will be the best moment of my life." He paused and got a mischievous grin on his face. "Well, it's going to be close to first, next to the first time I was between your thighs."

I attempted to grimace, but a smile curled my lips. His lips pressed against mine in a sweet kiss full of love. He pulled back and leaned his forehead against mine.

"I love you so much. I think I have since that crazy old lady laser tag bachelorette party."

"You loved my tits."

He shrugged. "Well, you shook them at me. How could I not want to dive into your cleavage and motorboat them?"

"I did not shake them at you. I just took a deep breath and I can't help they are still quite perky. They are my best asset, after all."

Bucky sobered. "They aren't your best asset. You're brilliant, beautiful, funny, sassy, and a complete pain in the ass." A scathing retort was on the tip of my tongue, but he kept talking. "You are the perfect woman for me. I couldn't have dreamed up a better match. Now, let's get out of—"

Before he could finish, the doors to the chapel swung open. Dolly clapped as a couple stumbled toward us. Bucky and I froze when we recognized them.

"Olivia?"

"Xander?"

Bucky and I said at the same time. They stumbled out of the chapel and onto the crowded sidewalk.

"Who do we have next?" Elvis the officiant asked from the chapel entrance.

"Did ya'll still want to get married?"

"What?" I blinked and looked back at Dolly.

"We've gotta go." Bucky pulled me out the door to follow Olivia and Xander.

By the time we had gotten our wits about us, they disappeared. We split and walked separately down a block and then back. They were gone.

"How did they disappear so quickly?" Bucky asked.

"Probably a taxi."

"Yeah. Any chance it wasn't them?"

"I guess anything is possible." I blew out a breath. "Let's head back to the hotel. I'm tired."

"Let's grab the monorail. That will be quicker."

"Lead on." I hooked my arm with his.

"Do you want to come in?" I smiled at him.

"Are you sure?"

"Get your hot ass in here." I pulled him with me and he pinned me against the wall by the door. His nose caressed the length of my neck, causing shivers through my body.

"Where's your room?" I pulled him toward my room but stopped.

"Hold on a second." I knocked on the door next to mine. "Olivia?" I leaned my ear against the door and didn't hear a noise. Hesitantly, I pushed the door open and held my breath. Immediately, I relaxed. No one was in there.

"Are they in there?"

"Nope." I could hear giggles and moans coming from the other two rooms and smiled. "Looks like the other two are getting a little lucky."

Bucky linked his hand with mine and dragged me into my room. "Let's see if you can as well."

Within moments, we were naked and kissing. I stopped when I remembered something. Pulling back, I took his hand and pulled him toward my bathroom. The light turned on as we entered.

"Holy shit. How did you land this?" Bucky wandered over to the large claw-foot tub.

"Teagan felt a little bad for Grayson overstepping. I didn't think I'd get to use it. Want to use it with me?"

A sexy smile curled his lips. "You don't have to ask me twice, but I want to use some of those smelly bubble things."

I laughed. "You want a bubble bath?"

He turned on the water and walked over to me. "I want to fuck you in the tub while I cover your gorgeous tits with suds."

"How can a girl say no to that?" I pranced over to the sink and grabbed one of the complimentary bottles.

The tub filled as Bucky caressed my body from behind. I was getting wet, and we weren't even in the tub yet. His fingers pinched my nipple, sending pleasure directly to my pussy. Bucky's other hand traveled to my pussy to find how wet I was getting.

"Damn. You're so fucking wet."

My teeth dug into my bottom lip as I nodded. "Let's get into the tub. You first."

He let me go and stepped into it. Sinking down, the water rose to the top. It was the most erotic sight I'd ever seen and I'm not ashamed to say I've seen many hot guys.

"Don't just stand there and gawk at me. Get that sweet ass over here."

I stepped into the tub and sat on the edge. For some reason, this made me feel vulnerable. I didn't get to focus on that too much because Bucky pulled me to him. Water sloshed over the edge and wet the floor.

"You made a mess." I straddled him.

"I don't give a fuck. You looked too good sitting there and I plan on making more of a mess."

"You do?"

Bucky's hand slid under the water. He found my clit and pinched it. I squeaked with surprise. "I plan on doing a lot. Now slide forward. I need to be inside you." His hand grabbed my ass and pulled me forward. His hard silk-covered steel slid against my clit.

With my hands on the sides of the tub, I pushed up to settle his cock at my entrance. I sheathed him in one move. We both moaned. Leaning forward, I captured his lips with mine. As our kisses deepened, our hips moved in tandem. Water splashed everywhere as we got more and more frenzied without lovemaking. I broke off our kiss to lean back and enjoy the feeling of his hard cock moving in and out of me. Bucky's hand went straight to my clit. He pinched it once again, which sent me over the edge of pleasure.

"Fuck me!" I shouted.

"That's right, baby. Come all over my cock."

Stars shot through my vision as my orgasm overcame me. I clamped around him as I rode the passion wave. Squeezing his cock inside me pushed him over the edge and I felt him come inside me. I collapsed against his chest as mini tremors continued to rack my body. We relaxed together in the bubble bath. Bucky drew lazy circles on my back. The silence in the room was comfortable. It was a first for me.

"Babe, maybe we should get out," Bucky mumbled into my hair.

"I'm comfortable right here."

"Believe me. I don't want you to leave my arms, but the water is getting cold. If you get out, I promise we can lie just like this in that big bed."

I blew out a breath. "Fine."

Standing up, I felt the water sluice down my body. Gingerly, I stepped from the tub. There was water everywhere. I tiptoed over to the towels and wrapped it around me. As I turned, I said, "Be careful there's—" I didn't even get the sentence out when I saw Bucky go flying. "Oh shit. Are you...ah!" As I rushed over to help him, my own feet flew out and I landed right on top of him.

"Ow," he breathed out.

"Oh my God. I'm so sorry." My body slid off his and I realized my knee had actually landed in a very sensitive spot.

"It's...okay."

"Let me help you." I stood and held out my hand.

Bucky shook his head and crawled naked across the bathroom to the towels. My teeth dug into my lip as I held back a laugh. He looked ridiculous, but damn, did his ass look hot.

"You better not be checking out my ass." He reached the counter.

"Damn right I am." I smacked his ass just before he could cover it with a towel.

"You're gonna pay for that."

I squealed as Bucky stalked toward me. I took off into the bedroom and he tackled me onto the bed. My towel disappeared along with his.

"If this is how you're gonna make me pay, I'm ready and willing."

Bucky leaned down and nipped my ear. "This is only the beginning. That ass is going to be red when I'm done with it."

He flipped me onto my stomach and gave my ass a smack. My body shivered with excitement. This punishment was going to be so enjoyable.

45

Fucking Plausible Deniability

Hi there Angsty Aimee!

I can't believe I'm still writing to you. But I wanted to share how wonderful my life has become. I'm back with Bucky. Don't be a jealous bitch. I know you are. After his surprise striptease, the boys partied with us the rest of the weekend. Well, most of them. Olivia disappeared after that night. She sent a cryptic text saying she got called in about an exclusive story. Bucky and I knew better. However, she didn't say a damn word about marrying Xander. As for Xander he stayed with us but checked his phone a countless amount of times. He was so mopey he ruined his cosplay costume by being the saddest my little pony. Bucky made more than one crack about dressing him up like that sad donkey from the children's story. It didn't improve Xander's mood. Grayson and Teagan were inseparable. If those two don't have a surprise in the oven before the wedding, I'd be surprised. Bucky and I weren't too different from them. The only difference is I have an IUD. I don't think Teagan is using anything.

The night after our tub sex, Bucky freaked out. He remembered we hadn't used any protection during our tub time and was so worried we were going to have a baby. His mood swung from worry to elation and back. When he finally settled down, I clarified why there wasn't any reason to stress. My heart broke slightly when his face fell at the idea of us having a little one was dashed.

Maybe one day I'll pop out one of his pups. Definitely not today. If you ask Beaty, my uterus is drying up from unuse. I'll tell you what I said to her...fuck off.

Well, gotta go. I have lunch with Nomi and then work at the daycare.

Check ya later...

"What's that?" Bucky rolled onto his side and stared at me.

I shut the journal and peered down at him. "It's just a journal."

"I wouldn't have thought you were a journaling kind of person."

"Well, I wasn't until the girls made me. Now it's become a bit of a habit."

"Can I read it?"

A snort escaped me. "You aren't ready for that kind of trauma." I held up the journal in my lap. "This is direct insight into how my brain works. We just got to a good place in our relationship. No need to ruin things by showing you exactly how fucked up I am."

He grinned and sat up. His lips pressed against my shoulder. "You're probably right. No need to read about what a rockstar I am in bed and how I'm the best boyfriend in the world and how you want to have all my babies. That is too much to handle. I might get the idea you're a stage five closet clinger."

Using the notebook, I smacked his gorgeous six-pack. "You're an idiot."

Swiftly, he pulled me on top of him. His lips took mine in a passionate kiss that made me moan. Then his hands began wandering down my back to my ass. With a slight pull, I could feel he was aroused again.

Breaking the kiss, I drew away slightly. "I need to meet Nomi in forty-five minutes. Also, I need to take a shower and get dressed."

Bucky groaned. "Can't you just stay in bed with me all day?"

"Don't you have to work today?"

"So. I'm the boss. I can do what I want and if that is staying in bed with my gorgeous girlfriend and her smoking hot body, then so be it."

"Uh-huh. I heard Edna and the other naughty grannies were going to be at laser tag today."

He groaned again. "Fuck my life. I hate when they come. I mean, don't get me wrong, I love that my grandmother supports me, but damn, do they always have to cause a scene?"

"Apparently. Now get up and go to work, loser."

I swiped his discarded shirt off the floor next to the bed and threw it over my head. Slinking from his bed, I grabbed my duffle bag with all my essentials. With a glance over my shoulder, I saw the most heart-stopping sight of my life. Bucky was laying there with the sheet barely covering his hips. Every atom in my body tried to charge right back to bed and ride him like my life depended on it. Mentally, I slapped my overactive vagina and opened the door.

"Seriously, Ember?" Nomi said as I jogged into the little cafe.

"What?" The words whooshed out in heavy breaths.

"You're an hour and a half late."

"No. I can't be." I knew I was. Bucky and I had sex on more than one surface of the bathroom. One of the most incredible things about that man was his bounce-back ability.

"Don't play stupid. Let's order. We have shit to discuss, and I have places to be."

"Sorry. Time just got away from me."

"Yeah. Yeah. You have a sexy boy toy now. I don't care."

My brow furrowed. "What's going on? You're really cranky."

"I don't want to talk about it," she mumbled.

"It was good seeing you, garden gnome." A handsome Latino man stopped at our table.

"Fuck you very much, Romeo," Nomi spat.

He gave her a wink and a megawatt smile. People in the cafe murmured and took their phones out to take pictures. What the fuck was going on?

"Nomi..."

"Ignore him. He's a fucking idiot. Now let's order." Nomi waved at a waitress.

We each placed our orders and sipped our drinks. Nomi looked around to see if her mystery man was still around. I watched as he looked over his shoulder at Nomi. She stiffened and refocused on me.

"Are you ready?" Her voice snapped out like a whip.

"Sure. Is this about Olivia? We should probably talk to her about Vegas."

"Huh? What's wrong with Olivia?"

"Uhm..."

Nomi waved her hand dismissively. "I can't worry about her. We need to talk about your dad."

"What about him?" Unconsciously, I began rolling my napkin in my lap.

"About the house."

My entire body relaxed. "Oh. Jesus, Nomi. You scared the shit out of me. What's going on with the house?"

"Oh sorry. Didn't mean to be so dramatic. He has it back."

"Wait, what?"

"Yep. It seems that these cult people don't like the idea of lawsuits or the authorities checking out the workings of their little operation."

"Oh my God! That's wonderful news. So, Dad can move back in?"

"Absolutely." She smiled for the first time since I'd sat down.

I jumped up from the seat and knocked the tray out of the waitress's hands. The crash was deafening. I cringed and looked. "I'm sorry." Kneeling, I began picking up shards of broken dishes and food.

"It's okay." The waitress stood to retrieve a broom.

"All right. I've had enough of you two." A manager charged out from the back.

"Uhm...what?" My eyes met the angry manager.

"You and your friend are no longer welcome here. Leave before I call the cops." He moved toward me, but Nomi stepped between us.

"I wouldn't do that."

The manager crossed his arms over his chest. "Leave."

"Come on, Ember." Nomi grabbed my purse and shoved it at me.

"I don't—"

"Just come on. I'll explain after we leave."

"Okay." I followed Nomi. Eyes of all the patrons followed us as we passed table after table.

When the door shut behind us and we walked toward Nomi's car, she was doing her lawyer thing where she kept her head up and acted like nothing could ever rattle her.

Pulling her to a stop, I asked, "What the hell happened back there? I mean, it was an accident. I'm sure I'm not the only person to have accidentally bumped into a waitress before."

Nomi sighed. "I may have caused a scene with Romeo."

My eyes widened. "What do you mean by a scene?"

"I may or may not have thrown my glass of water and yours in his face."

"So, you did. Why?"

"I've known him for a very long time. He's done some things that he needs to atone for."

"You thought you needed to do something to speed it up?"

"Yep."

"Okay." I started walking toward the bus stop.

"You aren't going to ask me what he needs to atone for?" Nomi called.

The bus pulled up, and I turned toward her before getting on. "Aren't you a lawyer? Plausible deniability is a girl's best friend." With one last wave, I boarded the bus to get to the daycare.

46

Don't Be a Used Tampon

"Excuse me? Can you say that again?" My jaw hung open as I stared at Corrine and Cole, her lawyer husband.

She let out a deep sigh. "We need to let you go."

I started wringing my hands in my lap. This wasn't fucking happening again. I did everything right. I even have a damn boyfriend now.

"Can I ask why?"

Corrine looked at her husband and then back at me. "You don't belong here."

Tears gathered in the corners of my eyes. "Oh, I thought I was doing a good job with the kids. I'm sorry to have wasted your time." I glued my eyes to the floor as I stood from the chair.

"Ember, wait."

"I'm sorry, Corrine. I am barely holding it together, please don't ask me to stay."

"Please listen before you go." She held her hand out for me to regain my seat.

I nodded but kept my eyes away from her.

"When you were in Las Vegas, Cole and I had a little party. We filled it with quite a few influential locals. In fact, I believe you knew one couple."

My blood froze. There was only one couple who was influential that would know me. Stan and Eve Lane, my previous bosses.

"I can imagine they had some colorful things to say about me."

Corrine smiled. "I knew who they were when we invited them. You see, Ember, Cole and I were so impressed with what you did to our house that we knew what your real calling was. So, we hatched a plan."

"I'm so lost right now."

Cole smiled. "I work a lot of high-profile cases. A lot of people owe me."

"Okay. I'm not sure what this has to do with me."

"You will. As I was saying, we had an enormous party and people were remarking on how wonderfully organized the house was. They asked which company we hired. After one of the woman's excitement about your organization of the kitchen, Stan and Eve overheard."

"Oh Jesus," I muttered.

Corrine giggled. "This is one of the best parts. They had the nerve to ask if their company did it. That the work looked so familiar."

A loud laugh burst from me. "You're kidding me."

"Nope. I told them proudly that they had nothing to do with this. That it was the Get Your Life Together Company...owned and operated by Ember Tyler."

"What?"

"You should have seen their faces. They went pale and then red. Stan walked away while Eve tried to enlighten me about you. Before she could say one bitchy word, I cut her off. I told her everything you'd already told me and that they were both assholes and she blamed the wrong person when she fired you out of malice."

"I'm sure Eve loved that."

"She sputtered like a fish out of water. It was fantastic. The only thing that would have made it better would have been if you'd been there." The three of us laughed.

I wiped away my tears from laughing and sobered. "I appreciate what you did but I'm not sure how this affects me."

Cole pulled something out of his briefcase and slid it over to me. It was a manila envelope with my name scrolled across it.

"What is this?"

"Open it." Corrine nodded toward the envelope in my hands.

I looked between the two of them, then opened the clasp holding the envelope closed. A paper-clipped packet was inside. Sliding the packet out, I flipped it over to read the cover page. My eyes widened.

"Is this for real?"

Corrine smiled. "Absolutely. I wasn't lying when I said this job isn't for you. You are actually a wonderful teacher." My eyebrows rose, and she laughed. "I had some doubts when you first started. We even had a pool going on who was going to break you."

"Nice, boss."

"None of them did, so I won."

"You didn't think any of them would break me?"

"Nope. You're too tough. You remind me of me." Corrine laughed again. "However, you are much more suited to be a professional organizer."

"I still don't really understand why."

Corrine moved to explain, but Cole shook his head. "Look, Ember, we talked extensively about this. Corrine and I believe you can be incredibly successful. If we thought differently, we wouldn't be offering to be investors in your business. I understand you will want to have Nomi look over the paperwork. Would you like me to take it to her when I go into the office?"

I shook my head. "No, thank you. I need to think about things and talk to Nomi about all this."

"We understand, Ember. I need you to know that if you choose not to accept our proposal, you are still welcome to teach here. But I really hope you quit and take us up on our proposition."

I grinned. "I'll let you know tomorrow."

"It better be I quit," Corrine yelled as I left her office.

A laugh bubbled up inside me as I walked past the classrooms. The clamor of the children made my heart sink. If I started my own business, I'd never see those kids again. My thoughts swirled. How was I ever going to make this decision?

Midnight Sun was busy for a Monday night. The crowd comprised a lot of financial bros, businessmen, and a few sports fans excited about whatever game was going on. Christmas lights glittered around the room, reminding me how close it was to the holiday. My friends and I sat at our usual table. Nomi focused on the papers I'd given her, Olivia stared out the window and Teagan was blissfully unaware we were all pre-occupied.

"Aren't you done with that?" I asked Nomi.

She barely looked up and said, "If you had let Cole bring it to me earlier, then I wouldn't be doing it now."

"Sorry, Nomi. With everything you've done for me lately, I shouldn't even be asking you to look at that. Hand it back and I'll find someone else."

"What do you mean? What has she done?" Teagan asked as she took a sip of her drink.

Nomi looked at me with one eyebrow raised. "I guess I forgot to tell you. She's a superhero. She shook down Dad's former cult and got his house back."

"Seriously? That's fantastic!" Teagan exclaimed.

"I know. I can't—"

"Hello, ladies. Can we buy you drinks?"

I looked up to see a group of the finance bros hovering near our table. "Uhm...thanks but we're good." My tight smile barely contained the 'fuck you' I wanted to say.

"Aww. Come on, sweetheart. I don't see guys lined up here for you. You should take what you can get."

My nose wrinkled in disgust. Why did men always think women had to be happy just to get attention from them? They just assumed that we should meet any attention they gave with utter reverence.

"Excuse me. What is your name?" I asked sweetly. My friends knew this wasn't a good sign for this guy and his friends. Nomi looked up from the papers, Teagan stopped sipping, and Olivia finally tuned into what was happening around her.

"I'm Gary, sweet cheeks. Now, why don't you give me a smile? Women always look so good when they smile. I'm sure you have a great one."

If his condescending comment wasn't enough to piss me off, the fact that he was saying all of this to my tits really fueled my rage. Just as I was about to tell him exactly what he could do with his fucking smile, I noticed the men behind him. Bucky, Xander, and Grayson glared at the group of used tampons.

I smiled, but not because jackass Gary told me to.

"Good girl. Let's go outside and I can show you what else you can do with those lips." He placed his hand on my upper arm.

"I'd remove that hand before I break it off and shove it up your ass," Bucky growled.

"Excuse me? We were here first."

"Did you just call fucking dibs on these ladies? They aren't a fucking seat in a car. Look, you're lucky I'm here to rescue you, buddy."

"What?" Gary scoffed. "Rescue me?"

"Yes. If you continue to touch my girlfriend, I will let her do exactly what she wants to do."

Gary looked at me. "What exactly do you want to do?"

My maniacal smile curled my lips. I stood from my seat and leaned close to Gary's ear. "I would break off one of the stool legs and shove it so far up your ass that you'll be spitting toothpicks for a month. Then when you think I'm done, I'll take that little spoon and slowly and methodically saw your dick off. Don't worry, I'll shove it in your pocket for safekeeping."

Gary paled, and Bucky's lips curled in a smirk. Gary and his finance bros left our table without another word. I threw my arms around Bucky and gave him a passionate kiss. Just like with all his kisses, my world blurred and only encompassed the two of us. The kiss ended too soon, and I saw Grayson and Xander had found their way to the bar.

"The guys and I are going to watch the game. I promise we won't interfere with your girl time." He kissed me on the cheek and whispered in my ear, "You are fucking hot. You're tying me up tonight."

A blush colored my cheeks as I sat back down with the girls. The three of them gave me warm smiles. Well, two of them did. Olivia's eyes were focused on Xander at the bar. Their little secret was still well and truly hidden. I knew they had to work that out between them.

Nomi went back to the papers, but I pulled them away. "You're done for the night. Time to have a drink or two."

She blew out a breath. "Fine, but you're giving them to me before we leave. I'll let you know what I think tomorrow."

"Okay. I want to propose a toast." I held up my drink.

"Seriously?" Teagan looked at me skeptically.

"Okay." Nomi shrugged and held up her glass.

"What's going on?" Olivia was finally back to the four of us.

"Shut up and raise your glasses, bitches." They raised their glasses. "Hot mess isn't a description. It's a way of life. Our way of life." Our glasses clinked, and we all took sips.

When we put the glasses down, Teagan looked at me. "That was a fucking weird toast. I hope you don't plan on saying that at the reception."

I grinned. "Oh hell no. I'm totally roasting your ass. All the dirt is coming out."

"Fuck you." Teagan grinned.

"Fuck you too." I couldn't help the grin that curled my lips as the four of us laughed.

Come Along on the Hot Mess Express

The papers on my desk started to make my eyes cross. I'd been trying to diagram a closet organization for a prospective client, but it just wasn't working. I dropped my head on my desk and moaned.

"Ember?"

"Mnnngh..."

Kinsley laughed. "Not a clue what you just fucking said, but there is a delivery here for you."

I sat up and rolled my neck, hearing the vertebrae pop. Kinsley cringed at the noise. "What is it now? Please tell me it isn't something else from Mr. Sanchez. I'm glad he's happy, but if he doesn't stop sending taco bouquets, I'm going to be a thousand pounds."

"I'm pretty sure this isn't from Mr. Sanchez." Kinsley left the office.

I sighed and stood from my desk. Glancing at the clock on my wall, I realized I hadn't stood in two hours. Who would have thought owning your own business was so consuming?

I grabbed a folder off the desk for Kinsley to organize for the presentation for the client.

"Here you go, Kins. I'll have the rest of the diagrams ready by tomorrow. Where is this—" My words cut off when I saw a gigantic bouquet of roses. It was so obnoxiously big that the poor delivery boy was hidden.

"What in the world?" Gina, my apprentice, joined me staring at the flowers. "Is it your birthday, Ember?"

"Not that I know of." I glanced over at Kinsley. "Am I dying? Did someone send me a funeral arrangement?"

Kinsley snorted. "Not that I know of."

The phone rang, and Gina walked over to her desk in the corner. "Hello. Hot Mess Express Organizing. This is Gina. How may I help you?"

I vaguely heard Gina directing someone to look at our website to schedule an appointment. She hung up, then rejoined Kinsley and me.

"Hmmm. Well, if you can hear me in there, you can put the flowers in my office." I directed the delivery boy toward my office.

"Do you even have room in there?" Gina asked.

I snorted. "Probably not since it's the size of a porta potty."

"Smells like it some days too," Kinsley added.

After Nomi took the night to look over Cole and Corrine's proposal, she advised everything was on the up and up. That was good because I'd stayed up all that night dreaming about the business I could create. The idea of having business cards again made me giddy. Bucky tried his damnedest to take my mind off it, but I'm slightly ashamed to say that while he was pounding me from behind, I was making a list of everything I'd need to do to get things up and running.

Nomi joined me for coffee that morning while Bucky slept in my bed. We chatted about everything I needed to do to start a business. My head spun with ideas. I'd been so focused on my dream that I almost missed my stop for the daycare. The bus screeched to a halt and my head almost landed in a lonely old man's lap. With pep in my step, I walked in and resigned. Corrine was in my classroom and began squealing and jumping. The kids didn't understand and began doing the same. She pulled me into a giant hug and then dragged me to her office.

The following months whipped by as I set up the business. I rented a small office space, hired Kinsley, and went to the university to find an interior design student interested in home organization. That was how Gina came into my life. The office was drab, and I did most of my work meetings in a restaurant or at the client's home, but it was functional. But more importantly, it was mine.

It wasn't just the business, but my personal life as well. Dad moved back into the house. Aunt Beaty reluctantly moved back with him as well. The menagerie minus Cuddles the porcupine went with her. Bucky had bonded with the spikey bastard. Dad swore off dating for a while, but when he met Xander's mom, Jocelyn, he felt he needed to act fast. They were currently on a 50+ cruise around the Mediterranean.

As for my relationship with Bucky, we haven't been able to spend much time together lately. Our individual business ventures have become all-consuming and when we do see each other, we fall asleep on the couch watching a movie. We've become one of those boring couples. In the past, I would have run fast from that. Now I can't imagine my life not having him in it.

I grabbed a bottle of water from the mini fridge in our office and started back toward my office. "Kinsley, I'm going back. I'm determined to finish these damn diagrams."

"Uh-huh." A smile painted her words.

I ignored her weirdness and walked into the office. The delivery boy was still arranging the flowers. How long did that take? He took his delivery very seriously. However, I didn't have time to wait for an overzealous delivery boy wanting a good tip. I had shit to do and a boyfriend to cuddle with.

"That's fine. Thank you. Stop by Kinsley's desk and she can give you a tip out of the petty cash."

"No need. I'd like to give you my tip."

The voice made me jump. "Bucky?"

"If you have to ask, we really haven't been around each other."

I dropped what I was holding and stepped into his arms. His cologne and powerful arms enveloped me. Our lips crashed together in a passion-filled kiss.

"Did you come for a quickie?" I asked. "We don't have blinds yet, so you have to be okay with your sister watching us."

"I'm not okay with that," Kinsley shouted from her desk.

Bucky laughed. "As appealing as that sounds, I have come to kidnap you."

"What?"

"I'm kidnapping you. I booked a cabin and we are going to spend the next four days fucking, eating, and sleeping. All in that order."

I blushed. "I can't. I didn't even bring a bag."

"Teagan packed you a bag. It's in the car. Cuddles is at your dads with Beaty and Kinsley has assured me she cleared your schedule until Tuesday. Nothing is keeping you here."

My eyes found Kinsley leaning on the doorjamb of my office. "You knew about this."

"Of course. You don't actually think that idiot came up with the cabin idea all on his own, do you?"

"Nice, Kins," Bucky muttered.

"Am I lying?" Kinsley raised her eyebrows.

"It doesn't matter. Are you serious right now? Four uninterrupted days. Just you and me?"

"Yep. Now get your sweet ass in gear." He smacked it, making me yelp.

"Keep it in your pants, Bucky. You can at least wait until you have a bedroom." Kinsley left my office.

I placed my papers on the desk and grabbed my laptop and purse. "I'm ready."

"Nope. That's not coming." He pointed to the laptop.

"I don't want to leave it, plus if I get ideas, I need to act on them."

"Got that covered too. There are three empty spiral notebooks in the car. Kinsley will take care of your laptop."

I shrugged. "Okay." Placing the laptop back on my desk, I linked my arm with my hot boyfriend's arm.

We swept out of the office. When we got in the elevator, the sexual tension filled the confined space. The moment the doors opened, Bucky dragged me from the elevator. Our hurried steps only belied our feelings toward one another. Each of us needed the other and not for a good nap on the couch. Goose flesh pebbled my skin. Anticipation and excitement filled me. I wish I could say it was just the thought of having time alone with my boyfriend, but in reality, the most thrilling thing was the prospect of my future. The world was wide open, and the possibilities were endless. I would always be a hot mess, but I was finally happy with my mess.

Acknowledgments

This book was a journey. It took me a lot longer to get Bucky and Ember's story just right. A lot longer was pretty much two plus years. Granted in that time there was a global pandemic that tested everyone's mental and physical health.

My primary cheerleader eager to read any and all of my pages is the wonderful Leanne Burkholder. Without you I could have possibly given up writing all together when the words woudn't come.

Another huge support has been Michelle with Cupboard Maker Books. You took a chance on an unknown indie author and have been such a support that I want to keep coming back to see you guys and the kitties.

Of course I can't forget my family. My husband, Heath, who loves that I write so we can go travel to all the book signings. My kids, Brayden, Sam and Shalee who are ever my inspiration and assistants at those signings. Finally, my mother, who reads all my books. Just don't ask me to explain anything.

THANK YOU

Thank you for taking the time to read Caution Hot Mess Ahead. If you have a moment, please leave a short review. I'll love you forever.

To stay up on all my books, events, and other craziness, I'm up to sign up for my newsletter at www.jackiepaxsonauthor.com

If you haven't read Teagan and Grayson's love story, continue for a taste.

A Work in Progress

Dawn of a New Me

I never dreamed that I'd be looking down the barrel of 40 years old and still be a virgin. You may be asking yourself how in the world does something like that happen. Was I kept in a dungeon most of my life? Did I live in a nunnery? Was I brought up in such a strict household that I wasn't allowed to be around boys? That would be a no for all of those. I've had boyfriends and dates but never pulled the trigger. Somehow, I've managed to meet every shitty guy out there. None of which I'd wanted to give my flower to. Though it's more like a wilting bud rather than a flower.

The flames that came off my birthday cake illuminated the singing faces of my best friends Olivia, Ember and Nomi. I am the first in our group to be only one year away from forty. As their off-key singing ended, I knew exactly what my wish would be. Blowing with all my might, I snuffed out each candle only for them to relight. The bitches that were my friends laughed like lunatics.

"Gotcha!" They yelled together.

They thought they were so funny. I pasted on a fake smile, but inside I was stabbing them with the cake knife.

"Uh Oh...Teagan has her fake smile on again," Nomi said, pulling the knife toward them.

"Chill out, Teag," Ember said next to me.

"You guys just think you're so funny. Well, you three aren't much further away from becoming crazy cat ladies than I am," I huffed.

Olivia rolled her eyes. "Oh puhlease. Here comes Tegan's pity party."

I narrowed my gaze at my supposed best friend then straightened. It was time I told them my plan for the final year of my thirties. "I've decided something."

"Here we go. What are your plans now?" Ember asked, cutting the cake and handing out slices.

"This year will be the year of Teagan. I will leave my thirties accomplishing the things I have been putting off. I will finally finish my novel. I will get in shape. I will adopt an animal that is not a cat." I stood with my shoulders back in an overly dramatic pose.

"And lose your virginity?" Olivia mumbled past the cake she'd shoveled in her mouth.

"I guess that can go on the list." I shriveled a bit with that.

"That is a must for that list. I refuse to let my best friend die a virgin," Nomi declared.

"I think you're being a bit dramatic there, Nomi. I'm not ancient and I'm not dying."

"You never know. You could walk outside to work and bang!" She pounded the table. "You're pushed into traffic by a bicyclist but manage to dodge an oncoming bus only to trip over your feet and knock yourself unconscious on a curb rolling into a puddle and drown while people watch."

"What the hell, Nomi?" I exclaimed.

"Seems feasible for you," Ember said with Olivia nodding.

I needed to find new friends.

"Anyway, this year will be a new Teagan. I refuse to let the next year pass as every other year has passed."

Ember, Olivia and Nomi stared at me. Ember lifted her glass of wine and said, "We are with you, Teag. We pledge to make sure you don't become a virgin crazy cat lady without a published book."

"I second that!" Olivia said, raising her glass.

"I third that!" Nomi raised her glass.

I rolled my eyes but smiled at the best friends a girl could have. Well, really, I could probably find better, but they've been around a while, and it's a lot of work meeting new people when you hate people. So, I raised my glass with theirs.

"Here's to taking thirty-nine by storm," I said, clinking my glass with theirs.

Teagan's ~~Get Laid~~ Bucket List

1. *Lose virginity/have mind blowing sex*

2. *Ride in a hot air balloon*

3. *Ride a mechanical bull*

4. *Go on a yacht*

5. *Go to a casino*

6. *Get a pet (not a fish, lizard or bird. Must be furry and cuddly)*

7. *Sing karaoke*

8. *Hike to a beautiful waterfall*

9. *Make-out under the stars*

10. *Do something selfless*

11. *Do an escape room*

12. *Teach a class*

13. *Run a ~~marathon~~ mile*

14. *Have cake for breakfast*

15. *Get lost on purpose*

Have sex! Have sex! Have sex! (added on an unknown date by Ember, Olivia and Nomi)

About Author

Jackie is the author of the Dirty Laundry series, a romantic comedy series featuring sexy movie stars and the feisty women who put up with them. Her love of writing stemmed from her love of reading which began with the Sweet Valley High series. She'd conveniently start a new book when she was supposed to clean her room. When she's not writing, she's busy with her husband, three kids, and two fur babies, Cady and Oberon. In those rare moments between family, writing, and her day job, she is busy posting sarcastic/too honest posts on Instagram. Finally, in that sweet spot between utter exhaustion and an overactive brain, she enjoys reading until the kindle slaps her in the face.

To stalk Jackie, find her on Instagram, Facebook, and Tik-Tok @jackiepaxsonauthor